BOOKS BY LEE WILLIAMS

IN HIS BLOOD
2009

SINS OF THE FATHER
2011

THE GOVERNOR'S MAN
2013

NIGHTHAWK

LEE WILLIAMS

NIGHTHAWK by Lee Williams

Copyright©2020 by Lee Williams

This is a work of fiction. Names, characters, places, and incidents either are the product of the author's imagination or are used fictitiously. Any resemblance to actual persons, living or dead, events, or locales is entirely coincidental.

Cover Portrait: Ret. IRS Special Agent Brenda Viteri

Book and cover designed by Ellie Searl, Publishista®

ISBN-13: 9781734005202

LCCN: 2019913386

LW Publishing Enterprises
Westmont, IL

Acknowledgments

To the men and women in law enforcement who unknowingly contributed to this story and all the other first responders who sacrifice their safety to make our daily existence possible. In addition, I'd like to thank the members of the Room Seven writer's group who without their patience and constructive criticism this novel would not exist. Thanks to the members-Frederick Meek, Pat Camalliere, Michael Cebula, Luisa Buehler, Pam Holtman, and Rod Brandon. I would be remiss if I did not mention Ellie Searl whose classy artwork is displayed on the cover of every novel I have written, and Brenda Viteri who is a retired special agent and is the face of Gloria Nighthawk on the cover of this book. Finally, to my significant other, Debbie Geary, for fine tuning my errant commas and periods and expanding my consciousness of a woman's behavior in my attempt to write from the perspective of a female protagonist.

CHAPTER 1

Baghdad, Iraq
September 4, 2004
11:00 p.m.

IN THE THICK HEAT OF the night, sweat rolled down IRS Special Agent Gloria Nighthawk's forehead as she lugged her duffel with both hands, an M-4 carbine slung on her back. Her black hair stuck to her face. A slender woman, barely over five feet tall, she swung the duffel into the back of the Humvee like an Olympic hammer thrower. Gloria and her partner, Jim Abbott, put on their sand-colored, bulletproof vests and helmets and hopped into the back seat of the vehicle. They laid their carbines between them and fastened their seat belts.

Gloria noticed Jim glance at her. She thought about her relationships and the hope that during this 90-day assignment, she would have gained some clarity about where her life was going. Were events controlling her, or was she herself out of control, like Iraq, like her relationships, like anything she touched?

Pulling a tube of lotion from her pocket, she squeezed a palmful and rubbed her hands together. The only thing she knew for sure she had gotten in Iraq were cracks in her cinnamon-colored hands from the dry desert heat. She gave Abbott a meaningful glance and he turned away, staring out the window at nothing. He seemed to be creating distance between them. Did he feel guilty about their relationship, or was it something else?

The vehicle bolted out of the Green Zone. Heavy steel gates closed behind it. The headlights were on high beam, blinding anyone sighting a weapon on them. An Army Ranger was behind the steering wheel with an H & K 416 at his hip. His partner in the shotgun seat had an M-4 across his chest.

In a minute, the Humvee was tearing down the street at fifty-five miles per hour. Gloria leaned forward between the front seats. "Take it easy, Sarge. Jim and I want to get to the airport in one piece. I don't want to go down in a traffic accident before I can get back to Chicago."

Sergeant Phillips, in his early twenties, looked over his shoulder. "Ma'am," in a voice respectful of his fifty-year-old passenger, "I'm in my second tour and the goal of everyone here is to get back home in one piece. The longer we're on the streets, the more the odds are against us. A fast-moving target is a lot harder to hit."

Gloria swallowed and hung onto a safety strap suspended from the ceiling as Phillips slowed down and took a turn at thirty-five, within arm's reach of three Ali Babas. She glanced at her partner and shook her head. Her dark eyes were charged with energy. She saw ambivalence in his.

"We got two-and-a half clicks on Route Aeros and then the fun starts. Five clicks on Route Irish and the risk increases substantially before we hit Baghdad International Airport," Sergeant Phillips said.

She saw the kid in the passenger seat glance at their travel orders, then turn and face her. "Nighthawk, what kind of name is that?"

She checked his name patch. "I'm Cherokee, Private Daniels."

"An injun? And you live in Chicago?"

She clenched her teeth. *Just a kid,* she thought. "It's Native American. We were on the land long before your ancestors. I was born and raised in Oklahoma. I was a cop there and I came to Chicago when I got the job with the G."

Daniels nodded. "Good thing you weren't there when the federal building was bombed."

She didn't respond and tried to squeeze the painful memory of the fallen Murrah Federal Building out of her mind. Daniels turned and faced the windshield. She had met that quiet stillness before, every time the fallen building came up in conversation.

"Ma'am, I just got to the sandbox a week ago, but I'm ready to go home. You think you can squeeze me on your flight?" Daniels said.

"Wish we could take all you guys back with us, but I'm only an IRS agent. I don't have that kind of pull."

"IRS? What're you guys doing here?" His forehead furrowed.

Abbott put his hand on the back of Phillip's seat and pulled himself forward. "Saddam's supposed to have seven billion tucked away. They want us to find it."

"I hope you guys are working on commission." The sergeant laughed. "One click to Route Irish. Be there in four minutes."

"Commission, why didn't I think of that?" Gloria joined in the laughter.

"So, you find anything yet?" Sergeant Phillips asked.

"We've tracked a little over a million in cash here and frozen a billion in assets he tried to hide in dummy corporations around the world," Abbott answered.

"Wow, you guys are gonna pay for the war," Daniels said.

"It's not just the two of us. We've got six special agents here," Nighthawk said. "Two more coming to take our place."

"We'll be at Checkpoint One in a minute," Phillips shouted as the Humvee squealed around a corner. Everyone leaned to the right on the hard turn. The Humvee reached the checkpoint and fell into line behind a supply convoy also heading to the airport.

Fifty GIs and Iraqi soldiers were checking the IDs and vehicles. Phillips pulled the Humvee between the giant blast walls and waited. In ten minutes, they had passed the checkpoint. He headed onto the entrance ramp for Route Irish. His knuckles whitened as he tightened his grip on the steering wheel. "We've got six overpasses to go under. Each one is a shooting gallery, a gift to the terrorists."

The Humvee's engine groaned as Phillips got the beast up to top speed. At seventy miles per hour, it bounced across the lumpy pavement. Inside the cabin it became silent. Every muscle tightened. Their heads swiveled from side to side, looking at the traffic ahead and behind. In the darkness, silhouettes of tree stumps, remnants of trees blown away by improvised explosive devices, appeared in the median that separated the four-lane highway. Carcasses of charred vehicles sat on the side of the road.

They approached the first underpass. "Have to watch out for vehicles coming down the wrong way on the exit ramps. They're vee-bids looking for a head-on collision." The sergeant zigged-zagged the Humvee out from the underpass.

"Vee-bids?" Abbott asked.

"Vehicle-born improvised explosive devices," Phillips said.

The PFC checked the ramp and the sides of the road, looking through the night vision scope on his helmet. "All clear."

Phillips relaxed his grip on the steering wheel.

A few minutes later they approached the next overpass. "There's some activity up there," Daniels said. "It looks like a woman pushing a cart."

Gloria found herself holding her breath as they went under the overpass. She exhaled as they broke from under the cement road overhead, thinking suddenly about her children, Darius and Adsila, teenagers searching for direction in their lives without her. *What a waste of time, but I'll be with them soon.*

They followed the convoy to the next overpass. The truck ahead of them flashed its searchlight.

"There's a man up there with a phone. Call it in, Daniels," the sergeant ordered.

The private picked up the two-way and notified the base station. They went under the overpass. The sergeant deliberately swerved the Humvee into a serpentine path as he stepped on the gas and roared ahead.

A rocket hit a supply truck in front of them. The one-and-a-half-ton vehicle flew into the air in a blast of flames, illuminating the night. It landed sideways across the road, blocking their way. Gunfire drummed the sides of their Humvee.

A fiery blast hit their vehicle and it did a three-sixty, colliding with a burnt-out chassis on the side of the road. Their passenger door was flush against the wreck. Smoke filled the air. Rapid machine gun fire ripped across the heavy steel armor. Another blast and the windshield shattered into pieces. Shards of glass rained into the cabin.

Blood oozed down Daniels's forehead. He wiped his sleeve across his face, clearing the blood off his eyes. The Humvee's headlights caught two mujs firing their AK-47s at the vehicle. Phillips and Daniels shoved the barrels of their weapons into the opening left by the blown windshield and returned fire. In the darkness, an orange-yellow blaze flashed from the muzzles of their barrels.

The insurgents fell to the pavement, blood spilling from their chests. Four more continued firing.

Daniels yelled into his two-way radio. "Under fire west of overpass three. Send support."

Sergeant Phillips fired bursts of three rounds, emptying his thirty-round magazine in fifteen seconds. He ejected it, ripped a new one from his vest, slammed it into place, and kept on firing. The flash burst from the muzzle of his machine gun and a muj's head exploded. The body waited an eerie second before it collapsed to the pavement.

Gloria's ears rang from the gunfire. She grabbed her carbine but couldn't safely fire with Phillips and Daniels in front of her.

The private threw the radio to the floor and squeezed the trigger on his M-4. Ten rounds blasted out in seconds. Another insurgent fell, but two more came out of the shadows. Daniels wiped his sleeve across his eyes again. A bullet grazed the sergeant's left shoulder, but he kept his weapon firing down range. Two more Ali Babas crumbled to the pavement.

She saw Daniels jerk back in his seat. Blood spurted from the private's neck like oil gushing from a rig. Fear writhed in her intestines. She leaped between the seats with her M-4, braced under her arm, and fired at two attackers charging the Humvee. They spun to the ground. She dropped the rifle, turned, and clamped her hand on the private's throat. The blood seeped between her fingers, but the bleeding slowed. "Jim, shoot between us."

There was no response.

Another Humvee screamed up Route Irish, screeching to a stop next to Phillips's. Four marines jumped out. Two mujs came out of the darkness under the overpass. A barrage of bullets screamed from the marines' rifles. The targets curled to the pavement before they could get a shot off. The copper smell of blood and pungent odor of gunpowder filled the air. Stillness descended.

A marine came to the sergeant's side of the Humvee. "You okay in there?"

"Get a bandage for the private's neck and get him to a hospital. He's lost a lot of blood." Gloria said. She glanced to the back seat but didn't see Abbott. "Jim, Jim, you okay?"

There was no answer.

Sergeant Phillips opened his door and stepped out, ignoring his wound. A marine rushed in, applied a wrap to the private's neck, and helped carry him from the Humvee.

Gloria jumped into the back seat. She dragged her hands down her vest, wiping off Daniels's blood. Abbott hung forward, strapped in by his seat belt. She pulled him up. A black shadow surrounded the bullet hole in the middle of his vest. A string of blood and saliva hung from his mouth. "What the fuck?" She placed her hand on his neck and felt nothing. "Jim, stay with me. Jim! Medic! Medic! Get a medic here, *fast.*"

A marine jerked the rear door open.

Gloria moved to the side and leaned back on her haunches. What she saw would stay with her forever.

The marine checked Abbott's pulse. "He must have been hit early in the firefight."

She slammed her fist against the window. "But the vest, why?" she said.

"It's not the first time. They're good for shit." The marine dropped his fingers from Abbott's neck. "Sorry, Ma'am."

Gloria saw sympathy in the marine's eyes. There was nothing that could be done for Jim. It was she who had convinced him to come to Iraq so they could explore their relationship. Could they give up their marriages and start a new life with each other? Now, he was dead.

Her eyes welled, and, with the gentle touch of her fingertips, she closed his eyelids. It felt like a spike driven into her heart. She closed her eyes, and for a moment, in the darkness, she was sure this was a dream. Then the report of another shot rang in her ears, and her eyes jolted open. Jim was dead. *Please, God, forgive me, again.* Tears rolled down her cheeks.

CHAPTER 2

Baghdad, Iraq
September 4, 2004
Midnight

THE MARINES RUSHED GLORIA INTO another Humvee. She looked out the window, saw them drop Jim Abbott into a body bag and zip it close. *Please wake me up from this nightmare.*

The Humvee joined the rest of the convoy and zig-zigged down Route Irish. They made it to the airport without any further incidents. A C-130 was waiting on the tarmac, its four propellers spinning.

She ran up the rear ramp into the chassis. In the aft of the plane were fifty soldiers in fatigues, sitting in red canvas seats. One row against each wall faced the interior and two rows in the center faced the seats against the walls, so the GIs sat looking at each other. Farther in, two Humvees were strapped end to end to the floor.

In front of the vehicles, Gloria found a seat between three empties. An unconscious soldier on a stretcher, with an IV dripping morphine into his arm, was secured to the floor in front of her. Gloria glanced at the sheets wrapped tightly around his body and numbly registered the fact that both his legs were missing below the knees. A female nurse dressed in fatigues stood next to the stretcher, felt the man's forehead, and sat down next to her. Gloria closed her eyes, wanting only quiet and for time to pass. In fifteen minutes, the plane taxied down the runway for the two-hour journey to Doha International Airport, Qatar. ETA: 3 a.m.

About halfway through the flight, Gloria felt the nurse move as she rose to check on her patient. Gloria opened her eyes and watched as the nurse felt the GI's forehead again and then shifted her hand to his neck. The nurse placed her stethoscope on his chest and then turned off the IV. Her chin dropped. She exhaled with a sigh and collapsed into the seat next to Gloria.

Gloria placed her hand on the nurse's. Her skin felt soft and smooth. She noticed the gold wedding ring on her finger. "He's gone?"

The nursed nodded. "I feel so helpless. There are so many dying, or going home with brain damage, missing limbs, awful stuff, to lives that will never be the same. The people at home, how will they cope?"

Gloria brushed the nurse's brown hair off her shoulder and put her arm around her. "I don't think I could ever do what you do."

Silent tears ran down the nurse's face.

"Where're you going, Doha?" Gloria asked.

"I was supposed to escort the private to the medical facility at Landstuhl, Germany, for more surgery. Now, they'll be sending him home from Doha in a body bag, and I'll go back to Baghdad on the next flight. What about you?" The nurse straightened up, and Gloria lifted her arm from around her shoulders.

"I'm going home, back to Chicago."

"Good for you. I hope you never have to come back. I don't mean to be rude, but I'm going to try to sleep." The nurse closed her eyes and curled away from Gloria.

The Herc landed, taxied to a military gate, and the GIs filed off. Gloria and the nurse stood as two GIs hurried onto the plane for the soldier on the stretcher. The nurse shook her head. No need for haste now. Another crew hustled into the plane and started to remove the straps that secured the Humvees.

The nurse stood next to the GI on the stretcher and lightly caressed his forehead. She looked at Gloria. "If you have a connecting flight, you better go."

"Yeah, I guess so. Good luck." Gloria marched through the plane, down the ramp, and searched for the Lufthansa gate to pick up the next leg of her flight. On the walk through the terminal, she passed by GI's on stretchers and wheelchairs. She thought how their lives will never be the same for them or their families. Jim's family will be devastated. She thought about how he changed. Was she so wrong persuading him to come to Iraq? What changed him?

The layover in Germany and the long plane ride home gave Gloria a lot of time to weigh the events of the past few months. She contemplated the marital counseling that had appeared to be making no headway for either her or Jim, and the surprising evolution of the emotional intimacy between them that had both exhilarated and unnerved them.

This assignment was supposed to help them both decide what the future held, for them and their families. At first, they were determined not to consummate their relationship, knowing it would only complicate matters, but this was not the first time in history that the daily threat of violence and death changed everything. Lust won over, and the physical aspect of their relationship, driven by fear and the ravages of the war around them, became all-consuming. At the end, *No surprise*, she thought, guilt had crept in. They found themselves in separate beds.

Now, on the last day of the assignment, her confidant, her confessor, her best friend, was gone, and her future was an enigma. Gloria was glad the lights in the cabin were off; the darkness was comforting. She leaned her face against the cool window, listening to the hum of the engines as they flew somewhere over the Atlantic Ocean. Tears rolled down her cheeks and rested on her lips. She rolled her tongue over them, tasting the salty remnants of her emotions. In addition to grief and guilt, she was conscious of a growing anxiety as she contemplated her homecoming and her husband, Judge Robert Carlton. Would he be waiting at O'Hare Airport for her? She wasn't sure. Would he be perceptive enough to realize what had been going on the last few months? She didn't think so, but still....

The plane landed at 11:30 p.m. and taxied to the gate ten minutes later. She waited for the crowded aisle to empty, blew her nose, and before leaving the plane, hastily applied makeup to hide the redness around her eyes. She passed through the baggage terminal, not knowing whether her duffel still existed after the firefight in Baghdad. She breezed through customs and saw her husband waiting outside of security. He was a hard man to miss, six feet, six inches tall, and in all his blackness, wearing a green, orange, and red African Kufi cap.

He met her exiting customs and gave her a polite kiss on the cheek. "I'm sorry about Jim." His voice was deep, the words sounding like they came from a preacher man. She had called him during a layover in Germany and had told him of Abbott's death.

"I know, you told me." Gloria looked down at her sand-colored boots. She knew he wanted to say something like "How long will it take you to get over it?" but had thought better of it. That made her happy, as though she had control over their conversation. Then he came through as expected.

"Is this going to be an issue for you?"

She pursed her lips, wanting to avoid conflict.

"I asked you a question."

"How can you be so insensitive? I just saw a...a close friend die in front of my eyes and you're asking if it affected me?"

"All I'm saying is there's nothing you can do about it. You knew it was a dangerous assignment, but you had to do it, for whatever reason. Now you're facing the worse possible situation. But you've got your kids, your job here, and...and your marriage to deal with. This is your real life, not some screwy adventure that left us all hanging here without you for three months."

She shook her head. "I really don't believe you." She resented that control he exerted over everything, as though he brought his judicial aura home rather than leaving it in the courtroom on the twenty-fifth floor of the Dirksen Federal Building.

"Well, I'm just saying," he exhaled. "Never mind, we'll talk later. I badged the cops. They let me park right outside the door."

"That's convenient." She didn't feel like testing his ethics. She just wanted to get home, hug the kids, have a glass of wine, and listen to some soft music. Maybe put on a Luther Vandross CD, or maybe not. On second thought, maybe it would be better to have that wine and just go to sleep. Maybe this will all be a nightmare. She would wake up, still be in Baghdad, and see Jim's face on the pillow next to hers.

"Mrs. Abbott called. The service for Jim is on Friday."

His voice brought her back to reality. "Do we have to talk about this now? One minute I was sitting next to him and the next he's gone. His blood on my hands."

"Have it your way." They stepped out of the terminal into the warm summer evening.

A policeman was resting against the front fender of the judge's black Lexus. "Have a safe trip home, Your Honor." He stood and opened the front passenger door for Gloria. The judge climbed into the driver's seat and they drove off.

"If you don't mind, I just want to sleep and get this behind me."

"Put the seat back. I'll wake you when we get home."

Gloria leaned back and rolled onto her shoulder, turning her back toward the judge. Every time she drifted into sleep, she was haunted by the reoccurring vision of Jim lying in the back seat of the Humvee, the black stain of his blood soaking his bulletproof vest.

CHAPTER 3

Chicago
Tuesday, September 7, 2004

A T SEVEN THIRTY IN THE morning, Gloria felt the soft touch of someone's hand on her shoulder. She shook her head, not sure of where she was, for a moment thinking it was Jim Abbot. She looked into the dark eyes of her fourteen-year-old daughter Adsila. Her cinnamon skin color, pug nose, and high cheek bones matched Gloria's. She wore skinny pants and a moss-green, long-sleeved T-shirt with a jungle print. A gold charm hung from a chain around her neck. Gloria sat up in bed, looked at her daughter, and wrapped her arms around her. "Honey, it's so good to see you. You grew so much this summer! You look like you're eighteen."

"Mom, I'm so glad you're home. I missed you so much." They both cried.

"I missed you too. I'm never leaving you again."

"What about me?" Darius asked.

Gloria glanced at the other side of the bed. Her seventeen-year-old son, Darius, sat there. He was the image of his father, tall and lean, with chocolate-colored skin. He wore a Bulls jersey, number 23, over a gray pullover, Levi jeans, and Air Jordans.

Gloria reached across the bed and dragged Darius toward her. They had a three-way hug. "I love you both so much. We have to do something special to make up for the time we missed this summer."

Adsila lifted a smoothie from the nightstand. "I made this for you."

Gloria grabbed the drink. "Thanks, Honey."

"Mom, we have to go. I've a zero-hour chemistry class and the bus will be on the corner in five minutes," Darius said.

She kissed them both. "Okay, but think of something we can do together, something special."

Darius rushed out of the room.

Adsila waited a second and held on to her mother's hand. "Mom, I'm sorry about Mr. Abbott."

"Thanks, Baby. It was terrible." Gloria shook her head, avoiding Adsila's eyes.

"I have to catch the bus, too." Her hand slipped out of Gloria's. "Love you," Adsila said, rushing out of the bedroom.

"Me too, Baby." Gloria put the smoothie on the nightstand, laid down, and pulled the cover over her head. *She mentioned Jim. I wonder if she sensed something?* She heard the shower running in the bath. *The judge preparing for another day in his kingdom.* Her eyes closed and she fell back to sleep.

At eight o'clock, the phone rang. Gloria raised her head from the pillow. Her husband ran in from the bathroom. His crisp white shirt hung unbuttoned over his blue boxer shorts. He picked up the receiver. "Hello," he said, then extended his arm toward Gloria. "It's your chief."

She sat up in bed and took the phone. Her husband returned to the bathroom. "Hi, Tony."

"How're you doing?"

"I can't believe what happened. Tell me we never left Chicago. That it was all a nightmare, and Jim and I are teaching the money laundering seminar to a group of cops today."

"I wish I could. Take all the time off you need. You must be tired. I mean with the jet lag and stress of dealing with everything. I wanted to let you know the Secretary of the Treasury is flying in for Jim's service on Friday. The following Friday, the Under Secretary of Defense for Intelligence will be presenting medals to Jim's wife and family and to you. The company that supplies some of the military hardware is starting a college fund for Jim's kids with a check for $10,000 and picking up the cost of the funeral. They have a reputation for supporting the GIs."

"That's really nice, Tony. I'm sure it will be a great relief for Janice Abbott, though I suspect she's not thinking about college right now. I'm tired, but if you don't mind, I'll be in later. If I stay home, I won't be able to stop thinking about what happened. Going to the office will give me something to focus on."

"It's up to you. If there's anything we can do, let us know."

"Thanks, Chief. See you later." She hung up the phone.

The judge stepped out of the bathroom, lifted his tailored navy suit coat off the gold valet stand, and slipped his arms into the sleeves. His silver tie was in a firm Windsor knot. "I've got motion calls on five cases at ten. Will you be all right?"

"The kids came in to see me before they left to catch the bus." Gloria pulled the cover up to her neck. "I hardly had a chance to see them last night. I wish they were off from school."

"They missed you. Too bad you were gone for the whole summer. But we had some good times—concerts, ball games, and stuff." He cocked his head. "Now you're back, but you can't expect everybody to accommodate your schedule, you know. With school just starting, I'm sure you don't want them to fall behind."

You're so adept at pushing my buttons. "I do know, and of course I don't want them to fall behind. I'm going to the office in a little while." She told him about the service on Friday and the Under Secretary of Defense's coming the following week to present them with medals.

He straightened the lapels on his suit coat and brushed a gray hair off his shoulder as she talked. "That's impressive. Ten years in the prosecutor's office and fourteen years on the bench and the Under Secretary of Defense never came to see me."

Gloria pulled the cover over her head, knowing that what she was thinking was better left unsaid. *Is he serious? The biggest risk he ever had was getting a paper cut.*

Gloria heard the bedroom door close. Fifteen minutes later, she pushed herself from under the covers, put on her white terry cloth robe, and headed downstairs to the kitchen. She pulled a mug out of a glossy white cabinet and sat down at the black granite countertop island. She poured a cup from the coffee maker, took a sip. Usually she loved that first cup of coffee in the morning but today it tasted bitter.

She dumped it into the sink.

An hour later, wearing a gray suit and a white blouse, Gloria walked into the offices of the Internal Revenue Service, Criminal Investigation Division, on the twenty-fourth floor of Kluczynski Federal Building in downtown Chicago. The floor was filled with typically gray cubicles, each populated by one special agent, one government-issue file cabinet, and one desk. There were twelve agents in each group. The managers' offices were positioned along the walls, convenient for supervision.

Gloria stopped at a window on the way to her cube, gazing down at the Calder statue in the center of the square. Most people considered it an abstract version of a giant orange flamingo, but whatever it was, she liked it. The sounds of ringing telephones and cacophony of conversations were the white noise she needed to help pass the time. Intermittent visits from fellow agents giving their support helped, too.

Settled at her desk, Gloria's eyes drifted to the photo of Adsila and Darius. It seemed like she had missed a year of their lives, not only one summer. She thought about Jim Abbott's kids, who had lost their father forever. His life had come to an end because of a faulty bulletproof vest. In her mind, she saw Jim in those final moments, the dark shadow of blood in the center of his body armor. *What was it that marine said about the vest? 'They weren't worth shit.' How could that be?* She tried to shut out his words, but they pounded in her head, and she could feel the flare of anger igniting in her chest. She was sure the Army was paying top dollar for those vests.

Her mind drifted to her husband, holding court in the Dirksen Building across the street. *Is he thinking of me at all today? What I have been through? What I am feeling? Did he have any concept of what might have been?* She didn't think he did. Now the secret would forever remain a secret.

Gloria sighed, swiveled around in her seat, pulled a file drawer open, and lifted out a handful of files on the Henderson case. It had been on hold while she was in Iraq. She read the suspicious activity report filed by the car dealership's bank and shook her head. *More than three hundred thousand dollars in cash deposits, each under ten thousand. Not too crafty.* She opened her IBM laptop, turned it on, and clicked on the case file. The sound of pants legs swishing together as someone approached her cubicle interrupted her.

"Hi, Gloria." Tom Stephens, her supervisory special agent, looked into the cubicle. He carried just a bit of extra weight. He wore a tan, short-sleeve, button-down shirt with a matching tie.

She nodded. *One of the guys on the fast track. What did he work, five or six cases before he was promoted?*

"I bet it's good to be back. Sorry about Jim."

She nodded again. *Why don't you go back into your cubbyhole?*

Stephens stood there silent, using all of his people skills, making her as uncomfortable as hell.

She decided to break the silence. "It was a terrible tragedy." *When is he going to tell me this case is over age? Should have been out of here two months ago.* She saw his eyes drift to the files on her desk and then to the case name on the monitor.

"I'm glad to see you're working on the Henderson case. You know that was over age two months ago."

Gloria cocked her head, "Really, how time flies. I would've gotten it done sooner, but I was putting in sixteen-hour days in Baghdad. Well, except for Sundays, only eight hours then."

"Oh, I know. I'm just saying. Well, it's good to have you back. Always nice to talk to you." Stephens stepped back, tripped over a wastepaper basket, and braced himself against the cubicle wall. "Let me know if I can help you with that report."

"Oh yeah, definitely." She couldn't help but laugh at his awkwardness. It helped her deal with the annoyance she sometimes felt towards him. *Yeah, if I need to fill out a form, you'll be the first one I ask. But if I need help on a case, you'd be the last person I'd ask.*

Her fingers danced across the keyboard as she started typing her recommendation: Seize the funds in the business's bank account and prosecute two of the corporate officers. *If I can prove that they knew this was drug money, they'll get more jail time.*

Her phone rang and she picked up the receiver, "Criminal Investigation Division."

"Is this Agent Nighthawk?" It was a scratchy connection. The man spoke with a middle eastern accent.

"Yes, can I help you?"

"I got your business card from Agent Abbott. He said that if anything happened to him, I should call you."

"Where are you calling from? You know what happened, sir?"

"The attack was planned. I know about the cash and the bribes. I am in Baghdad."

Gloria heard the sound of traffic and the chatter of conversation in the background. She pushed her computer to the side, pulled out a yellow legal pad from her file cabinet, and reached for a pen. "Can you speak louder? It's hard to hear you. What's your name and telephone number?"

"I can't talk louder, someone might hear." There was a groan, yelling in Arabic, "Allahu Akbar." She heard the sound of flesh pounding flesh, then the thud of a body being slammed to the ground. "Let go of me. I know nothing." The phone went dead.

Gloria raised her voice. "Hello, what attack? Hello? Hello? Shit." She dropped the receiver.

Stephens thumped down the aisle and swung into her cubicle. "My God, what's wrong now?"

"What's wrong? Somebody 6,000 miles away who wanted to help just got…pummeled, maybe worse. Something happened in Baghdad. That's what's fucking wrong." She slammed the file cabinet closed and crossed her arms across her chest.

Gloria tightened her fist, her fingernails biting into her palms. *A planned attack, why? Did they know who we were? Who Jim was?* In a controlled tone, she said. "I have to…have to get some fresh air." *I need to figure out what to do.*

CHAPTER 4

St. Mary's Church
Oak Park, Illinois
Friday, September 10, 2004

AFTER THE VISITATION, JIM ABBOTT'S casket was taken to St. Mary's. Abbott had been on the job for twenty years and had worked joint cases with just about every local, state, and federal agency. The rustic church's pews were filled, and people were standing in the back and along the sides.

Gloria stepped up to the heavy wooden doors and pulled them open. She did not want to join anyone else riding from the funeral home to the church because she didn't know if she could maintain control. After all the secrecy, she couldn't risk being unusually emotional. She tiptoed into the church and stood between two men behind the last row of pews, peering between their shoulders at the priest.

Father Dugan said the mass. A spider web of veins creased his shiny red nose. Deep wrinkles stretched from the corners of his eyes, and a thick shag of silver hair hung over his ears. Janice Abbott and her three children were seated in the first row.

"I know there can be no words of comfort to ease the pain you and your children are suffering," Father Dugan told Mrs. Abbott. "But if you can, look around and realize what we all know. Jim Abbott was not your usual man. This is reflected by the love, respect, and admiration evidenced by the turnout here today. God knows this church hasn't been this full in decades." The priest spent some time highlighting Abbott's career achievements and contributions to his community. Several others followed, adding anecdotes of their own, awards he received, noting his coaching his sons' little league teams, and testifying to Abbot's integrity and to the strength of his values.

Gloria felt she knew him better than anyone else other than, probably, his wife, and knew that what was being said was true.

After the mass, Gloria was the first to leave the church. She waited behind the three-deep crowd on the sidewalk as the pallbearers carried the bronze casket down the stairs to the hearse. She looked down at her black pumps and thought, *Army Intelligence keeps track of attacks. They might have something about the man that called. He might have information on why Jim was killed. Why didn't I think of that sooner?*

She looked up and saw Janice Abbott stepping down the stairs with her arms wrapped around their three children, Katie, Josh, and Jim, Jr., Katie the oldest at ten and the boys eight and six. They were all dressed in black and faces were grief stricken. The funeral director opened the rear door of the limousine and Janice herded the children into the car. She turned around, an attractive woman with blonde shoulder-length hair. Janice's glazed eyes searched the crowd and then fixed on Gloria. She stepped away from the limo and walked in Gloria's direction.

Gloria swallowed and took a step back. She thought about what Jim had told her. *Janice is bipolar, hates the way her meds makes her feel. When she's off them she can be explosive and violent.*

Janice kept coming.

Gloria took another step back and forced herself not to run away. Her heart pounded. *What was she doing? What did she want? Did she know?*

Janice approached the men and women standing in front of Gloria. They parted and Janice stopped in front of her. Gloria felt the woman's eyes drilling into her. She averted her eyes from Janice. Her stomach fluttered and head swiveled, looking at everyone watching them.

"You were my husband's partner," Janice's voice was low, but strong. "You spent more time with him than I did. You knew him better than anyone. I need to talk to you. Come to my house tonight at seven. My sister will have the kids. Come alone." She turned around and walked back to the limo.

Eyes turned to Gloria and she could hear murmured conversations in the crowd, people wondering about the conversation. Then the moment passed, the crowd dispersed, and cars lined up behind the hearse and the limo for the funeral procession.

Gloria took a deep breath and decided to avoid the potential for any contact with Janice Abbott at the cemetery. She went back to the office to call the agents in Baghdad.

The office had only a skeleton crew to man the phones. She was glad for the quiet. She sat at her desk and glanced at her watch: 11:00 a.m., which made it 7:00 p.m. in Baghdad. *Nothing to do there but work. Someone will be at the phone.* She pulled up the address book on her cell phone and pushed the button for CID-Baghdad.

"Criminal Investigation Division, Agent Musgrove."

"Bill, it's Gloria."

"What the hell are you doing, calling here? Didn't you get enough of this place?" After a pause he added, "I'm sorry about Jim."

"Thanks, Bill. It was a hellish experience. I just left his funeral mass. A few days ago, I got a call in the office from an unidentified man in Baghdad. He said he knew about the attack, about money and bribes. He was assaulted before he could say anything else. I don't know if he was killed, kidnapped, or what."

"So, you want me to do what?"

"Find out who he is…or was?"

"You know how many hundreds of men have been killed since you left Baghdad?"

"I know, but if you can, would you check with Army Intelligence and the CIA and see if they have any information on an incident that happened last Tuesday morning around ten-thirty Chicago time?"

"Gloria." Musgrove said, sounding like his patience was being taxed.

"Bill, please, do it for Jim."

"Okay, but realistically…."

"I know, the chance of getting anything is slim. But it's all I've got."

"Okay, give me a couple of days. I'll let you know."

She hung up the phone, chewed on the inside of her cheek and thought, *Janice, seven tonight,* and blew out a deep breath.

CHAPTER 5

Janice Abbott's House
Oak Park, Illinois
Friday, September 10, 2004

GLORIA CIRCLED THE BLOCK ONCE. The sun was low, its golden rays breaking up from the horizon. She looked at the house where she had picked up Jim Abbott hundreds of times to go on interviews, execute search warrants, or whatever else they were doing. It was a two-story white frame with a large porch. The lawn was patchy and the shrubbery a little overgrown.

Misses Jim's care. He loved taking care of that house, Gloria thought, as she adjusted her holster that held her P226 semi-automatic Sig Sauer. She parked her black Chevy Blazer in front of the house and headed up the sidewalk. She wore jeans and a lightweight black jacket that covered her holster.

Gloria perused the house, shades drawn, lights off, with a Big Wheel on the porch. She took the three steps up to the porch and listened for any sounds coming from inside. Total quiet. She tapped on the screen door and thought about what Jim had said, *violent when she's off her meds,* and remembered the glazed look in Janice's eyes at the church.

Maybe she crashed, or she decided to be with her kids. Gloria stood there twisting her wedding ring on her finger. *Jim's kids will never see their father again.* She grimaced and bit her lip. Turning to walk down the stairs, she made to leave, then said to herself, "Fuck, she wanted to see me. If there's something I can do that'll help her, I owe Jim that much."

She did an about face and pressed the doorbell but didn't hear the chimes she had heard in the past. *The house is definitely missing Jim.* She opened the screen door and knocked louder on the interior door. The sun was going lower and it was getting darker. She pressed her face against the glass of the door.

The porch light flashed on, and Gloria jumped back. She automatically adjusted her feet to a defensive stance, left foot forward, right foot back, hand near her right hip at her holster, and waited. The curtain inside pulled away, and Janice Abbott's eyes stared at her.

The door creaked open.

"Hi, Janice." Gloria swallowed. Janice was in a pink bathrobe. Her eyes were red and shiny. She nodded, turned, and walked away from the door into the living room. Gloria stepped into the house, closed the door, and followed. The room was furnished with a green sofa tired from the wear of three kids, a brown recliner opposite a television, and an armchair with tan stripes.

Janice sat on the sofa and nodded at the recliner. "That was Jim's chair, always sat there for the Bears, Bulls, and Sox games." She pointed at the armchair. "Why don't you sit there?"

Gloria nodded and sat down. There was a coffee table separating them. She could feel the tension filling the room.

"I didn't know Jim was going to Iraq until a week before he left. When did you know?"

"It wasn't firmed up until about then. You know with the government, many times it's almost a last-minute thing. You remember when they sent us to Georgia to teach at the training center, and notified us on Thursday that we had to be there on Monday?"

Janice nodded, "Yes, but you weren't going to a war zone that time. Christ, this was so fast, so dangerous."

"I know. I'm so sorry for what happened." Gloria exhaled and began to sense that she was just there to help a grieving wife process her feelings—that Janice had no idea what she and Jim were contemplating.

Janice picked a Kleenex from the box on the coffee table and dabbed her eyes.

Gloria felt her eyes well. "Can I have one of those, too?"

Janice pushed the box toward her. Gloria rose from the chair, pulled out a tissue, wiped her eyes, returned to her chair, and curled her lips. She was sitting across from her lover's widow and couldn't get the image of Jim Abbott with a bullet hole in his chest out of her mind.

Janice folded her hands and rested them on her lap. "I don't think he would've gone if you weren't going."

Gloria swallowed. She crossed her legs and her top foot started bobbing. "He was very patriotic. He felt it was his duty."

"I'm sure he told you about my…my problem and how…how I can get sometimes." Janice blinked her eyes. "He would get worried that I might hurt myself or maybe even the kids. Of course, I would never hurt the kids. I promised him that I would take my meds while he was gone. I hate how dead they make me feel. I stopped taking them yesterday."

Gloria shook her head and lied. "No, he never brought that up. Maybe we weren't as close as you think." It seemed like the right thing to say, to calm her down. She could sense emotion building in Janice.

"There's something I want to give you. Wait here," Janice stood and walked out of the living room to the kitchen.

Gloria heard drawers sliding open and slamming shut. She slid her hand back to her holster and unsnapped the keeper. She couldn't believe what she was contemplating—shooting the widow of the man that a few days before she thought would change her world. It made her feel nauseous. She heard the shuffling of Janice's slippered feet returning. Gloria's swinging foot went still.

Janice turned the corner from the hallway and entered the living room. Her right arm was at her side and in her hand was Jim's Sig Sauer. She scuffled between the coffee table and the sofa and sat down, holding the pistol in her lap.

"Janice, why don't you put the pistol on the coffee table?" Gloria's eyes focused on Janice's right hand.

She turned her head and looked out of the corner of her eye. "You don't think I'm going to hurt you, do you?" She smirked.

"No, it's just that a pistol is a dangerous thing. You have to be very careful. If it hasn't been cleaned in a while and checked by a gunsmith, the trigger pull can lighten. It could go off."

"I'm sure Jim took real good care of his pistol. You should know how he took care of everything that was important to him." She looked at Gloria and smiled.

"He always talked about you, the kids and this house. How he loved to work around the house to make it nice for his family."

"And he did," Janice raised her hand and gazed at the Sig. "I hated it when he would take his jacket off and I would see this black pistol hanging on his belt. I would get really mad at him when he did that in front of the kids."

Gloria sat back in her chair, leaned her left side forward, and slid her hand back to the grips of her pistol. "Why don't you put the pistol down on the table?"

Janice bent at the hip, lowered her hand to the table, and tilted her head, gazing at Gloria. Then she released the pistol.

Gloria leaned forward and grasped the gun. "I'll take this back to the office for you, so you don't have to worry about the kids playing with it." She slipped the pistol into her waistband.

"Thanks. There was one more thing I wanted to show you." She reached into the pocket of her robe.

Gloria's hand shifted back to her Sig.

Janice paused and removed a letter-sized envelope. She laid it on the coffee table. "I found it in Jim's desk. I don't know what to do with it."

Gloria's brow furrowed. She grasped the envelope, opened it, and saw that it was stuffed with one-hundred-dollar bills. "How much is in here?"

"Ten thousand dollars."

"Good grief! Do you have any idea where this cash came from?" Gloria couldn't hide her surprise.

"No, I haven't worked for ten years, since the kids were born. We just live on Jim's salary. You know how much that is. We're not rich. With five mouths to feed, we barely had enough to pay the bills and maybe go out to eat once a month."

"I've seen enough crap in the world. If that money can do a single good thing, you keep it and don't tell anyone. You and the kids deserve it. I'm going to take the first bill, the last one, the plastic wrap, and the envelope. I'll get back to you if I find anything out." She rose from her chair, hugged Janice, and left.

CHAPTER 6

G LORIA HOPPED INTO THE BLAZER and pulled a clear plastic evidence bag
out of a box on the back seat. She placed the hundred-dollar bills, the
shrink wrap, and the envelope into the bag and sealed it. She didn't want to
think about what that money in Jim's possession might mean. She headed to
Harlem Avenue, entering the Eisenhower Expressway westbound instead of
heading east to her house in the Bronzeville section of the city. She picked up
her cell phone and hit the speed dial for Bill Ramirez.

When he answered, Gloria said, "Hi, Bill, it's Gloria Nighthawk. I just
picked up some evidence that I need checked for prints. Do you mind if I stop
by your house and drop it off?"

"This can't wait until Monday?"

"It's a special situation. I'll explain it when I get to your place."

"You like pepperoni pizza? I'll save you a slice, that is if the kids haven't
devoured it by time you get here."

"Thanks, Bill. I should be there in about twenty minutes."

Gloria merged from the Eisenhower to I-88 westbound and exited south
on Highland Avenue into Downers Grove. The man she was going to see,
Special Agent Bill Ramirez, was assigned to the IRS forensic lab. In a few
minutes, she pulled into the drive of a brick ranch house with a two-car
attached garage and parked behind a familiar-looking government vehicle, a
2001 dark green, four-door Ford Crown Victoria. She rang the doorbell and

hoped Ramirez could hear it over the laughter of kids and the booming of the television. The door opened, and Ramirez stood with a slice of pizza in his hand. His hair was thinning, with gray intruding on the black. He wore a black White Sox T-shirt and blue jeans. "Come on in. Welcome to my version of the insane asylum."

Gloria stepped in and saw three boys and a girl in their early teens at the dining room table, laughing and eating. *Joan of Arcadia* was on the television and being completely ignored. "Kids, say hi to Ms. Nighthawk." There was no response. "See how they listen to me? Fortunately, they're not all mine." He glanced at the evidence bag in her hand. "Let's go to the kitchen so we can talk."

They sat at the kitchen table. Gloria paused, thinking that she just spent ninety days in Iraq away from her kids and now, the first Friday after she'd returned, she's away from them again. She put off thinking about her priorities and placed the evidence bag on the yellow Formica tabletop. The appliances and cabinets showed some age but weren't quite ready for replacement. It was a homey kitchen, lived-in and welcoming.

"That was tough news about Jim," Ramirez said.

"That's part of the reason I'm here."

Ramirez's brow furrowed. "That was in Iraq. How can I help about that?"

"Bill, we've known each other for, what, fifteen years? I have a favor to ask of you. This is very sensitive. Normally, I would go through channels, but I can't, not at this time, anyway."

Ramirez shook his head and scratched his temple. "I don't understand."

"If you can just do what I ask you to do and not ask me why, you're better off. I promise you when the time comes, I'll explain it, and you'll agree this was the way it had to be done."

He leaned back in his chair and tilted his head. "Does this have to do with Jim's death, with Iraq?"

"The truth is, I don't know." She slid the evidence envelop toward him. "I'd like you to check these two bills, the plastic wrap, and this envelope for prints."

"I can do that, no problem. But if you want the prints identified, then they have to go to the FBI lab. You know that requires an official request."

"If you can just tell me how many prints are on them? How many individuals might have handled them? Maybe I'll know more by then and can request identification."

"How many individuals? That's a shot in the dark. Unless I can say that the prints are from a certain finger and they're on the envelope in several places." Ramirez shook his head, grabbed the bag, and tapped it on the kitchen table. "I'll do what you ask. Obviously, this is between you and me." His tone lacked enthusiasm.

"Of course."

"One more thing." He paused and gave her an evil eye. "Do you want me to see if there's any pizza left?"

"I'm good. Thanks, Bill."

"I'll call you Monday afternoon."

"Thanks." She left, heading back to the city.

CHAPTER 7

IRS-CID Office
Chicago
Monday, September 13, 2004

GLORIA WAS AT HER DESK, focused on her work. She wore a blue, cap-sleeve T-shirt, khakis, and Merrill boots. Her Sig was holstered on her hip. She didn't dress to impress. She was reviewing a spreadsheet she had prepared that listed eighteen vehicles purchased from Henderson Luxury Autos, each paid for with more than thirty thousand in cash. They were Cadillacs, Lexuses, Porches, Corvettes, and other high-priced cars.

"Got to find out who really owns these," she mumbled, and looked up to gaze at the photo of Darius and Adsila. She moved the gold frame so her children's eyes faced her. Touching the photo gave her a warm feeling. She sighed. *Back to work.*

She pulled out a group of folders that contained the deal jackets and copies of titles for the vehicles. The first folder was for a 2002 Corvette convertible, purchased in the name of Versie Bambridge, a sixty-three-year-old African American woman who lived on the west side of Chicago and, according to the sales invoice, paid $40,000 cash for the car. Her tax returns indicated that she worked at a daycare center, never earned more than $20,000 a year, and had no bank accounts. "Versie, you're going to get a visit from your friendly IRS agent, namely me."

"Hi, Gloria," Tom Stephens said.

Gloria looked up and saw her supervisor. Behind him stood an attractive, tall young woman.

"Gloria, this is a Special Agent Lauren Ashberry. She finished her year in the training group, just returned from the training center, and she's been assigned to our group. Lauren, Gloria is one of the best agents in the division. I'm sure you'll learn a lot from her."

I yelled at you and you get even by saddling me with a rookie agent. Gloria drew in a deep breath, released it, stood, and shook hands with Lauren. "Nice to meet you." Lauren was a head taller than Gloria, blonde shoulder-length hair, slender, fair skin, and blue eyes. She wore a navy-blue pants suit, white blouse, and matching open-toe pumps, revealing red nail polish on her toes. *She's dressed to impress, but will she work?*

Gloria's eyes shifted to Stephens's. "Tom, I'm meeting an informant on the west side in half an hour, and then interviewing some of the buyers from Henderson. You sure you want to subject Lauren to that right off the bat? She's dressed very nicely, and we might end up in some places that aren't too nice. I can get another agent to go with me today, and she can go out with me on another day."

Stephens shook his head. "We want Lauren to get right into the swing of things. I'm sure she wants to jump-start her career and gain the experience of working with an agent like you. See how things are done by the book. That'll be perfect."

"Yes, Mrs. Nighthawk, I really would like to go out with you," Lauren said.

Gloria paused, then thought of another reason not to be saddled with the rookie. "We might be out late. Is she on premium pay?"

"No, she's not, but I'll give her comp time if necessary. I'm sure things will work out fine." Stephens nodded and sauntered off.

Gloria pinched her lips together and stuffed the deal jacket into her black leather briefcase. She swung the strap over her shoulder and said. "Lauren, around here we're all partners. There's no Mr. or Mrs. It's Gloria."

"Yes, Ma'am. I mean Gloria." Lauren said., correcting herself with a little laugh.

"Yeah, let's go. Marvin will be waiting for us."

They headed out to the federal garage; a six-story gray cement building tacked onto the twenty-eight-story federal lock-up. They hopped into the Blazer and went west on the Eisenhower Expressway.

"I heard you just got back from Iraq. I was on my way here from training, so I missed the funeral. I'm sorry about Agent Abbott," Lauren said.

"It was tough." Lauren's mention of Jim Abbott sent Gloria's thoughts once again to why he had had ten thousand in cash stowed in his desk. But there was no one to talk to about it and only one thing to do now, change the subject. "Are you from Chicago?"

"Yes, I grew up in Morton Grove. Went to DePaul."

"Good. I know a lot of new agents are assigned offices anywhere in the country. You must have done well at the training center to be assigned in your hometown."

Lauren nodded and held her head high. "I was first in my class."

"You did a lot better than me." *I'll probably be working for her when Stephens gets promoted,* she thought. "Working in the field can be a lot different than in the classroom. Anyway, we're going to be meeting one of my informants. He's worked for me about five years. He did some time on a drug charge and that gives him credibility with some of the druggers. I want to bounce the names of the cash buyers from Henderson's car dealership off him." Gloria took a minute to fill Lauren in on some of the case details.

"Anyhow," Gloria continued, "the dealership didn't prepare any 8300 forms documenting the cash payments over ten thousand, and then they structured the bank deposits so there was never more than ten thousand in a single deposit. Obviously, the dealership hoped that the bank wouldn't file currency transaction reports, which they didn't. But they did file a suspicious activity report detailing the cash deposits. If the informant can identify any of these buyers as straw purchasers, it'll help us lock up Henderson's officers for a lot longer."

"Sounds like you're about to nail this one," said Lauren. She paused, looked out the window and then back at Gloria. "If you don't mind my asking, how long have you been an agent?" Lauren asked.

"You're testing my math skills. Let's see, twenty-four years."

"That's a long time."

Gloria sighed, "Tell me about it." She looked at the line of red brake lights dancing off and on in front of her. It was the beginning of rush hour traffic.

"Sorry, I didn't mean to get too personal."

"No problem. You're going be asking people questions a lot more personal than that. You seem more like a CPA type. What got you interested in being a special agent?" Gloria stepped on the brake as the traffic slowed to a crawl.

"I worked for my dad at his accounting firm during summers and holidays. But I hated accounting, majored in it only because of him."

"Didn't he want you to become a CPA?"

"I am a CPA, took the test my senior year while the accounting was fresh in my mind. But I had an uncle who was a federal agent and that sounded a lot more interesting. So here I am," Lauren said.

"What's your uncle's name? Maybe I know him."

"He's the black sheep of the family. He went to jail. I haven't seen him in years. He's my mother's brother, Frank Mazini."

"Yeah, well, you don't want to make it that interesting. Maybe I'm the one who's prying a little too much." She remembered the name but didn't want to go to such a dark place on their first day together.

They exited at Austin Boulevard, headed north, and turned east on Jackson Boulevard into Columbus Park, pulling to the curb behind a late-model yellow Cadillac Fleetwood. A black male in his late forties got out the Cadillac and looked around. He wore all black, an FUBU hoodie pulled over his face, baggie slacks, and canvas shoes. He climbed into the back seat of the Blazer and lowered his hood, his diamond stud earrings sparkling in the sunlight.

Gloria turned in her seat and faced her informant. "Marvin, this is Agent Ashberry. She's assisting me with a case on the Henderson dealership."

Marvin smiled, showing off a diamond in his one front tooth. "Cool, never met with two woman agents before."

"It's a new world, Marvin," Gloria said.

"That it be."

"Marvin, there've been a lot of cars purchased with cash at the Henderson dealership, and some of the deals don't make any sense. There's no way some of these people could come up with the amounts of cash paid for these cars." She handed Marvin her list of the eighteen high-priced cars and their buyers. "Any of these names mean anything to you?"

Marvin held the sheet in his hand, glanced at it, and laid it on the seat beside him. A black Cadillac El Dorado slowly pulled by. Rap music blasted from it, and eyes gazed at them. Marvin pulled his hood up and sank down in the seat.

"You know those people?" Gloria asked.

"No, but don't pay for Marvin to be seen. Haven't seen you in a while. Where you been?"

"I was out of town, just got back."

"Where'd you go?"

"On assignment, you know, can't talk about it."

"Yeah, some top-secret shit." He waved his hands in front of his face. "I got that, but you know, Marvin could use some cash."

"I don't have any cash on me. I can get you some in a couple of days. You know it takes a few days to get it approved."

"Well, that don't help me none. I need cash now. Lost my job and need money to feed my kids."

"Marvin, I can give you some of my personal cash, but you'll have to sign a receipt for it when I give you the G's money. You know I'll take my money back out of the G's."

"Fuckin' works for me."

Gloria took her credentials out of her pocket, opened them and pulled a hundred-dollar bill out from behind her badge, and handed it to Marvin. He grabbed the bill, stuffed it into his pants pocket, and picked up the list. "This Bambridge lady, you don't know who that is?"

"Educate me, Marvin," Gloria said.

He spread his hands out, palms up. "Shit, that's got to be worth five bills alone."

"Two hundred is all you're getting, unless you know who the shooter was on the grassy knoll."

He sat erect; eyes wide. "Marvin don't know, but for a few more Benjamins he can find out."

Gloria's eyes shot to the ceiling. "Who's Bambridge, Marvin?"

"That's Jim Dandy's grandmama."

Lauren pulled a palm-sized spiral notebook out of her pocket and scribbled the name.

Gloria took a deep breath and released it. "Who's Jim Dandy?"

"Willie Jordan, man. He's got the spot in K-town, on Kedvale, couple blocks north of Madison. All those boys slinging dope belong to him. You don't know 'bout him? That's gotta be worth somethin'."

"You know where Bambridge lives?"

"Jim Dandy bought a house for her. It was made by that guy that designed them houses in Oak Park."

Gloria drummed her fingers on the steering wheel. "What guy?"

Marvin scratched the back of his head. "You know, that White guy."

"Wright, Frank Lloyd Wright," said Lauren.

"Yeah, that's the guy. Your new sidekick here – quiet, but she got some smarts." He gazed at Lauren. Gloria raised her eyebrows. "Oh, yeah, the house. It be on Central, just north of Madison. It be painted mellllow yelllllow." Marvin laughed

"That's good. Anybody else you know?"

"Yeah, this guy, Wilson. He's one of Spencer McElroy's homies. You know the Gangster Disciples? Call themselves the GDs. Well, McElroy's a real GD honcho, you know, high up. Wilson's a janitor at a grammar school. He ain't got no money. How much they say he pay?"

Can't tell you how much because you talk too much, Gloria thought. "Where's Wilson live?"

"Don't know, but he works at that school on Franklin, couple blocks north of Chicago."

"Anyone else on that list you know?"

He lifted a pack of Juicy Fruit gum from his pocket, pulled out a stick, rolled it into a ball, and placed it in his mouth, as if buying himself time to think of something else that might be worth money. "No, that's it. Don't know anybody else."

"You did good, that helps."

"So how much you gonna get for me?"

"I'll get you another hundred."

Marvin leaned back into his seat. "Ah, come on, this worth more than two hundred. Gots to feed my kids."

"I know, Marvin. What you gave me is good, but it's only worth two hundred and you know it. You get me more, I'll give you more. You want to testify?"

"Shit no, that's not our deal."

"Then that's all you get."

"Shiiit." He opened the door and left, doing his pimp stroll back to the Cadillac.

"Lauren don't put anything about the hundred, or anything at all about money, in your notes. Technically I've got to have Stephens approve it before I can get the cash out of an imprest fund."

Lauren ripped the page out of the notebook and crumpled it up in her hand. "I'd rather not leave any evidence of not following procedures. It's a little too early in my career to do that."

Gloria opened her hand and Lauren dropped the ball of paper into her palm. *Learns fast. A little snotty, but smart.* "Sometimes you have to skirt some of the policies to get things done on the street."

"Yes, Ma'am, I mean, Gloria."

"Don't tell Stephens either. He wouldn't understand."

Lauren tossed a strand of her blond hair off her face with a shake of her head. "I figured you didn't want anything in my notes, you wouldn't want me to tell him about your way of doing things by the book."

Gloria started the Blazer and shook her head. "Who would paint a Frank Lloyd Wright house yellow?"

"I took an architecture course. That house is not actually a Wright design. It was designed by one of his students, very similar, but not the same."

"Well, that's a different story. Let's go see if we can find Versie Bambridge."

CHAPTER 8

West Side of Chicago
Monday, September 13, 2004
4:30 p.m.

GLORIA HEADED EAST ON JACKSON, driving parallel to the fairway for the first hole of the Columbus Park district golf course. Three young black kids bolted out of the woods, grabbed the golf balls that had been hit onto the fairway, and disappeared back into the woods.

"Did you see that?" Lauren asked.

"Boys will be boys," Gloria said. "They'll sell the golf balls back to them on the sixth hole for a quarter apiece." She turned north on Central Avenue, past a few graffiti-covered six-flats and a couple of burned-out buildings, and crossed Madison. The yellow Frank Lloyd Wright look-a-like was on the west side of the street.

Gloria glanced at her watch, hoping to get rid of Lauren. "It's four-thirty, your day is officially over. If you have some plans, I could drive you home. This interview could take a while."

"I've got nothing happening that can't wait."

"No boyfriend waiting to take you out for dinner?"

"Nope, no boyfriend. He got a job in San Francisco. Didn't take long to find out that a long-distance relationship wasn't going to work. Especially when he came up with a new girlfriend in two weeks."

"Sorry about that. Man problems can be a life-long plague. If I drop you off at your place—"

"Don't have a place. Live with my parents and they left yesterday for a three-week vacation in Europe. I've got the whole house to myself."

"Peace and quiet, that sounds nice." Gloria gave up and glanced at the house. "No sign of life in the front. Let's head down the alley." She turned west on Washington and then south down the alley. "Look at that, can't beat dumb luck." A gray Chevrolet Cavalier idled in front of the garage as the door rose. The car pulled into the garage and Gloria eased the Blazer forward. They saw an elderly woman, built like a boxcar, exit the driver's seat, grab a cane out of the car, hobble toward the service door, and press a button. The garage door eased down. "Think it's safe to say she's not driving a Corvette around town. Let's give her a few minutes to settle in before we knock on her door."

Gloria parked on Central. Minutes later she and Lauren stood at the front door. Gloria knocked. "Take good notes for this interview," Gloria said.

Lauren cocked her head. "You sure?"

Gloria sighed. "You sure you don't have to get home?"

The door creaked open, and the lady from the garage stood there. "Can I help you?"

"Yes, Ma'am," Gloria said. They presented their badges and identification. "We're special agents with the Criminal Investigation Division of the IRS. We would like to ask you a few questions. Can we come in and talk to you?"

The woman had short-cropped gray hair, wore a dark-green, short-sleeved, dress that hung on her like a tent, and white canvas slip-on shoes. "IRS? Lord, what's this about?"

Gloria said. "You're Mrs. Bambridge, right? We'd like to come in."

"Yes, all right, come in." She backed away from the door. "You can sit here." She pointed to a black leather sofa.

Across from the sofa was a wall-mounted, flat-screen TV. A glass dining table with six matching black leather chairs and a matching sideboard were visible in the dining room.

"Your house is decorated very nicely," Gloria said.

"It's my grandson. He treats me real good. I wish he wouldn't be so loose with his money. I tell 'im, you've got to save for a rainy day. Would you like some iced tea?"

"No, thank you. We won't be long. We don't want to keep you from your dinner."

"I usually take a nap before I fix dinner. I work at the daycare center and those kids just poop me out." She waved her arm, and the fat jiggled as she plopped into a recliner across from the sofa.

"We are looking into the Henderson Luxury Auto dealership. I've got a bill of sale for a 2002 Corvette that was purchased in your name." Gloria stood, moved toward the recliner, knelt next to it, and showed her the bill of sale. "Is this your car?"

Mrs. Bambridge reached for the invoice and held it close to her eyes. "A Corvette," she laughed. "Could you see me getting in and out of that car?" She handed the document back to Gloria.

"Did you pay for it with your money?"

"What was the price, that car?" Mrs. Bambridge asked.

"Forty thousand dollars." Gloria said.

"All I got to my name is three hundred dollars in a cookie jar."

"Is your grandson Willie Jordan?"

"He's my grandbaby, raised him since he was two." She held her hand out, knee high. "What's this got to do with him?"

"Isn't this car his, and wasn't the money used to purchase the Corvette his money?"

A creaking noise came from upstairs.

Gloria glanced at Lauren, alerting her to the unknown.

A voice called from the upstairs, "Hello, grandmama."

"Down here, Willie."

A dark-skinned man stepped into the room. He wore black leather pants and was tucking a black knit shirt into his waistband. "Who are these people?"

He yawned, but Gloria felt his eyes drill into her and then shift to Lauren. Lauren looked up from her notebook.

"We're with the IRS." Gloria stood and flashed her badge. "We're conducting an investigation of Henderson Luxury Auto, and we were asking your grandmother about a car that was purchased in her name."

"Which car?"

Lauren moved her jacket away from her right hip.

"A black 2002 Corvette convertible."

"Well, what she say?"

"I'm not allowed to tell anyone what a witness says," Gloria said.

Gloria saw Willie's eyes veer toward his grandmother, "What you say—"

"That's your car isn't it, Willie?" Lauren said.

Gloria's head swiveled and she stared at Lauren. She tried to control her expression. *What the hell is she doing?*

"Yous the tax police. I ain't got to answer your questions. I got rights." Willie lapsed into serious street talk.

Gloria's gaze swung back to Willie. Wanting to reestablish control, she held her hands up and said, "Calm down, Mr. Jordan. You're not under investigation, the dealership is. So why wouldn't you answer my questions?"

Lauren stood and pointed at Jordan. "That was your cash, wasn't it?"

"I ain't talking to you no more and neither is my grandmama. You all can leave right now." He marched to the front door and opened it.

Gloria curled her lips and felt her face flush. "Come on, let's go." She stomped out of the house. Lauren followed, and Gloria felt Jordan's eyes on them as they climbed into the Blazer.

Gloria slammed her door, put the SUV in gear, and squealed away from the curb.

Lauren leaned toward Gloria. "Why didn't you press him more?"

Gloria raised her hand, palm facing Lauren. "Don't say another word. Where the hell did you learn to interview? You ever hear of contact agent and cover agent? An interview isn't a race between agents to ask questions. What in God's name are they teaching in training nowadays? Next time, if there is a next time, keep your mouth shut." Gloria all but ground her teeth. *Some partner*, she thought.

Gloria's cell phone rang. She yanked it from her belt and practically shouted, "What!"

"Gloria, its Bill Ramirez. If this isn't a good time to talk, I can call later."

Gloria shifted in her seat away from Lauren and slowed the car down. "Sorry, Bill. Go ahead."

"Got some info for you. There were several prints on the envelope, the plastic wrap, and the two bills. Some were on all four docs, but it's not possible to really tell how many people the prints were from."

"Thanks, Bill, I appreciate your doing that for me. I'll be in touch if something else—"

"Hold on. I did find out one interesting thing. An old college buddy of mine works for the New York Federal Reserve. I gave him a call because of the shrink-wrap with New York Fed printed on it. He checked the serial numbers of the two hundred-dollar bills. Get this, those bills were part of a cash shipment of 2.4 billion dollars sent by the Fed to Iraq on June 22 for the Oil-for-

Food Program. Let me repeat that: It was all in cash. One hundred thousand dollars in each shrink-wrapped package."

"How much did you say was in each package?"

"A hundred grand."

Gloria's eyebrows rose. *Janice said there was ten thousand in that envelope. What was she doing? Did she have a whole package? A whole hundred thousand dollars? Was she looking for my reaction?*

"You still there?" Ramirez asked.

"Yeah, sorry, Bill. Go ahead."

"My buddy said that the Fed has shipped numerous pallets full of cash over there because Iraq doesn't have a central bank to process financial transactions, so everything is paid for by cash. Gloria, one more thing. We have a set of employee fingerprint cards. I'm pretty sure that one of the prints was Jim Abbott's. How did Jim Abbott get ahold of those bills?"

Gloria froze. "I don't know how he would have gotten those bills. I might have to talk to your friend at the Fed. Can't talk right now. I'll call you later." She closed her phone. *One hundred thousand in each package, and I told her to keep what was left from the envelope she gave me.* "Unfucking believable," she mumbled.

"What's that about?" Lauren asked.

"It's confidential, on a need-to-know basis, and you don't need to know." Gloria was still angry. She relented a bit and added, "It's not related to the Henderson case." The image of Jim Abbott dead in the back seat of the Humvee shifted to one of him holding a hundred grand in his hands. She wondered whether Abbott had had his own agenda for going to Iraq, a mission that had nothing to do with their relationship.

CHAPTER 9

IRS-CID
Chicago
Tuesday, September 14, 2004
7:30 a.m.

G LORIA ARRIVED AT HER DESK, and before she could set down her nearly empty Starbucks and drop her black leather satchel, Tom Stephens was there.

He leaned against her cube's partition. "How did things go with Lauren yesterday? I think she has the potential to be a really good agent."

Gloria lifted the satchel strap from her shoulder, placed the bag on her desk, unzipped the top, and pulled her Sig out of the built-in holster. "She did all right for the first time out in the field." Gloria thought, *she'll learn.* She unlocked her file cabinet and gun safe and stashed the pistol.

"Good. I'm glad it worked out between you two."

"You could say that." Her eyes rose toward the ceiling.

"Let's have a meeting as soon as Lauren gets in to discuss yesterday's contacts."

"If you don't mind, I'd like to get settled and get another coffee." Gloria took her first real glance at Stephens and noticed he was wearing a matching blue shirt and tie in contrast to his previous matching tan ensemble. *No problem mixing or matching for this guy. I bet everything's planned for the week and today even his boxers are blue.*

"Sure. Whenever you're ready, just bring her in." Stephens did an about face and marched to his office.

A few minutes later, Lauren showed up at Gloria's desk. She was wearing a cranberry-colored pants suit, a black blouse, and pumps. Gloria looked down at her Merrills, tan khakis, and green pullover. "You must have spent your allowance from daddy on clothes." Gloria noticed Lauren glance at her boots.

"I like to look professional." She cocked her head.

"Stephens wants to see us to talk about how things went yesterday. You remember what I told you about your notes and the money."

"Don't you remember? I gave my notes to you. I don't know what you did with them."

"I'll meet you in his office. I'm getting more coffee." Gloria went to the coffeemaker in a cubbyhole not far from her desk, and then to Stephens's office. Lauren was sitting in one of the two chairs in front of his desk. Gloria sat down, brought the cup to her lips, and frowned at the aroma. She placed the cup and the imprest fund request on Stephens's desk. "The informant identified two nominees that were used as straw purchasers on two of the vehicles bought from Henderson's."

Stephens picked up the request. "Two hundred dollars seems like a lot of money for a little information."

"We didn't have any positive information on the purchasers until the CI gave us this."

"Have you prepared the memorandum of interview?"

"Not yet, Tom. The interviews were late yesterday afternoon."

He slid the request back to Gloria, "Why don't you give this back to me with copies of your memos and then I can better evaluate your request."

"This informant has worked for me for five years. Whether you agree with the amount for the information he gave or not, we want to keep this relationship going," Gloria said, thinking, *Wish I had a supervisor I didn't have to explain this to.*

"The informant was very helpful, and he could be in a very precarious situation, "Lauren said.

Gloria glanced at Lauren. *That's a turnabout.* "We corroborated the validity of his information when we interviewed Versie Bambridge." Her eyes shifted from Lauren to Stephens. "The CI identified Bambridge as the grandmother of a drug dealer by the name of Willie Jordan. We interviewed her yesterday, too. She gave us enough testimony to prove she was a nominee, and for us to get a money laundering count on Jordan. In fact, we could even get one on old Versie herself, if we want to put pressure on Jordan."

Stephens leaned back in his chair and put his feet on his desk. He raised an eyebrow and gave a thumbs up. "That's great. I'm glad everything worked out so well. I knew it would be a good experience for Lauren to work with you. I think I'd like to see you two be partners. You know, Gloria, you'll need a new partner anyway. Give me both memos of interview when you return the imprest fund request. I really think that a hundred would be adequate for your informant." Stephens slid his chair back and grabbed his phone off his credenza, signifying the end of the meeting. Then he cradled the phone. "You two only have one case between you. Gloria, I want you to take over the currency transaction report project. The printouts are in the file cabinet against the wall outside of my office. We need to generate more cases. Our inventory is getting low." He picked up the phone again and mumbled, "Could affect my merit pay."

Gloria shook her head. *Lauren's a rookie, but she's coming around, and Stephens is an inexperienced manager; I can deal with them. But, Janice Abbott, what're you up to?*

CHAPTER 10

Arlington Cemetery
Arlington, Virginia
Thursday, September 16, 2004
3:00 p.m.

JACK NESTOR TOOK A DEEP breath, inhaling the sweet aroma of freshly mown grass at Arlington National Cemetery. He stumbled through the sea of white headstones until he found his father's grave. He pulled a stainless-steel flask from his suit pocket, unscrewed the cap, and took a swig. It was not his first drink, and liquor often made him talk to himself.

"Jack Daniels, Pops, or do you still want me to address you as Colonel Braxton Nestor? You son of a bitch." He scowled and took another gulp.

"I could have beaten that court-martial. They didn't have shit on me. One witness, James Abbott, who said I went against orders when I told those boys to go ahead. Who knew that sandstorm would fuck up everything?"

He took another swig. "You said that I had to protect the family's reputation. We had spilled Nestor blood from Gettysburg to Da Nang. Resign and our name will be protected from the public embarrassment of a court-martial. Fuck them and fuck you. Fuck all you dead bastards." Nestor jammed the flask into his pocket. He scanned the cemetery and saw visitors at nearby headstones. *If they weren't here, I'd piss on your grave.*

"I got the best of everyone. They say the best revenge is living well. That's what I do better than anyone else in the Nestor family. Got millions in cash from the Department of Defense. Joke's on them. The ones who were going to court marital me are the same ones that are lining my pockets."

Nestor stumbled a quarter of a mile toward the late afternoon sun and stopped at a lone tree, a Cedar-of-Lebanon. He heard a cardinal's song and looking into the bright rays of the sun for the bird, could only make out its silhouette. Shielding his eyes, he looked to the ground and read the plaque memorializing this tree to the 'Beirut Victims of Terrorism.' Guilt seized him, but he continued toward his intended destination, the Iran Rescue Mission Monument, a bronze plate mounted on a white stone marker. He took another hit from the flask, then folded his arms across his chest. "Operation Eagle Claw was going to bring home the fifty-three hostages held by the Iranians. Once again the Nestor name would be honored on the battlefield." He spat at the monument. "Instead, a few fuckers made me their scapegoat."

He glanced at the names of the three marines and five airmen who had died in the fiery collision of two aircraft. From a distance, the sorrowful cry of taps brought a tear to his eyes despite himself, and he flinched at the volley of a twenty-one-gun salute for a recently fallen soldier. "You guys haunted me every day of my life until I figured out you were just collateral damage on the way to my goal—living well.

"Then what happens? My old second-in-command, James Abbott, comes back into my life."

His vision blurred and the words on the brass plaque fuzzed out. "Well, Jimbo, now you're collateral damage. The joke is tomorrow, when I watch his old lady get a medal for her old man's courageous deeds, and I give her ten grand to ease my conscience." He lifted the flask out of his pocket and drained it. "Good to the last drop. Adios, Jimbo."

———◇———

September 17, 2004

Friday morning in the Chicago CID conference room, Chief Tony Spagnola was behind the podium in a charcoal-gray suit. Directly behind him was a portrait of President George W. Bush, and next to it the stars and stripes. To the far left and behind the chief, Gloria Nighthawk sat in a chair on the stage. She felt feverish, a bead of sweat trickled down from her eyebrow, and her muscles ached. She wore a black pants suit and had unbuttoned the top button of her white blouse, loosening the collar around her neck.

Seated on her right was the Under Secretary of Defense for Intelligence, John Blanton, wearing a navy-blue pinstripe suit. To the right of the president's portrait sat Janice Abbott and her three red-eyed children, once again all dressed as though for a funeral. To the right of the Abbott family sat a man Gloria didn't know. The audience, composed of agents, secretaries, clerks, and Gloria's children, filled all the seats. People stood in the back and along the sides of the conference room. The chief spoke of the bravery and patriotism of Nighthawk and Abbott, about the important work they had volunteered to do, the attack, and how Nighthawk had saved PFC Daniel's life and killed two insurgents.

The words were white noise to Gloria. Her eyes were locked in a frozen gaze. She saw the faces of her son and daughter and the empty chair next to them for her husband. It seemed preposterous to her that, in a way, this event was a celebration of death.

Her mind drifted to the only death she ever celebrated, Timothy McVeigh's execution on June 11, 2001. Last June she had popped a cork from a bottle of champagne with Jim Abbott in Iraq. The irony hit her then that McVeigh's execution was three months to the day before the 9/11 bombings that led to the invasion of Iraq in March 2003, and to her being there fifteen months later.

But this only reminded her that her parents would be alive if her mother hadn't found that job in the daycare center of the Murrah Federal Building. She had argued with her mother once again over why she had left Oklahoma City and had chased the agent's job to Chicago. The next morning, that terrible Wednesday, Gloria had overslept, so her father had driven her mother to work instead.

A click from the microphone brought her back to the moment. She turned her head toward Janice Abbott and the three children. Blanton leaned forward and gave her a smile. *He thinks I'm looking at him. Fool.* She shook her head, bent at the waist, and watched Janice, who was wiping a tear from her eye with a white handkerchief. Her children sat in a daze.

The chief put his notes down and turned to Blanton, who went to the podium and shook Spagnola's hand. Spagnola sat on Gloria's left. Blanton settled in at the podium and spouted on, basking in the glory of having this opportunity to present the medals. He opened a brown leather box containing the Secretary of Defense Medal for Valor.

"This medal is given by the Defense Department only in situations where private citizens have exhibited amazing bravery. It is a five-point star laid on top of a laurel wreath inscribed with the word, "Valor." On the reverse side of each medal is inscribed the names of today's recipients, James Abbott and Gloria Nighthawk. Below their names are the words, "FOR EXHIBITING BRAVERY." The medal is suspended by an ultramarine ribbon. On either side of the ribbon are two stripes of old glory red, and inside the red are two thin stripes of white. Now I call Mrs. James Abbott and her children to the podium."

They trudged together in a protective huddle. Blanton babbled on and presented the medal to them.

Gloria's emotions were running rampant. She felt powerless in the grip of her subconscious. There were images that could not be exorcised from her mind. She saw herself crumbling to her knees at the ruins of the Murrah Federal Building when she saw the rear of her father's red pickup truck under the debris. Fraught with guilt, her sobs so loud she could barely hear the words spilling out of her mouth, "God, no. God almighty, no." Then the image of Jim Abbott flashed in front of her eyes. He was leaning against the seat in the back of the Humvee, the bloom of blood on his bulletproof vest. On the stage, she gasped for air; she smelled the cordite and felt the fear once again.

Gloria wiped the tears welling in her eyes, sorry for the pain Janice and her children were feeling, even sorrier for being the reason Jim had been in Iraq. She felt his blood on her hands. She had put her parents in death's way and had gone through the grieving process, but now the grief returned. And now, some man in Iraq she didn't know had likely been murdered for calling her. *My body count is mounting.*

The chief nudged her. She looked at him and swiveled her head toward Blanton, who was standing at the podium holding her medal. Her bottom lip trembled. Her grief had been lurking in the shadows. Now, it was a roaring hurricane that picked up strength, whipped ashore, and devastated everything in its path. Her stomach roiled; she dropped her head into her hands, then jumped up, ran across the stage, and exited through a side door.

There was a pause, and Lauren saw the chief step up and accept the medal on Gloria's behalf. Lauren went to Gloria's children, and escorted them out through the rear exit into a smaller conference room. "Wait here. I'll find your mother and bring her back to you." Stephens joined them, and Lauren left to search for Gloria.

Lauren first checked the room where the ceremony was taking place to see whether Gloria had returned. Her seat was empty. The chief was introducing the man seated to the right of Abbott family.

"Ladies and gentlemen, we have one more person to introduce: Jack Nestor, former US Army colonel and president of Standard Armor & Supply. His company produces, supplies, and transports many of the weapons, armament, and other materials used by our troops to protect and defend themselves. There is a side to the company of which most Americans are unaware. When tragedy strikes, Standard Armor & Supply is there to do whatever they can to ease the burden for our soldiers and their families."

Lauren watched, mesmerized, as Nestor rose from his chair. He was greeted by polite applause, shook the chief's hand, and nodded at Blanton as if he didn't know him. He stepped to the podium. Barely a head taller than the podium, Nestor stood with a tight military posture and a GI haircut. His physique was hard and lean, cheeks sunken with a red burn scar on his left cheek. He had blue eyes. He wore a pressed black suit, crisp white shirt, a red tie, and spit-shined shoes.

He turned to Janice Abbott. "My mission today is to let Mrs. Abbott know that she's not alone. The people of Standard Armor & Supply will be available to help you in any manner we can." He turned back to the audience. "We've started a scholarship fund for the Abbott children with an initial deposit of ten thousand dollars. Anyone wishing to contribute to the fund can contact Chief Spagnola."

Lauren thought, *Something too oily tongued about him.* She left the conference room to resume her search for Gloria.

Stepping into the bathroom, she heard Gloria sobbing in one of the stalls. *What is wrong with her?* "Gloria, its Lauren. Your kids are waiting in the small conference room. I told them I'd bring you back there."

"Thanks, Lauren."

"I'll wait here until you're ready to go see them."

"Why don't you keep them company? It was probably scary for them to see me run out of the presentation. I'll be there in a minute." Gloria retched.

Lauren opened the door and stepped into the hallway. *I can't leave her like that, not until she feels well enough to get out of here.* Lauren stepped back into the bathroom waiting to see if she was going to vomit again, and then thought, *Maybe she'll feel some comfort if she knows I'm here and her kids aren't alone.* "I'll wait here until you feel better. Stephens is with your kids."

"Go ahead, tell them I'll be with them in little while." Gloria retched again. She came out of the stall, wiping her mouth with toilet tissue. Her eyes were red.

"I understand how difficult this is for you. If you want, I'll drive your kids home and you can rest here for a while. I'll come back for you."

Gloria shook her head.

I'll try to be sympathetic, but I wish she would get hold of herself. Lauren put her arms around Gloria's shoulders, "Have you seen a doctor? Are you sick?"

Gloria took a deep breath. "I need you to help me."

Lauren pulled her closer. She swallowed. *She always seems so strong. What could she need that I couldn't handle?* "Of course, I'm your partner. I've got your back."

The words seized up in Gloria's throat, but she was desperate for help. She forced them out. "I'm...I'm pregnant."

CHAPTER 11

IRS-CID
Chicago
Friday, September 17, 2004

L AUREN AND GLORIA LEFT THE bathroom and walked down the hallway past the open door to the stage. They saw Jack Nestor speaking to the audience. He hesitated and glanced their way. Lauren pulled Gloria by her sleeve and they headed to the small conference room.

They entered and Adsila and Darius rushed to her. Lauren drifted to the background.

Adsila grabbed Gloria's hands. Her eyes filled with concern. "Mom, are you all right?"

Darius put his arm around Gloria's shoulder and nestled his head next to hers. "You feel warm, Mom."

Gloria was unable to look into their eyes. She knew that the truth was something they would never, and could never, know. "I think I have a slight fever. I just need to go home and lie down for a while. Lauren will drive us home."

"I've got a set of keys to Dad's Lexus. I can drive us home," Darius said. "He can take the CTA."

"I don't think your father would go for that," Gloria said.

Adsila shook her head. "He should have been here to see you get that medal. That was important."

Darius waved his hands. "He has a case on trial. He can't just walk away."

Adsila pleaded. "He could have continued it for a day. The defendants are locked up anyway, so what difference would a day make?"

"Due process, due process," Darius puffed his chest out. "Haven't you learned anything from him?"

Gloria glanced at Lauren and rolled her eyes. "Okay, that's enough. Lauren will drive us home and your father will drive himself when the trial is over for the day. He's probably got motions to read and rule on, so he wouldn't be coming home until late. I'm sure he wouldn't want to take the CTA at night, and frankly, I'm getting really tired of listening to you two argue."

Lauren drove the Blazer to Bronzeville. The Carlton home was an old two-story Greystone that had been gutted and remodeled. The fifteen-minute drive was a continuation of the argument between Darius and Adsila, both of them scoring points and neither one winning. Gloria finally called a cease-fire five minutes from the house, as their behavior came closer to Marquis of Queensberry rules than to courtroom etiquette.

Darius and Adsila jumped out, slammed their doors shut, and once away from their mother, continued their argument as they went up the walk to the front door.

Gloria turned to Lauren. "Thanks for your help today. She diverted her eyes from Lauren, "I may have a favor to ask of you."

CHAPTER 12

September 17, 2004

AFTER THE MEDAL PRESENTATION, BLANTON and Nestor took an elevator to the bowels of the federal building and entered a black stretch Cadillac limousine leased by Standard Armor. They settled into the spacious back seat as the limo headed up the ramp to Clark Street.

Blanton lifted a Cuban cigar out of his inside suitcoat pocket, removed it from a glass tube, and snipped off the end. He lit the stogie with a gold-plated Dunhill lighter. A cloud of smoke floated from his mouth as the tip glowed red. "You have to take care of the little people. Know what I mean? I'm not belittling them, but in the big picture, it's a diversion so we can keep things right."

"Right for us." Nestor laughed and waved his hand, disbursing the smoke.

Blanton held the cigar between his forefinger and index finger and pulled it from his mouth. "That was a nice touch, setting up that fund for Abbott's kids."

"Thanks. I thought of that myself and it's just a fraction of the cash we'll pocket from Iraq. And of course, no taxes! I don't know if I told you that this was the second time for me and Abbott. He was in Intelligence back in 1980 during Operation Eagle Claw when we tried to rescue the hostages from the embassy in Iran. He was a troublemaker back then, too. He came in with the weather report telling me the helicopters wouldn't be able to fly, some bullshit about a haboob sandstorm. The Army put the blame on me for the eight men who died and washed me out. That ended my career and would have ended my family's legacy."

"I heard your old man took it hard." Blanton examined the cigar and wondered why Nestor was telling him this.

"The Army was going to court martial me. My old man, he pulled some strings so the family's reputation would stay untarnished. He offered the fuckers my head on a silver platter. They cut the deal. I could resign without all that shit going public in a court martial. The old man wouldn't have it any other way."

Blanton placed the cigar between his lips. Another puff of smoke drifted from the stogie. "Too bad we can't make these in the States. Well, one thing about Abbott. A dead motherfucker can't hurt you."

Nestor waved at the cloud. "Sometimes the little people can cause more trouble than they're worth. He was a man we had to get rid of. Fortunately, the insurgents did it for us."

"There's the unknown. What did he do with the hundred grand he extorted?"

Nestor shook his head. His face reddened. "How many times are you going to bring that up? I've told you it wasn't in his things in the Humvee. I had one of my men search it, and if you think I pocketed the cash, you're fucking wrong."

Blanton raised his hands, palms facing Nestor. "Take it easy. I never implied that. I think he sent it home. Or that other agent found it, the one that was supposed to get her medal but ran out. What was that about?"

"Broads, who knows? But I agree with you, either his wife or that other agent, Nighthawk, has the cash. I think he was fucking her." Nestor smiled. "She does have a tight ass for an old broad."

Blanton glanced out the window at the traffic and decided it was time to drop his own bomb. He looked back at Nestor and took a deep breath. "There's an issue that's going to change things."

Nestor narrowed his eyes. "What do you mean? Change what things?"

"Bush signed the Syria Accountability Act. It imposes tighter economic and diplomatic sanctions because of Syria's support for terrorism, involvement in Lebanon, weapons of mass destruction programs, and the destabilizing role it's playing in Iraq," Blanton said, ticking off each point on his fingers. "You've got to figure out a new way to get the cash out of Iraq. My contacts in Syria aren't going to be useful anymore."

"Don't give me the political bullshit verbiage. What're we talking about that directly affects us?"

"The sanctions are meant to stop Syria's illegal importation of Iraqi oil and the illegal shipment of military items to anti-US forces in Iraq. That means you can't sell your body armor to Syria anymore."

"Well, I think I can get around that. All the body armor was billed to and paid for by the DoD in cash we received in Baghdad. Then some of the merchandise was diverted to Syria, and we got paid again for the same armor by the Syrians."

"Double billing, that helped the profit margin. But that'll be too risky to do anymore. There's going to be a lot of limitations on any products made in the US that're shipped to Syria. You get caught diverting product to Syria, you're going to get a lot of scrutiny from the government. It's not worth the risk."

"Fuck. Anything else?"

"Forget using the Commercial Bank of Syria. No American bank will be allowed to have any transactions with it. You try to divert funds from Syria to another country and then to a domestic bank, you're looking for trouble. It will draw too much heat."

"That's going to cause a lot of problems. I just want one more deal. I'll figure out some way."

The limo sped to O'Hare International Airport and the Standard Armor Lear jet waiting to fly both of them back to D.C.

CHAPTER 13

Washington, D. C.

NESTOR SAT IN THE BLACK plush recliner in the passenger section of the Lear. He looked at Blanton in the matching recliner on the other side of the aisle, his legs splayed, belly expanding with each breath, and snoring so loudly that Nestor put on headphones to shut the noise out. *What a sad state of affairs, that leeching bureaucrats like Blanton are in positions of power. I have to be careful he doesn't fuck things up.*

He weighed his options of where to go next: to Standard Armor's corporate headquarters in Potomac, Maryland, or to his home in the quiet suburb of Lanham, Maryland.

At home, his wife and five kids were waiting for him. After five kids, he hated to admit that she didn't hold the same physical attraction that she once had. He shook his head and decided on the happy medium between office and home. He grabbed the satellite phone to call the condo bought by Caribe Armor, a subsidiary of Standard Armor. It was pretty snazzy: a half-million-dollar pad, perfectly suited to his needs. His wife had never heard of Caribe. She thought he spent lonely nights sleeping on the couch in his office. He punched in the number.

"Hello." Her voice was deep and throaty.

"I'm coming to spend the night with you."

"Ah, my white prince, I look forward to seeing you. It's been much too long."

"Yes, it has. I've been working too hard traveling all over the world."

"You must slay your lions so that we can enjoy the feast."

Nestor laughed. "We'll be feasting in about forty-five minutes."

"Excellent, my prince."

Her name was Ifede Adebayo. She was three inches taller than Nestor, lean, with skin as black as the night. She went by the name Cherry Jubilee when she danced at the Stiletto Gentlemen's Club. She said her ancestors were Nigerian royalty.

The plane landed, and Blanton and Nestor went their separate ways. Blanton took a cab to his office. A limo dropped Nestor off in front of the Watergate. He took the elevator up to the ninth floor, inserted his key in the lock, opened the door. There she stood, her hands and feet outstretched touching both walls of the hallway. She wore only a black leather G string and the gold necklace with the one carat diamond he had bought for her. It dangled between her breasts as her hips undulated. The feast was about to begin.

CHAPTER 14

Chicago
Friday Night, September 17, 2004

GLORIA SAT DOWN AT THE black marble kitchen island and placed the just-delivered Due's pan pizza on it. In the time it took her to lift the lid, Adsila and Darius had three settings of plates and silverware ready and slid onto their seats.

"Is Dad going to join us?" Darius asked.

"No, after work he's playing round ball with some of his attorney friends. He's reliving the good old days at DePaul; except there he rode the bench until they were behind by twenty points." Gloria laughed, trying to make light of the situation, but her Tuesday morning abortion appointment preyed heavily on her mind. She felt guilt creeping in.

Darius reached with his plate-sized hands and grabbed two pieces of the pie.

"What a gentleman." Adsila shook her head.

He separated the pieces, placed them on two plates, and put one in front of his mother and the other in front of his sister.

"Nice recovery," Gloria said.

"What do you mean? Don't I get credit for anything around here? Geez." He grabbed two more slices and set them on his plate, picked up his knife and fork, and put them down just as fast. He grabbed a slice and chomped down on it. Tomato sauce ran down his chin, and he smiled. "That's the way Dad eats it."

There was a moment of silence while they all enjoyed the first bite. Gloria glanced at the highboy against the window. On it sat separate gold framed photos of Adsila and Darius, taken when each was only months old. They were wrapped in pajamas that covered them from neck to toe. The word abortion lingered in her mind and in her soul, like an anchor buried so deep in the sand it was impossible to move. She put her fork down, took a deep breath, and exhaled while she contemplated what she was going to tell her children. *I have to lie to my angels.* "On Tuesday, I have… I…I have to . . .." She paused, looked at the photos again and exhaled. "…to interview witnesses in San Francisco."

Adsila froze, holding a forkful of pizza in front of her mouth. "Mom, you just came back from Iraq! Can't someone else go?"

Even Darius stopped eating, a string of cheese connecting his mouth to the pizza in his hand. "It's not fair, Mom."

"I'll only be gone a few days, should be back by Friday at the latest." Gloria pushed the slice of pizza around her plate with her fork. *Lying to my kids. I'm reaching new lows.*

By ten she was in bed reading *The Power of Intentions* by Wayne Dyer when her husband entered the bedroom, holding a slice of leftover pizza. She set her book on her lap. "How was your game?"

"I haven't lost my touch. Three pointers were fallin' through the net." He held the pizza in his left hand and flicked the fingers on his right hand. "Swoosh."

"You played so long ago they didn't have three-point shots."

"If they did, I could've made the NBA."

"Back to reality." She took a deep breath, gaining the courage to tell the lie one more time. "I have to leave for San Francisco on Tuesday to interview some witnesses."

"What? You're kidding! I thought when you got back from Iraq you said you wanted to do something special with the kids to make up for the lost summer. You always pick your work over your kids." He shook his head and entered the bathroom, closing the door behind him.

Gloria closed her book and looked at the closed bathroom door. *No, I don't pick my work over my kids. I just have to make the lies I tell you credible.* She turned off her reading light and rested her head on her pillow, wondering again whether she could trust Lauren, and what she would say to all this, particularly to the favor she was about to ask.

CHAPTER 15

Washington D.C.
Saturday, September 18, 2004

FRIDAY NIGHT WAS A REPLAY of Nestor's and Cherry's afternoon delight. The morning came in a flash and Nestor woke. The satin bed sheets were ripped off the mattress. His red silk tie was wrapped around his right ankle and secured to a bedpost. His black leather belt looped around his other ankle and was tied to the opposite bedpost. The pillows were strewn across the room. An upside-down bottle of 1996 Dom Perignon jutted from the ice bucket that lay on its side next to the bed. Cherry lay there. He could see the muscle tone in her naked body, but her face revealed she was enjoying the innocent sleep of a newborn baby.

Nestor sat up and freed his ankles, rolled onto his side, and rested his feet on the lush white carpet. He saw his navy-blue boxer shorts lying under the ice bucket, rose from the bed, pulled his shorts out from under the ice bucket, and slipped them on. His body trembled. "Still a little cold," he mumbled.

His body felt like it had done two rounds with a wild beast. He groaned and headed toward the bathroom. Bracing his hands on the sink, he gazed into the mirror, admiring the reflection of his fifty-year old body—Napoleonic in stature, but with the muscle tone of a younger man. Nestor pulled in his abs and pumped his biceps. "Look at those pipes." He gritted his teeth and smiled. Turning his body to a forty-five-degree angle to the mirror, he raised his right foot standing on his toes and flexed his quads. "Shit, man, thighs and glutes like

Arnold in his prime." Then he noticed the bite marks on his shoulders and scratches on his back. "No sex with the old lady, not with these trophy marks."

He ambled into the walk-in closet and closed the door behind him. He went to the end of a line of designer dresses and pushed them aside. Behind the dresses was a black Liberty safe that stood five feet high and two and one-half feet wide. He bent at the waist and spun in the combination, then turned the five-spoke wheel and opened the door. He reached in and yanked out a stack of hundred-dollar bills still in the original New York Federal Reserve shrink wrap.

Nestor stood and placed the package on top of the safe. He pulled open the jewelry drawer in the safe. It was filled with necklaces, broaches, and bracelets that sparkled with red, green, and white stones. He pushed those to the side, moved over a Glock 17, lifted a Swiss army knife, and a handful of rubber bands out of the drawer. He yanked the knife blade out from the red grips and slit the shrink-wrapped package open. He lifted the hundreds out and put them into three piles. The first thirty thousand was for Blanton. *Hope he has the sense to bury this money in his backyard or deposit it in an offshore bank account.*

The second thirty he would take for his Standard Armor slush fund. He needed the cash to bribe officials in Iraq and other places Standard Armor would be doing business in the future.

The third thirty he rubber-banded into ten stacks of three thousand each and lined them up next to Jubilee's designer shoes, primarily Louboutins, Blahniks, and Choos. Those three-thousand-dollar stacks were how Jubilee earned her keep. She would deposit the cash into ten bank accounts in various names set up at different banks to avoid the preparation of currency transaction reports.

The remaining ten thousand was his personal mad money. A wild weekend at the baccarat tables in Las Vegas, some time at a brothel, and maybe even a gift for the wife and kids. This was a stressful business and he knew his R & R would be beneficial for everyone.

Nestor locked the safe, hopped into a hot shower, shaved, and went to back to the closet, where he selected a white Greg Norman golf shirt, Levis, and Nike jogging shoes. He headed to the bed, where Cherry was in a deep slumber, her head under the pillow. He laid his hand on her shoulder and jiggled it. "Hey, Babe, I've got to go to the office and get home for a few days. Take my shirt, tie, and suit to the cleaners and deposit that cash I left out into the bank accounts."

"What?" She mumbled.

He lifted the pillow off her head, tossed it to the floor, and repeated himself.

She groaned, reached across the mattress, grabbed his pillow, and pulled it over her head.

He leaned over, lifted the corner of the pillow, lowered his mouth to her head, and used his military voice. "Did you hear me?"

Cherry turned facing him. "Go fucking home."

"I will, after I go to the office."

She exhaled and reached for his hand. "I'm sorry. I miss you. Come back after you finish your work?"

"I haven't seen my kids in a week. I need to spend some time with them."

She dropped her hand and turned her back to him. "Then you better go."

"You're going to drop my clothes at the cleaners and make the deposits?"

"Don't worry about it. I know what to do."

Cherry heard his footsteps leave the bedroom and the door click open and close. She hated feeling abandoned. *I've seen her picture. Why does he pick that fat blond over me? I'm not a whore he can fuck and leave.* She stayed in bed until nine thirty and then realized it was Saturday, and she was supposed to be dancing on the bar at Stiletto's by eleven thirty, working the lunch crowd. Marko, the Russian mobster running the establishment, demanded punctuality or else. She grabbed a quick shower and tossed the rubber-banded bundles of cash into a tan Louis Vuitton bag.

Dressed in skinny jeans, a black, long-sleeved V-neck T-shirt, and wearing no bra, Cherry slipped into three-inch heels and hopped into a cab. The club was in downtown DC, just around the corner from two of the banks that held some of the accounts. Out of the cab, she hustled into the bank.

The bank was a stately old building, with a thirty-foot rotunda ceiling above the three open teller lines, each with at least four gray-haired ladies patiently waiting. Cherry headed into the line that seemed to be moving, tapping her foot impatiently and counting down the minutes while she listened to an old lady provide her recipe for fruit cake, in agonizing detail, to the teller.

Finally, Cherry made the deposit. *Three thousand down, twenty-seven to go.* She left the bank, glancing at her Rolex. "Shit, 10:45," she mumbled. She crossed the street and headed into the next bank, located a short distance down the block from an auto dealership that she had previously passed many times on similar errands for Nestor.

She ran to the bank, her heels clicking down the sidewalk. Cherry stood in line behind an old man holding a social security check. It was a cool September day, and her nipples made an impression in the thin material of her top. The old man turned around, eyeing her up and down and shaking his head. Then he spent several minutes discussing the weather with the teller and debating whether he should get all fives or mostly twenties. "The grocery store doesn't like twenties." It was ten minutes after eleven by the time Cherry completed the deposit. *Six thousand down, twenty-four left. I'll never get this done in time. Can't take all this cash into the club.*

Cherry glanced down the street and her eyes caught the sign, "Certified Preowned Vehicles." She saw a red 2000 Mercedes SLK Kompressor convertible rotating on an elevated stand underneath the sign. The sun reflected off the hood, sparkling in her eyes

"I won't have to worry about taking the money to the club," she laughed. "If I can't have him, I'll get what I want. What I deserve." She walked into the dealership past two shiny black Mercedes sedans, and three salesmen charged toward her. She pointed at the oldest and fattest one. He wore a green shirt, the collar slightly frayed, and a black tie. The knot hung an inch below his collar. *I won't have to waste time ignoring his come-ons,* she thought. "I want that car," gesturing at the SLK in the lot.

"My name is Ted. Let me get the keys and we'll take it for a spin. A little red convertible would be perfect for a stylish young lady like you."

She caught his eyes focusing on her cleavage. "I don't have time. I have to go to work."

"You don't want to test drive it?"

"I don't have time. Can't I just give you the money? Oh, and I'll pick the car up at five today."

"We haven't discussed the price yet."

She slung one hip to the side and rested her arm on it. "How much?"

"Uhh…"

She swayed her hips to the other side. "How much?"

Ted blinked. "Ah, I have to talk to my manager."

"I'll give you twenty-four thousand."

"That should be okay. Sure, sure, should be fine." His eyes widened and a smile broke across his face. "Do you have a trade-in?"

"No."

"How much are you going to put down?"

"All of it."

"I have to make sure your check will clear for that amount before we can release the car to you. It's company policy—"

"I'll pay cash, all cash." The magic words got old Ted's attention.

He straightened his tie, blinked again, and pointed to a room in the back of the dealership. "My finance manager has to handle this. Come this way."

He waddled ahead and sat Cherry down in a paneled meeting room with a long wood table surrounded by ten chairs. On the walls were photographs of Mercedeses and Porsches. She glanced at her watch. Eleven twenty.

A man in his mid-thirties, wearing a gray three-piece suit, entered with Ted.

"Hello, I'm Jeremy Winchester, finance manager. I have final approval on all transactions."

Cherry put her forearms on the table and leaned over, flashing her cleavage. "I have to get to work. I'm an executive at Standard Armor and I have a meeting that I'm late for, so here's my driver's license and here's payment for the car." She dumped the Vuitton bag upside down, and eight rubber-banded packets of Franklins rolled onto the table.

Winchester picked up her driver's license. "OK, then, Miss... ah... Adebayo. We'll have your car ready to pick up this afternoon."

She grabbed the empty bag and left the room.

Winchester stood, waving his hand at her retreating figure. "Can I interest you in an extended warranty?"

CHAPTER 16

G LORIA WAS AT HER DESK waiting for Lauren to get in. She glanced at her
watch. It was eight fifteen, and she was due in at eight. She drummed her
fingers. *I need to talk to you today.* She heard the banging of a briefcase. She
sprang out of her chair and looked over her shoulder, only to see Stephens
rushing into his office. Gloria sat down again, but at every new sound she
jumped out of her seat, hoping to see Lauren.

Fifteen minutes later she heard, "Goddamn traffic." Lauren slammed her
briefcase onto her desk on the opposite side of the aisle.

Gloria stood, nodded, and Lauren came over with her overcoat still on.

"The Kennedy was a mess. From now on I'll take the train." She slipped
her arms out of the tan Burberry trench coat and held it over her right forearm.

"Let's go across the street to the Marquette for a cup of coffee." Gloria said.

"Why don't we just go to the cafeteria here?"

"I need to talk to you about what I mentioned Friday," she said in a hushed
tone.

Lauren took a deep breath and a step back, "Oh yeah...okay." She slipped
her coat back on and followed Gloria. It was a silent walk out of the federal
building, across the plaza with the Calder sculpture, and then across Adams
Street to the Marquette Restaurant. Gloria led the way past the crowded tables

and counter service near the entrance to the rear of the restaurant, which was almost empty.

They slid into opposite sides of a red leatherette booth in a dark corner. A waitress stopped at their table. Her fireplug build was squeezed into a black uniform a couple of sizes too small.

"Two coffees," Gloria said, holding up two fingers.

"Make that one coffee. I'll have tea, Earl Grey if you have it." Lauren glanced at Gloria. "I don't like coffee. That taste that stays in your mouth, yech."

"I guess if we're going to be partners, I'll have to learn more about you."

"I can be a picky eater."

"Well, anyway, what I told you in the bathroom Friday is true."

"Congratulations, but are you sure?" Lauren words trailed off. "I mean no offense, but aren't you kind of old to have a baby?"

"No offense taken. That's what I thought, too. I thought I was menopausal, and it couldn't happen. Stress, things at home and work stopped the flow. I was never on a regular schedule, not much, but I guess… it happened and…" She paused.

Lauren rested her chin on her thumb, curling her forefinger under her lip. "And what?"

"I need help."

Lauren's forehead wrinkled. "I don't understand. What kind of help?"

Gloria looked around for prying eyes and her voice quivered. "I need an abortion."

Lauren dropped her hand onto the table and her eyes opened wide. "Why? Have you talked to a doctor? What about your husband? Does he know you're pregnant?"

The waitress set down a cup of coffee and a cup of hot water with a tea bag on the saucer. "Will there be anything else?"

"No, thanks," Gloria said. She sipped her coffee, set it down, and pushed it away.

Lauren set the bag in the steaming water. "Did you see a doctor?"

"Once you've been pregnant, you know when it happens again. All the symptoms." She looked at the coffee. "Things don't taste right, tired, and nauseous."

"You have to see a doctor. And what about your husband? You've told him, right?"

"I'm seeing a doctor this afternoon."

"And then you'll tell your husband?" Lauren brought the cup to her lips.

Gloria lifted the coffee to her mouth, inhaled the aroma, and set it down without taking a sip. The words came out in a whisper. "It's not his baby."

Lauren dropped her cup to the saucer, the tea spilling over the side, and covered her mouth with her hand. "Oh my God."

Gloria slid a napkin across the table, wiping up the tea. "So, ah, you said that your parents are out of town for three weeks?"

"Yes." Lauren moved back against the cushion.

"I need a place to stay for a few days while I recover."

Lauren picked up her cup and sipped the tea.

Gloria noticed Lauren's eyes glance away from her. She tapped her fingers on the table waiting for a response. She blurted out, "I really need a place to stay while I recuperate. It would just be for a couple of days. This would be a medical abortion, no surgery."

"I don't get it—"

"If I can stay at your house, I'll tell my husband that I have to go out of town for a couple of days. When I'm back on my feet I'll go home. It's just for a couple of days."

Lauren looked down at her lap and then gazed at Gloria. She set both hands on the edge of the table and exhaled. "I don't know if I'm comfortable doing this. It would make me a party to your lie to your husband."

"Lauren, I understand where you might feel uncomfortable getting involved. You have a lot of years of life ahead of you." Gloria paused. "Things between married people can get very confused and complicated."

"Can't you go to counseling?"

"We've been doing that for a while, a long while, and things are just getting worse. If he found out about this, he would divorce me. If the kids found out I cheated on their father, it would tear them apart—and I'm sure he would tell them."

"Don't you have someone else, an old high school or college friend?"

"I'm not from Chicago. I went to school in Oklahoma and that was a long time ago." Gloria had to admit to herself that she could understand Lauren's reluctance. She curled her lips and let it out. "I guess in that respect I'm a lot like you, Lauren. I don't have anyone that I'm that close to," she paused, "anymore."

"You...you mean Jim Abbott?"

Gloria nodded. "I need to know if you're there for me?"

"Can I think this over? I'm really uncomfortable…"

"You can think it over…for a while. But my appointment for the abortion is ten tomorrow morning. Are you with me . . . or not?"

Lauren pushed herself away from the table. "This is against my beliefs. I'm really not comfortable." She paused. "I feel like you're not giving me a choice."

"I'm sorry. But you understand I only have a few more days that I can do this by pill rather than surgically. The recuperation would be more involved then, but even with the pill procedure, I shouldn't be alone."

"So, you're putting me in a position where if I say no, I'm the bad guy."

"If that's what you think, I'm sorry. I don't mean to do that. I'll take a cab and stay in a hotel."

Lauren grabbed her spoon and tapped it on the table. "I lose either way. If I help you, I'll feel guilty about the abortion. I really don't believe in that. And if something happens, I'm…fucked either way. I assume it's best if someone is there to care for you."

"That would be best in case something doesn't go right. My house tomorrow, 9:00 a.m.?"

Lauren kept her eyes on Gloria, dropped the spoon, and nodded.

CHAPTER 17

Carlton Residence
Tuesday, September 21, 2004

GLORIA STARED OUT HER FRONT window, waiting for Lauren. Her husband and kids had left earlier. She was living the necessary lie; she needed the privacy to recuperate and couldn't have them calling the office for any reason. She knew there were no alternatives. Abortion was the only logical, yet difficult, decision. Secrecy was the only option.

She had chosen a clinic in Crystal Lake, a suburb fifty miles northwest of Chicago. The likelihood of running into anyone there who might know her was remote at best. She had two appointments, the first at ten twenty this morning, the second in two weeks for a follow-up exam.

A charcoal-gray Audi A6 Quatro pulled up to the curb. The manufacturer's list price was still pasted to the passenger rear window. Gloria went out the door and down the front steps to the car, thinking, *The girl leads a pampered life.*

Gloria had told Stephens that she was taking the week off, going to Oklahoma City to visit old friends. Lauren had called in earlier today, taking sick leave.

Sitting in the passenger seat, Gloria gazed at the gray clouds rolling to the east. It looked like a storm was coming in, and the mood in the car seemed to match the increasingly gray sky. She could feel Lauren glancing at her.

"How are you?" Lauren asked.

"Scared, depressed, but otherwise dealing with it." She thought, *My death toll will soon be five. Five angels I will have put in heaven, now including an unborn child. If there is a God, please don't hold this against me.*

"I wish you had some other alternative—"

"Like disappear for nine months. That's not doable," she snapped.

"I know, I'm trying to be empathetic. I don't know what to say."

"I'm sorry. I know you don't want to be involved, and I appreciate what you're doing for me. What can I say? I hope you never have to deal with this kind of situation."

Lauren pulled the Audi onto the Dan Ryan Expressway and silence fell like an invisible cloak over the interior of the car. She headed northwest on the Kennedy. Gloria lowered her seat and closed her eyes. At ten o'clock, Lauren pulled into the parking lot of the Northwest Suburban Surgical Center. There were eight cars in the parking lot. It was a single-story, yellow-brick, nondescript building. The windows were covered in light beige curtains, making it impossible for anyone to see inside; the name was scripted on the glass door in black three-inch print.

They entered the waiting room. Posters of Monet's water lilies decorated the dull white walls. Six young girls with what looked like either their mothers or boyfriends were sitting on light gray sofas. A soft light glowed from the recessed light fixtures in the ceiling onto the colorless carpeting.

Gloria approached a sliding glass window. Seated behind was a girl barely over twenty in a white nurse's uniform, Julie, according to her name tag. The girl frowned and gave her a look that said, "You're too old, what are you doing here?"

"I have a ten o'clock with Dr. Iwasoki."

She handed Gloria a clipboard with a questionnaire. Gloria stepped away and sat on a sofa next to Lauren.

"Hey, Lauren, it's Julie." The girl behind the glass window waved.

Gloria lowered the clipboard and her eyes shifted to Lauren. Lauren shrugged and went to the window. She chatted with Julie for a few minutes and returned to her seat.

Gloria kept her head down and mumbled, "I don't f-ing believe it. Drive all the way out here and we run into someone you know."

Lauren leaned toward Gloria. "She's an old high school friend that I haven't seen in four years. She doesn't know where I work, so everything should be fine."

The door opened next to Julie's reception area. A nurse in a white uniform stepped out and looked at Gloria. "Next," she said, indicating the way with a nod.

Gloria rose from her seat, took the clipboard with her, and followed the nurse to an examination room. She sat down in a white plastic chair and the nurse took her blood pressure. "One-hundred-thirty-five over eighty-five, not bad. The doctor will be with you in a few minutes." She smiled at Gloria and left the room.

Ten minutes later, a young Japanese man entered and introduced himself. The doctor went over the alternatives with her, including keeping the baby. *I don't need to hear what I know.* She nodded. "Can we start this, Doctor? I've been over all the alternatives with my doctor. He said that this is the best choice for me, and it's what I want to do. He told me exactly what I can—" her lips pressed together, and she paused. "What I can expect." She swallowed hard.

The doctor removed a small paper cup from a dispenser, went to the sink, and filled it with water. He gave her a packet containing three pills. "Each tablet is 200 milligrams of mifepristone. This is the first part of your treatment." He handed her the cup. "Take these now."

She broke open the package and washed the pills down. Her eyes welled and her chin trembled.

He gave her a small bottle. "This contains two tablets. Each one is 200 milligrams of misoprostol. Take these in the next twenty-four to seventy-two hours. You will probably start cramping within twenty minutes of taking the misoprostol, and in the next six to eight hours you should miscarry. You won't recognize anything looking like an embryo." He said it like it was the thousandth time. "No intercourse for two weeks. The literature I gave you repeats what I just told you in more detail and describes what exactly is happening and the symptoms you're likely to experience."

Gloria nodded, looked down, and pursed her lips.

"You've an appointment scheduled in two weeks. It's very important. Don't miss it. Do you have any questions?"

"No, I just want to go."

"Okay, you have our twenty-four-hour number. There is always someone available, so don't hesitate to call for any reason, especially if you don't miscarry."

"Thank you, Doctor." Gloria joined Lauren in the waiting room. She paid the bill in cash.

Julie waved to Lauren as they headed to the door. She lifted her hand to her ear, thumb and little finger extended, and mouthed, "Call me."

An hour later they pulled onto a paver brick circular drive in front of Lauren's parents' home. It was a red-brick, four-bedroom colonial with an attached two-car garage bordered on both sides by tall junipers. The interior of the house was furnished in earth tones, a pleasing mixture of greens, browns, and maroons in leathers and pin-striped silks. Lauren showed Gloria to the guest bedroom with an attached bath, on the second floor.

"Why don't you get comfortable and I'll make you some tea," Lauren said.

"Thanks, that'd be nice." Gloria got into a green cotton nightgown, pulled down the white comforter, fluffed up the four pillows, and crawled into the bed. On the nightstand next to the bed were a few copies of *Good Housekeeping*.

Lauren knocked on the door and gently opened it. She held a tray with a small teapot, a cup on a saucer, several different tea bags, and a plate with wheat crackers. She placed the tray on the far nightstand. "Would you like me to pour tea for you? There's chamomile, Earl Grey, and cinnamon."

Gloria reached out and curled her fingers around Lauren's. "Thank you so much for coming through for me."

A small smile spread across Lauren's face. "Hey, we're partners. I've got your back and you've got mine."

"Right, I'd like chamomile."

"Coming up." She prepared the tea and handed it to Gloria. "How're you feeling?"

"I'm good so far, but I'm not looking forward to this. I think it's going to be tougher emotionally than physically."

Lauren could see the sorrow in Gloria's eyes. "I can understand that. Whatever you need, just let me know."

"I think I'll sip this tea and take a little nap."

"Sounds good. Your cell phone is on the nightstand. I'll be in the house. If you need anything, call. If I leave, I'll tell you before I go." Lauren walked to the door.

"Thanks. I put you on my speed dial."

Lauren nodded and closed the door behind her.

Wednesday morning Gloria took the misoprostol and by mid-afternoon she miscarried. The physical aspects were not easy, but the overwhelming grief and sense of loss were worse. Coupled with the devastating emotional impact that the deaths of her parents and Jim Abbott had had on her, it was pain that would be with her for the rest of her life. She came out of the bathroom as Lauren was entering the bedroom with a tray of fresh tea.

Gloria raised both hands and covered her eyes, as the tears cascaded down her checks.

Lauren rested the tray on the nightstand and embraced Gloria. "I understand why you did what you did. In your heart, you knew it was the right thing to do. You had to protect Adsila and Darius and give your family every chance to survive."

Gloria nodded and pinned her arms against her stomach. "Thank you, Lauren. Being able to go through this here with you made my recovery less difficult for me. I feel like…I don't know, like I lost a part of me." She lowered her head, took a deep breath and cried, *an essential part, the last part of Jim Abbott.*

"Why don't you lie down, sip some tea and rest. If you want to talk, let me know."

Gloria took a sip of the tea. "Maybe we'll talk later." She fluffed up a pillow and laid down.

Lauren pulled the comforter up to Gloria's chin, took her cell phone off the nightstand, and tiptoed out of the room. Exhaustion took over.

Thursday morning the bedroom door opened, and light from the hallway brightened the dark room. Gloria squinted at Lauren's silhouette. She heard a tray slide onto the nightstand. The aroma of fresh coffee, scrambled eggs, bacon, and toast danced into her nostrils. She heard the shuffling of slippers across the carpet. The curtains opened and sunshine blasted into the room.

Gloria sat up and stretched her arms toward the ceiling. "I feel good."

"You look good, and you should be hungry. You've hardly had anything to eat the last few days."

"You know what? You're right, I am." She reached for the tray and slid it from the nightstand onto her lap. She grabbed a strip of bacon and took a bite. "Nice and crispy, just the way I like it. I didn't know you could cook."

"I'd hardly call that cooking. You should try my beef wellington."

"You're kidding me, beef wellington?"

"My father made me take accounting. So, I took a few cooking courses to satisfy my need for creativity." Lauren set Gloria's cell phone on the bed. "You've got a few calls." Gloria reached for the phone, but Lauren swiped it away before she could wrap her fingers around it.

"Not until you're done eating."

"Okay, mother." Gloria finished her breakfast and played the voicemails. Lauren pulled up a chair next to the bed. The first was Adsila calling, wondering if she was all right. "You usually call as soon as you land. I'm worried about you."

Two messages were from her informant, Marvin, the first one on Wednesday evening. "Gloria, you said you were gonna give me another hundred and I ain't heard nothing from you."

Later Wednesday night. "I got more info for you on Henderson. You know he had a car purchased under a woman's name, Shiquita something or other? Marvin's got a photographic memory. He remembers that whole list. Well, that ain't her real name. I did some investigating. Undercover type shit, dangerous for Marvin. They bought that car under a phony name and the car was for one of the Gangster Disciples big players. That should be worth some big money for Marvin. I'll tell you her real name and the name of the GD when you pay me. Big money for Marvin this time."

And Thursday at two in the morning. A voice with an Arabic accent said, "My friend who called before is no longer available. Don't worry, I was the source of everything he was telling you, and there's more. Don't call me back. I can't risk getting a call from you under the wrong circumstances or I, too, will no longer be available. I will call you in a day or two."

"What's that last call about?" Lauren asked.

"Do you have a passport?"

"Of course, I spent the summer before my senior year in Europe."

"Of course, how silly of me to doubt that you would." Gloria giggled in spite of herself and shook her head. "You'll have to make an expedited request for an official passport."

"Why?"

"So you can accompany me to Iraq."

"Iraq? For what?"

"I'll tell you after this guy calls again. I assume you want to go."

"Shit, yeah. I mean, of course."

"In the meantime, I'm calling my kids. I'm going home tomorrow."

CHAPTER 18

Carlton Residence
Friday, September 24, 2004

THE JUDGE GOT HOME AT seven thirty. No one greeted him at the door. He dropped his briefcase onto a chair in the foyer and plopped down in dark-brown leather recliner in front of the 60" Samsung in the living room. "Somebody bring me a beer."

A few minutes later, Darius brought a bottle of Heineken. Beads of moisture dripped down the side of the green bottle. "Thanks, son. Hear from your mother?"

"She got home about thirty minutes ago. She's lying down. Said they had some late nights interviewing witnesses, and with the time zone differences and the jet lag, she was tired. How's the trial going?"

"I expect the jury to come back Monday morning with a verdict. Should be guilty on all counts for all the defendants. A couple of white attorneys were using some gangbangers from the west side to push some bad mortgages, and the banks got ripped off for a couple of million." He took a long draw from the beer. "Hits the spot."

Darius sat on the arm of the recliner. "How much time you going to give them?"

"I'm going to hit those white boys hard. They were the brains behind the operation and got most of the money. I figure twenty years each. The gangbangers, probably seven years. Their girlfriends, three years ought to do it. Have to teach them a lesson."

"Aren't you supposed to wait to decide until you get the presentencing reports from the prosecution, defense, and probation?"

"Technically, you're right. But after all these years, I can pretty much tell you what each is going to recommend. I give them what I want anyway."

Darius stood and flicked his wrist. "I'm gonna go to the gym and shoot some hoops."

"You're gonna or you're going to? Speak English—no ghetto talk in this house."

His eyes shot down and his shoulders rounded. "Yes, sir."

"Where's your sister?"

"She left a few minutes before you got home. She's at one of her study groups. Should be home by ten."

"Good girl. Don't forget to work on your three-pointers. You're not quick enough to be slashing to the basket. You're going to have to hit at least half your three-pointers if you want a chance to make the big time."

"Dad, I'm quicker than you think."

The judge yawned, "Three-pointers, Son."

Darius's mouth opened as if he wanted to say something, but then he lowered his head, folded his shoulders, and headed out.

The judge grabbed the remote and turned on the flat screen. He mumbled to himself. "Bulls preseason game against the Rockets. The chubby high school boy is going to be eaten alive by the Chinaman and Dikembe. Luol could be good." He finished his beer, and his eyes gradually closed. Twenty minutes later, he shook his head. "Bulls down by fifteen. Think I'll give Gloria another chance to make me happy. It's been a long time," he mumbled as he shut off the TV and extracted himself from the recliner.

Gloria lay in bed. She thought about the abortion. She knew those thoughts would linger for a long time. Did she do the right thing? What would have happened if she had kept the child? There was no doubt that once Robert found out, divorce papers would have been filed. If she were honest, would that really have bothered her very much? What would have been a problem, though, was what her kids would have thought of their cheating mother. What kind of rights would she have gotten to see them? He would have made that as difficult as he could. No, it had to be done. Her chest tightened.

Gloria heard the bedroom door open, the sounds of clothing hitting the floor. She was lying on the right side of the bed, her back to the center of the mattress. She felt the mattress sink from the weight of his body. His large hand stretched across her hip, raising her nightgown to her waist. "Gloria, it's been way to long. No ifs, and, or buts. I want you tonight."

"I'm really tired, Robert."

"I'm tired of being ignored." He tugged at her panties.

The doctor's instructions ran through her mind, *No intercourse for two weeks.* She grabbed her panties and held them tight. "Not now."

"You can't ignore me all this time and then tell me 'no' when I want it."

"I'm tired and I'm sick. I caught a bug in San Francisco, and I've been vomiting."

"Who'd you go with anyway, now that your boyfriend isn't around anymore?"

"Jim wasn't my boyfriend." Gloria jerked away to the edge of the mattress. She was glad he couldn't see her face. She wasn't good at denial. "I went with a new agent, a female agent, Lauren Ashberry."

"Gloria, how're you doing it? You used to like it on regular basis. I bet it's been a year, or damn close to it."

"I think we talked about this with the marriage counselor, or don't you remember?"

"What a fucking waste of time and money that was." He got out of bed, picked up his clothes, took a step toward the door, stopped, and did an about face. "I'm divorcing you. I can't take this any longer."

CHAPTER 19

Offices of Standard Armor
Hyattsville, Maryland
Friday, September 24, 2004

EARLIER THAT SAME DAY NESTOR sat in a black leather chair resting his feet on the glass top of his desk and enjoying the view out his window. White swans swam across a pond, leaving behind a ripple in their wake. The tall fir trees surrounding the pond reflected in the water like an impressionist painting. *Such a peaceful setting, and here I am making a grand living,* he thought, and laughed. *No, making a killing at war.*

His cell phone rang. Unidentified caller. *Got to be Blanton with his encrypted phone.* "Hello."

"Meet you at location three at one thirty today."

"See you there." The call terminated. *He's becoming a secret squirrel. I feel like I'm meeting Deep Throat.*

<hr />

At one thirty-three, Nestor hurried out of a taxi, knowing that Blanton would be waiting. Trotting up the stairs of the Lincoln Memorial, he looked at the twelve Doric columns ahead of him, stopped to catch his breath, and turned, facing the reflecting pool and the Washington Monument. Nestor drifted backwards, appreciating the shimmering image of the monument in the pool.

Turning, he saw Blanton standing near the back of Lincoln's statue, dwarfed by its nineteen-foot height.

Blanton jerked back the sleeve of his black trench coat and stared at his watch. The collar of his raincoat was turned up. A wide-brim fedora was pulled low over his face, and dark sunglasses covered his eyes.

Nestor laughed to himself as he walked to the corner of the statue, remembering his favorite childhood cartoon, Rocky and Bullwinkle. *He looks like Boris Badenov. I wonder if he has a Natasha Fatale in his life.* "Hi, John."

Blanton pulled his sunglasses down and looked over the rims. "No names. You're late."

"Sorry, just a couple of minutes. I wasn't thinking." He stuck his hands in the pockets of his sport coat.

Blanton looked to his left and his right. "Got an email from the Fed this morning. The next delivery of cash is set for four a.m. on October 10." He paused. "Four hundred million."

"Got it." Nestor turned away from Blanton and felt a tight grip on his elbow. He looked back over his shoulder. "What?"

"I want more," Blanton said.

He glanced at Blanton's hand on his elbow, and then shifted his glare to the man's face. Blanton's hand fell to his side. Nestor lifted his hands out of his pockets and pulled at the sleeve of his sport coat, straightening the wrinkle. "Obviously, you appreciate how risky this is. You're dressed like a CIA operative."

"That shipment in June was over two billion. You expect me to believe you only took a mil?"

Nestor stood there speechless. He thought about the five million he'd stolen. "At some point, there's going to be an audit by somebody, maybe even Congressional hearings on all this cash floating around. I'm the one that's flying around the world picking the money up and spreading it around so Standard Armor will be profitable for years to come. That means that the job I promised, you when you leave the government, will be there, and you'll reap the rewards in the future with no risk."

Blanton shrugged, "So take more money this time. If you took just one percent, you'd have four million. No one is going to miss such a small percentage or be able to trace it if there is an audit."

"If I took four, how much would you want?"

"Say a quarter, one mil."

Nestor shook his head. "All you do is advise me of the delivery, and you want twenty-five percent?"

"You wouldn't know about the deliveries if it weren't for me. You wouldn't be getting any cash at all without me." Blanton almost whined.

Nestor shifted from one foot to the other, wondering what prompted Blanton's sudden greed. "I do ninety-nine percent of the work and take all the risk." *I have to call his bluff,* he thought. "If you're not happy with our deal, you find someone else to steal the cash. Maybe they'll give you twenty-five percent, maybe they'll even promise you a job like I have."

Blanton rubbed his hands together. "I've got an idea. Set up a diversion. Yeah, a fire… like an insurgent's rocket hit where they store the cash. You can even burn some of the money. They'll never be able to figure out how much was destroyed, and you could even take more than one percent."

Nestor's face reddened. "What the fuck is going on? You've never had a hair up your ass before about how much you got."

Blanton looked down and mumbled, "Lost it."

"You *lost* it? Where? *How?*"

"I've got a mistress, gifts, hotel rooms, travel, and a million other things."

"I gave you $300,000, cash. You couldn't have spent it all on one broad!"

"I took her to the Bahamas, stayed at Little Whale Cay in the penthouse suite. She knew the people there." He got an impish grin on his face. "It was ten grand a night, and she lost a lot on the tables."

"Motherfucking bitch. John, didn't you see you were set up? She probably split her losses with the house."

Blanton's gaze went to the floor, "She called and left a message on my home phone."

"Sure, she's going to try to extort you."

"It's worse than that. My wife took the tape out of the answering machine and she's got some shark lawyer that's going to grab everything she can. They get the receipts from the casino, they'll push to find out where the cash came from. We've been married twenty years. She'll take alimony, half my pension, the house, and who knows what else. I'm staying in a hotel now."

"Move in with your lady friend."

"She was from an escort service. She left when the money ran out. I don't even know her real name. I fucked up big time."

"Natasha," Nestor mumbled, and thought, *I can use this to my advantage.*

Blanton's forehead furrowed. "What?"

"Never mind, I can't change the way of doing things. The risk is too big. On top of everything that's happened, you don't want your ass sitting in a federal pen for ten years or more. You're in a position of trust. If a prosecutor pushes it, a hanging judge will put you away for even longer."

"Yeah, yeah, I guess you're right. Let's just keep things the way they were. I'll lay low and get some cover story to tell my wife. I'll tell her the KGB is trying to blackmail me with false accusations. They want me to be a Russian spy. I'll tell her I'm cooperating with the FBI."

Nestor nodded, "Good idea, and while you're at it, tell her the FBI wants that tape so they can do some kind of voice analysis to try to determine whether the woman they've identified is a spy."

"That'll work. You know a lot of slime balls. Can you get some actor to play an FBI agent to contact my old lady's attorney?"

"Good idea. Let me work on that. We've been here longer than usual. You leave first, John." Nestor watched Blanton walk away. The Undersecretary of State's head was down, and his shoulders were hunched. Nestor ran his hand through his hair. *Blanton's weak. If his wife's attorney contacts the FBI and a prosecutor offers him a deal, I'm fucked. The four hundred mil will be my last chance to cash in, and then I'll have to take care of Blanton.*

CHAPTER 20

GLORIA SAT AT HER DESK SORTING through her mixed feelings. They ranged from guilt about aborting the child, to sadness that the last part of Jim Abbott was gone, to relief that her pregnancy was over. All she had left were the memories and the angst. Why did Abbott really go to Iraq? Was it about their relationship, or was that a cover story for him to get the hundred thousand? Did he really take it? Why and how did that come about? Did Janice Abbott have it?

Lauren leaned over the cubicle wall. "Are you going to call your informant?"

"Huh?" Gloria shook her head, coming back to reality.

"The voicemail on your cell, remember?"

"Yeah, time to get back into the swing of things."

Encased heating and cooling vents bordered the windows. Lauren slid into Gloria's cubicle and crouched down on the vent. "How were things when you got home?" she whispered.

"The kids were great. Happy to see me, making plans to do things. Adsila and I saw the movie *Shall We Dance*. Richard Gere and Jennifer Lopez, I needed something light. It was fun. We had such a good time."

"What about Darius?"

"Poor kid, his father is destroying his confidence, tells the boy that he's not quick enough on the court to get a scholarship to a big school. The kid practices and works out seven days a week. "'Mom, I've got to get stronger, but I can't gain any weight. I can't lose a step'. He's torturing himself.'"

"Speaking of the man, how was he?"

Gloria looked over her shoulder and leaned toward Lauren. "He wanted to have sex."

"You couldn't, right? Didn't the doctor say you couldn't do anything for two weeks?"

Gloria nodded, "I—"

Stephens turned into Gloria's cubicle and laughed. "Hi ladies. You two look like you're up to no good."

Lauren stood. "We're planning our week. Going to contact Gloria's informant, Marvin. He's got more information on the Henderson case."

"That case is getting better all the time. Don't forget, I want both of you to get on top of the currency transaction report project. Lauren, that includes the 8300 forms filed by businesses on transactions over ten thousand dollars, and the foreign bank account reports for persons taking or bringing more than ten grand in or out of the country. We should be able to generate some good cases from the computer runs. No one's looked at the reports for months. They've piled up in the file cabinet next to my office."

"What's your priority, the case or the project?" Gloria asked.

"That's easy. There's a branch meeting in two weeks and the chief will want to know how many prosecution cases we will be forwarding and how many cases we'll be able to generate from the project. So, the priority is both. Got to keep the stats looking good. Let me know how the meeting with your informant goes." Stephens stepped back, turned to head to his office, and stopped. "Gloria, your husband called the office last week looking for you. I thought you said that you were going to Oklahoma. Didn't he know? Anyway, let me know what the informant says." He stepped away.

Gloria put her elbow on the arm of her chair and rested her forehead in her hand. The muscles in her gut tightened like a twisted cord. "Oh, shit."

Lauren put her hand on Gloria's knee. "Did he say anything to you about your going to San Francisco?"

Gloria shook her head and mumbled, "Friday night he said he was going to divorce me. Now I know why he said that. He didn't want me to know he called the office. He's saving up the ammunition in case he needs it."

"God, I don't believe it. After what you went through last week. What're you going to do?" Lauren stood.

Gloria thought, *I'm fucked.* "I've got to get him off my mind. I'll call Marvin and set up a meet."

That afternoon Lauren and Gloria left the office in the black Blazer. "I've got the hundred that Stephens approved after our last meeting," Gloria said.

"You mean the other hundred you owe Marvin?" Lauren asked.

"Yes, I've been too busy to figure a way to reimburse myself for the first hundred I gave him. Stephens is so tight-assed, he won't authorize the payment."

Lauren giggled.

"What's so fucking funny?"

"I can see your husband finding out you're taking your personal cash to give to another...black guy, and on top of that, you're disappearing for a couple of days."

"Yeah, that's funny, ha ha, it sure looks like this broad has a boyfriend," Gloria said.

"Yeah, Marvin is your boyfriend. I'll testify that I saw you pull a C-note from your personal stash and give it to him for services rendered."

For Gloria, this conversation was getting a little too personal. "That's enough. I've gone through too much lately to become the subject of your jokes."

"Sorry, I didn't mean to—"

"No, I'm sorry, Lauren. I'm just stressed. I shouldn't be short with you," Gloria said.

She pulled onto Jackson Boulevard and parked near the fairway for the first hole at Columbus Park. A few minutes later Marvin's yellow Cadillac parked in front of them. The taillight on the passenger side was cracked. He got out of his car wearing a black, wide-brim hat pulled low over his face, a black warm-up suit, and matching Jordan's. Marvin did his pimp stroll from his car and got into the rear seat of the Blazer.

"Good afternoon, ladies."

"Hi," Gloria said, and Lauren nodded. "I was out of town when you called last week. That's why I didn't get in touch with you sooner. You said you had information on another straw purchaser the Gangster Disciples are using."

"Yeah, but I believe we have a financial matter that has accrued since our last meeting. Namely a hundred bucks you still owe Marvin." He smiled, the diamond in his front tooth sparkling.

Gloria pulled the bill out of a folder on the console. It was paper clipped to a receipt. She handed it over her shoulder, along with a Bic pen. "Sign the receipt, please."

Marvin grabbed the bill, stashed it in the pocket of his warm-up suit, signed the receipt, and handed it and the pen back to Gloria, who put the paper into the folder. "So, what's new?" she said.

"This is big. If the Disciples found out I was giving this to you, it be the end of Marvin."

Gloria looked at Lauren and raised her eyes. "What do you have?"

Marvin pulled a stick of Juicy Fruit gum from his pocket, took the wrapper off, and stuffed it into his pocket. He curled the stick and stuck in his mouth. Chewing around his words, he said, "That honcho from the Disciples I told you about last time. He's using his baby momma to buy cars and buildings under her name. On top of that, she's not using her real name. That's good stuff, right?"

"Yeah, if we can prove it," Lauren said. "What's her real name, and what name is she using to buy the cars and real estate?"

He grabbed the back of the bucket seats and pulled himself up between them, resting his hands on the console. "You got five hundred for Marvin?"

"I've got to run it past my boss. If what you're saying is true and we can prove it, I'll try my best to get you five bills," Gloria said.

Marvin crossed his arms. "This is good shit. You got to get me five."

Gloria clenched her teeth. "Look, Marvin, don't tell me what I've got to do. I've always gotten you cash. This is a new boss, and I've got to educate him. Last time I jumped through hoops to get you a hundred from the G and it cost me a hundred out of my own pocket, but I kept my word to you. I'm telling you that if what you're saying is correct, I'll do my best to get you five. I'm just saying it's not up to me alone."

"All right, all right, you've always been square with me. This lady is McElroy's baby momma, so you know that she's in tight with the man. This guy is a killer. He don't mess around. If he just thinks somebody is talkin' on him, they be gone. So, you gotta be careful how you handle this, 'cause only a few people know what I'm about to tell you."

"We always protect your identity. You've been helping me a couple of years and nobody's ever said anything to you."

"Yeah, I know, but this guy would waste me in a heartbeat if he thought I was doing him."

"So how did you find out about this?" Gloria said.

"I was doing some painting in a building they bought in East Garfield Park, an' I heard McElroy talking to some white guy. I don't know if he was a realtor or lawyer or what, but they were talking about this building and to handle it the same way. It's a big courtyard building, five floors with at least five apartments on each floor. They were in the kitchen, and I was in one of the bedrooms, painting. I stopped when I heard them talking, 'cause I didn't want them to know I was there."

"What did you hear them say?" Lauren asked.

"McElroy tells the white guy to put the contract in the name of Shiquita DuBonnet."

"Can you spell that?"

"Marvin can do better than that." He unzipped his warm-up jacket and pulled out a sheet of paper. "After they left, I went into the kitchen and found this on the floor." He handed it to Gloria.

"This is a faxed copy of an estimated closing statement. It's got a fax number printed on the top. I bet that's the white guy's fax number and the buyer is Shiquita, Shiquita with an S. If that's the alias, what's the woman's real name?" Gloria asked.

"Her name is Tamika Carlton."

Gloria laughed to herself, *Carlton.* "How do you know that Shiquita is the name that Tamika is using?"

"I heard the white guy telling McElroy that everything is set for Tamika. That they had credit cards and bank stuff in the name of Shiquita, so Tamika can act like she's Shiquita when they do whatever they have to do to buy the building."

Lauren looked up from her note pad. "Where does Tamika live?"

"She stays with McElroy. In that fancy building on the north side of Grant Park on Randolph. I painted that place, too. I saw her there. She picked out the colors I painted."

Gloria nodded to Lauren. She set the notepad on her lap and asked, "How many kids does she have by McElroy?"

"Just one, a baby girl."

"What's McElroy's first name?"

"Spencer, but he goes by Ghost on the street."

"Do you know the white guy's name?" Gloria asked.

"No."

"What does he look like?"

"Don't know. I didn't creep around lookin' at them. I was hiding so they wouldn't see me. Ghost see me there, he probably woulda killed me right then if he thought I heard them talking like they were."

"How do you know he's a white man?"

"Come on, you think he's a educated black man?"

"It's possible."

"I know a honky-voiced white man when I hear one."

"Anything else you can think of, Marvin?"

"No, except when do I get my five bills?"

Gloria sighed. "I told you I've to get it through my boss. As soon as I do, I'll call you. You're right, though, this is good stuff."

"I know, should be worth more, but this a special sales price for you." He pointed at Gloria and then nodded at Lauren. "And you, too." Marvin grabbed the door handle, jerked it up, and left the Blazer. They watched him strut back to the Cadillac.

"Coincidence," Gloria said.

Lauren's forehead wrinkled. "What is?"

"Tamika Carlton has the same last name as my husband."

CHAPTER 21

IRS-CID
Chicago
Tuesday, September 28, 2004

GLORIA NODDED TO HER, AND Lauren took her usual spot on the heating vent next to Gloria's desk. "Before we meet with Stephens, I want you to do a Soundex check on vehicle registrations under the names of Shiquita DuBonnet, Tamika Carlton, and Spencer McElroy. Also, check the land trust records to see if any of them are beneficiaries, and look at the transcripts of their income tax filing history. I want to corroborate as much information as we can to convince Stephens to authorize five hundred for Marvin and to open cases on McElroy and Carlton."

"Okay." Lauren stood, stepped into the aisle, and turned to face Gloria. "What're you going to do?"

Gloria rubbed her brow as though warding off a headache. "Don't worry, I'll write the memo of our interview with Marvin."

"Good. Then I'll get right on this stuff."

Gloria nodded and smiled. "I'm glad you approve, Chief." She watched Lauren walk away and, once again, admired her taste in clothing. Today's outfit was a maroon pants suit, matching pumps, and a navy blouse. Gloria looked at her own ensemble—jeans, a gray long-sleeve T, and Merrill hiking boots—and shrugged.

An hour later, Gloria put the finishing touches on the draft of the memo, hit the print button, and shut off her laptop.

Lauren got comfortable on the heating vent again, a yellow legal pad in her hand and a pen behind her ear. "Interesting stuff. DuBonnet is a beneficiary of land trust #2004-124 at DCCI-American Bank and Trust. The trust includes the luxury condo at 400 East Randolph, which must be where Marvin met Tamika, and an address in East Garfield Park on the 3500 block of Arthington, not a nice part of town."

Gloria pushed herself away from her desk. "Interesting, but nothing in the land trust files for Carlton or McElroy?"

"Nope, the real estate is all under Tamika's alias."

"What about vehicles?"

"Get this. DuBonnet was the registered owner of a '99 Bentley, and currently owns a 2002 Bentley and a 2000 Porsche 911."

Gloria leaned back in her chair. "What vehicles do we have on—?"

"Carlton's got a '97 Chevy Impala, and McElroy has a '99 Chevy Van. Checked their tax filing history, too. The last return filed for McElroy was in 2000, and he only reported four thousand in income. He filed the previous four years, but never reported more than sixteen thou. Carlton's last return was 2002. She reported six thousand in income, and never reported more than that in any prior year. There's no record of returns at all for DuBonnet."

Gloria nodded. "So, it looks like McElroy got involved with the GDs after 2000. He didn't need a legit job after that. Carlton probably hooked up with him in 2002 or 2003." Gloria nodded. "Everything's low profile under their real names. Did you check the CTR project?"

"Next thing to do. We get something there, and Stephens can tell the chief at the staff meeting how valuable the project is."

Gloria laughed. "You sound like you're management material."

Lauren smiled. "Not for me. I'll stay in the field." She walked to the file cabinet to get the CTR project documents. Gloria had spent a career looking behind other peoples' masks for the truth, and she knew that one day, Lauren's ambition would drive her to go after the chief's office suite on the twenty-eighth floor.

A half-hour later, Lauren returned with a printout from the project. "The cars under DuBonnet's name were all purchased from a dealership in the western suburb of Westmont. The first Bentley was purchased with a combination of twenty thousand in cash and thirty money orders totaling one hundred thousand. Total purchase price: one hundred twenty thousand. The 1999 Bentley was a trade-in on the 2002, and the balance was paid with money orders totaling forty thousand. The Porsche was an all-cash deal, fifty big ones. I ran McElroy through TECS," she said, referring to the Treasury Enforcement Communication System. He's been arrested three times on murder charges, but never went to trial. Dubonnet served a one-year sentence in 1980 for conspiracy to defraud the government. Nothing on her after that."

"Read between the lines. There had to have been witnesses lined up for those cases, and something happened to them. Let's talk to Stephens. We should expand the Henderson grand jury to include McElroy and Carlton, and go knock on their door," Gloria said, thinking that she could slip in an imprest fund request to pay Marvin and recoup the hundred of her own cash that she'd given him.

Fifteen minutes later, Gloria and Lauren sat in front of Stephens's desk while he read Gloria's memorandum of the interview with Marvin. She noticed the family photo of his blond wife and twin infant daughters. *Nice looking family,* she thought.

Stephens put the memo down. "This is interesting information. Do you have any corroboration?"

Gloria looked at Lauren. "Show him what you found in the CTR project."

Lauren handed him the printouts summarizing the payments made on the Bentleys and the Porsche.

"What's your plan?" Stephens asked.

Gloria knew what she was going to tell him would feed his appetite for fast-tracking his career. "I think we should number cases on McElroy and Carlton and go interview them." Gloria handed Stephens the imprest fund request for a one-thousand-dollar payment for her informant.

Stephens picked up the request. "A thousand? You just paid him a hundred, and now you want to give him a grand?"

Even Lauren blinked when she heard the request.

Gloria knew Lauren was surprised by the amount, when Marvin had only asked for five hundred, but she also knew that Lauren would soon learn how to deal with Stephens.

"He's dealing with an extremely dangerous person. McElroy's been arrested three times for murder, but never convicted." Gloria felt she had better educate Stephens, too. "That means something happened to the witnesses against him.

The CI's in a dangerous position, but he's willing to keep helping us—for a price."

Stephens nodded. "Good job, you two. All right open the cases, and I'll approve the informant's payment for seven fifty. When you go to interview McElroy, I want you to take backup. Losing an agent in Iraq is one thing. I'm not going to lose agents on my home turf."

Gloria's gut clenched at the reference to Jim Abbott.

"Sorry, Gloria. I didn't mean to…"

"I know, Tom. It's OK," Gloria said. "We'll get the paperwork started." She turned and looked at Lauren as they left Stephens's office. At least she was getting more than they had promised Marvin. Then her gaze turned inward. The image of Jim Abbott came to her, and she thought, *Backup, good idea. I don't want another death on my conscience.*

CHAPTER 22

Offices of Standard Armor
Hyattsville, Maryland
Wednesday, September 29, 2004

N ESTOR GLANCED AT HIS CELL. It was Cherry's number. "Honey, I told you not to call me unless it's an emergency."

"I miss my white prince."

"I miss you, too. Can't wait until I can see my lioness again. But I really have to go."

She purred.

"We'll get together soon. But I really have to—" Nestor said.

"We might be able to get together sooner than you think," she said.

"How's that?"

"Can you see the parking lot from your office?"

"No, because I'm the president and I have a better view than that. I'm on the second floor, overlooking a pond, trees, and swans."

"Why don't you come to the front and take a look at the parking lot?"

He felt his gut roiling. "Cherry, what're you doing?"

"Come to your lioness, white prince."

Nestor hung his head and shut off his phone. He jumped out of his chair and raced around his desk, bashing his hip on the corner. "Shit."

Nestor marched out of his office, past the other executive suites, through accounting, past several clerks, and stood at the window. The clerks stopped working and a couple of them craned their necks to see what caught the president's attention. Cherry, wearing a white warm-up suit, was sitting on the trunk of the Mercedes, her feet straddling the gearshift.

He felt her eyes catch him in the window. She waved vigorously, motioning him to come down to the car. He shook his head. She waved harder. He looked at the clerks, "Does anyone know who that is?" They shook their heads. Nestor pointed at his chest. "I'll handle it."

Cherry slid into the seat, shut the engine off, and opened the door. In one motion, she spun out of the car and began walking toward the office entrance.

"Oh, fuck," Nestor mumbled. He turned and saw his staff eyeing him. He nonchalantly walked to the stairway in the center of the office. Once out of view, he ran down the stairs and through the revolving glass doors, meeting her at the entrance.

"Hello, my prince."

He looked around, saw no one else in the lobby. "Cherry, are you fucking crazy?" he hissed. "Drive to the Denny's. Just go out of the parking lot, turn left on the highway, and I'll meet you there." He glanced over his shoulder, checking the foyer one more time.

She wrapped her arms around her bosom, accentuating her cleavage. "I'm cold. Can't we go to your office?" She took a step toward the stairway.

He slid in front of her and blocked her access to the stairs. "Absolutely not. You know better."

"I missed you and I wanted to see you." She pouted.

"Just call me anytime and I'll come to the condo."

"But you left me all alone. I was so sad, and you left me all alone. I felt you didn't care." Now she was whining, close to making a scene.

He turned his head, checking the lobby again, and turned back to Cherry. He had to get her out of there. "I'm sorry, I...I won't do that again."

"Are you sure?"

Nestor grabbed the zipper on the warm-up jacket and pulled it up to her neck. "That'll help keep you warm."

She grabbed the zipper and lowered it.

He grasped her hand. "Please, Cherry, come on! You know it's not good to meet here. Go to Denny's, and I'll be there in five minutes."

"Promise?"

"I promise."

He watched her strut to the Mercedes and hop into the car. The convertible top hummed up and over her. She smiled and squealed away.

Nestor looked up at the second-floor window and saw several clerks scurry away. He shook his head and went to his car.

Nestor pulled his black Mercedes CLK AMG into the Denny's parking lot. Women were driving him crazy. Blanton hustled by a pro from an escort service; Cherry fucking with his mind. And now that Nighthawk broad. Did she know something about the cash Abbott had extorted from him?

Nestor saw the red convertible parked near the entrance and pulled his sleek ride into a spot at the opposite end of the lot. He glanced in the rearview mirror and tightened the knot on his blue silk tie. Marching into the restaurant, he saw her sitting in a booth at the far end. He scanned the area looking for anyone who might know him, but the coast was clear, and he joined her.

Nestor realized he needed to use all his charm and manipulative skills to prevent this from ever happening again. Showing his frustration would not win the day. He reached for her hand and caressed it. "This was a pleasant surprise."

She laughed. "I thought by the look on your face you were going to shit in your pants."

He chuckled, raised his eyebrows, and cocked his head to the side. "You're so funny."

She pulled the zipper down halfway, revealing the swell of her breasts.

He let go of her hand and raised his, giving her the stop signal.

"I thought you liked my titties. You said it was the best investment you ever made."

"I love them, but I want to keep them as my personal pillows, not share them with everyone in Denny's."

She patted the space on the booth between her and the window. "Why don't you come over to my side of the booth? There aren't many customers. I'll give you happy times right here."

He reached out for her hand again. "Cherry, we need to…" He heard the soft thud of a shoe falling to the floor, and felt her foot massaging him between his legs. "Talk" squeaked out of his mouth.

She pulled the zipper of her jacket down a few more clicks.

A waitress in a black uniform approached the booth. She was skinny to the point of anorexia and wore a brown wig. A wisp of gray hair shot out near her ear. She slid two glasses of ice water onto the table, and her eyes focused on Cherry's cleavage. "Is there anything I can get you?" Her eyes wandered to Nestor. "Looks like you have everything you can handle."

"I'll just have water," he said.

"I'll have pancakes…and a sausage."

"I bet you will." She jotted down the order and walked away. Her heels slipped out of the backs of her tennis shoes as they slid across the floor.

"Baby, you know you're my *secret* love," Nestor said.

She tilted her head down and then gazed up at him. "Honey, you make me feel like I'm your secret whore."

"Don't I give you everything you want: designer clothes, jewelry, a nice place to live?" His real concern was the bank accounts she deposited his money into, and what he might have to do to change all that. And that fucking red Mercedes. One bet where the cash came from to buy that. "I'm your white prince and you're my African princess. Has anyone ever treated you better?"

She slid her foot down from between his legs and slipped it back into her black pumps. "You are the best man I've ever known, but sometimes I feel used."

"I'm sorry, Baby. You know I'm a busy man with a lot of responsibilities. You know that I trust you with things that I trust no one else with. That should tell you what you mean to me and how I feel about you."

Cherry's eyes teared up. "I'm sorry I came to your office, but I missed you so much, and I needed to see you."

"I love to hear you say that." He felt his charm taking effect.

The waitress came with the order and placed it in front of Cherry. "Are you sure one sausage is going to be enough? You look like you have a hearty appetite."

Cherry stared at her out of the corner of her eyes. "Yes, I'm good."

"I bet. Well, if you need anything else, give me a whistle. You know how to whistle, don't you? Bet you don't know what movie that was from." She left the bill on the table.

Cherry picked up the sausage, slid it halfway into her mouth, and caressed it with her lips.

Nestor pulled a twenty out of his pocket and laid it on the table. "Maybe we can get a room when you're done. There's a motel about a mile down the road."

She pulled the sausage from between her lips and they left.

CHAPTER 23

Downtown Chicago
Friday, October 8, 2004
6:18 a.m.

PREVIOUSLY GLORIA HAD INITIATED THE cases on Spencer McElroy and Tamika Carlton. A white van parked on Randolph, a half-block west of Lake Shore Drive, across the street from the luxury condo. The sign on its side read ACE Plumbing. PVC pipes the length of the van were fastened to the roof. Two unshaven men in gray coveralls and stocking caps sat in the front seats as the sun's rays broke through the gray horizon.

IRS Special Agent Louis Garcia shifted to Park and shut off the engine. "I should've put on long underwear under these work clothes."

Agent Steve Henderson slid his passenger seat back and rested his feet on the dash. "That your bulletproof vest in the back? Put it on. That'll help keep you warm. You should wear it anyway. From what they said, this guy is dangerous. I've got mine on."

"Good idea." Louis climbed into the back of the van and sat on the chair in front of the array of equipment: two-way radio, four monitors, a printer, and a VCR. He unzipped the top of his coveralls, lowered it to belt level just above his sidearm, and strapped on his vest. "Is this your first time in the surveillance van?"

"Yeah," Henderson said.

"I'll show you how this works. There's four cameras, one each out of the back ends and front ends of PVC pipes on the roof." He turned on the monitors.

"Each camera has a monitor. You can freeze a picture and print it. The front camera on the driver's side has a shot of the garage entrance and exit for this building."

Steve gazed up at the forty-story glass tower. "She said that this guy has a condo on the twenty-eighth floor. Can you believe a mutt like this living in this kind of luxury, and he's only thirty years old?"

"It's the lifestyle. They don't know how long they're going to live, so they spend it as fast as they can." Garcia paged through the background summary Lauren Ashberry had prepared. "Between him and his girlfriend, they've got four vehicles. One of them is a black Porsche 911. This guy is six foot two and weighs two eighty. He sure won't be driving that. So, keep a lookout for a '97 Impala, a '99 Chevy Van, or the 2002 Bentley. They're all black, except the van is tan."

"I don't know why we had to get out here before dawn. No gangbanger will be going out at this hour. If anything, he's coming home about now," Henderson said.

"What they want to know is whether he's going or coming. The game plan is to catch him leaving, so they can go in and interview the girl. The guy's a honcho in the GDs. He's not likely to talk, but she's only twenty or so. Maybe she will."

"2-0-8 from 1-7-4," came over the two-way radio.

Henderson picked up the mic. "That's Gloria." He keyed it. "Go, four."

"2-1-0 and I are in position. Let us know if there's any activity."

"Ten-4, it's all quiet. We've got an eyeball on the garage access, so we'll let you know if we see anything."

By ten thirty, all they had seen was a parade of Mercedeses, Jaguars, and BMWs leave the garage, and stretch limos that pulled into the circular drive to pick up passengers.

Henderson keyed his mic. "1-7-4 from 2-0-8."

"Go," Gloria said.

"Do you have a time limit in terms of how long you want to wait on this guy?"

"Negative. Do you have any commitments?"

"Only mother nature calling. I've emptied my thermos of coffee, and I prefer not to use the bottle if possible."

"Why don't you 10-7? We'll take your place in the meantime."

"10-4." Garcia started the van, waited until he saw Gloria and Lauren park behind them in the Blazer, and then pulled away.

Fifteen minutes later, Henderson radioed them. "1-7-4, we're going to grab a couple of beefs. Do you want us to pick up anything for you and your partner?"

"Sounds good." There was a pause. "One with sweet peppers, the other with giardiniera and mozzarella."

"Good choice. Who's going with the giardiniera and mozzarella?"

"That's my partner. She's a bit of a gourmet – pretty picky with her preferences."

"Definitely has good taste. We'll see you in about twenty minutes."

"10-4."

Ten minutes later, Lauren turned on the radio to an oldies station; Isaac Hayes was singing *Shaft* just as the Bentley emerged from the underground garage.

Gloria looked at Lauren. "*He's a bad motha and no one understands him but his woman.*"

"That must be his woman in the passenger seat, holding the baby. That's got to be Tamika."

"We'll follow them, see if he drops her off someplace, and we can interview her there. Radio the guys and let them know we're moving."

Lauren keyed the mic. "2-0-8 from 2-1-0, we're moving south on Lake Shore Drive with both subjects in the Bentley."

"10-4, we're stuck in the drive-through. Keep us informed and we'll catch up with you."

"Lauren, did you get a good look at them?" Gloria asked.

"It was definitely the Ghost. The guy took up half the front seat. But the female was wearing a hat. Couldn't get a good look at her face, but we don't know what she looks like any way."

"Give Steve our 10-20," Gloria said.

"2-0-8, we're still on LSD, heading south passing Monroe Harbor."

"10-4, we're east on Taylor. We'll parallel on the Ryan. Give us some landmarks so we know where you are."

Lauren transmitted, "We passed Soldier Field, passing the 18th Street exit." She went on for the next ten minutes, calling out landmarks and exits:

McCormick Place, Stevenson Expressway, and then, "Exiting west on Oakwood."

"Shit, he's coming into my neighborhood," Gloria said.

"The subject turned south on Indiana," Lauren radioed Henderson and Garcia. They passed a mix of gentrified greystones. "East on 43rd and north into an alley. He stopped at the third garage on the west side of the alley." Gloria pulled the G car forward just enough to give them an eyeball down the alley.

Lauren broadcast, "He's out of the car. Opened the garage door. It's covered with graffiti. Pulled the Bentley into the garage."

As the garage door closed, Gloria pulled the Blazer into the alley, and they saw McElroy and the woman walking up the gangway to the house.

"He's carrying the baby, and she's walking with a cane. That's an old lady, not Tamika. Tell them to get down here and keep an eye on the garage. We're going back to the condo and see if Tamika's there."

Lauren radioed the other agents with the instructions. She gave Gloria a darting glance. "Isn't this close to your house?"

"About two blocks away," Gloria ran their faces through her mind. *Have I ever seen them before? I don't think so. Had McElroy ever seen me before? I don't know.* "I've never seen him in the neighborhood. Maybe they're just visiting someone." She returned to Lake Shore Drive and headed north. The traffic was light, and in fifteen minutes they parked in the circular drive of McElroy's condo. They exited the Blazer, carrying their briefcases. Both were dressed in suits, Gloria in blue and Lauren in gray. They walked through the revolving front door, their pumps clicking across the white marble floor, and stopped at a large counter in the lobby.

Standing behind the counter was an African American man with gray hair, wearing a black jacket, white shirt, and blue tie. "Can I help you, ladies?"

Gloria pulled out her badge. "I'd like to take a look in the garage."

"What would you be lookin' for?"

"Just want to see if a car we're looking for is in."

"Whose car?"

Gloria swayed from one foot to the other. "You know I can't say, but I'd really appreciate your cooperation."

The man leaned over the counter. "Ma'am, you can trust me. I used to be on the job, Austin District, Tac unit. Retired ten years ago."

Gloria paused. "This is really important."

"I'm good for it."

Gloria sensed that this man was solid. She looked at his name tag. "Mr. Green, do you know Spencer McElroy?"

"You can call me, Lucius, ma'am. I don't like him." He narrowed his eyes and clenched his fist. "You can tell he's a bad dude. He left about an hour ago, driving that black Bentley."

Gloria nodded, thought they had found an ally, but tested him. "Was he alone?"

"No, he had his mother and the baby. Usually, when he leaves, he's gone for the day. Not always, but usually."

"How about his lady?" Lauren asked.

"I haven't noticed her leave, but sometimes I'm dealing with a delivery man or on the phone."

"Lucius, can you let me into the garage? I want to see if his cars are still there," Gloria asked.

"Yup, I sure can. Come with me."

Gloria looked over her shoulder as she followed Lucius to an elevator. "Lauren, stay here. Keep an eye on the garage entrance in case he returns."

Lucius pushed a button, an elevator door opened, and he held it for Gloria. "Press G, when you get down there, go to the left. They've got parking spots 28108 through 28111."

"Thanks." She pressed the button, the doors closed, and in five seconds she was stepping into the garage. She walked to McElroy's spots. Three of them were taken by the van, the Chevy, and the Porsche. Gloria walked to the vehicles and put her hand on the hoods of the Chevy and then the van. They were cold. She walked to the Porsche and placed her hand on the rear of the car. It was warm. "Looks like our girl went out this morning and came back already," she mumbled.

"You always talk to cars?" an African American woman in her early twenties asked. She was dressed in black leggings and a gray warm-up jacket, and she carried a green yoga mat. Her skin was coffee-colored, and her hair was parted in the center. It was shoulder-length and in tightly braided corn rows. She had to be nearly six feet tall and had a lean athletic body.

"Nice car," Gloria said.

"It's mine, and as you could guess, I'm on my way out. So, if you unhand my car, I'll be going."

"You Tamika?"

She put her hands on her hips. "Who wants to know?"

Gloria reached inside her coat and flashed her gold badge and identification. "I'm Gloria Nighthawk, Special Agent with the Criminal Investigation Division of the IRS."

"What do you want with me?"

"Need to ask you a few questions."

"Obviously, I'm on my way out. Why didn't you call to make an appointment?"

"I'm busy, too, was in your neighborhood, so it was convenient to drop by." Gloria shrugged and held out her right-hand palm up.

"Sounds like bullshit to me. Who let you down here? Was it Lucius?"

Gloria ignored her question. "I'm sorry if it's not convenient. I only need about fifteen minutes of your time and then you're free to go."

"What do you want to talk to me about?"

"Can we go to your condo? I have some papers to show you." *Then I can see the interior, where I'm sure you spent a mint.*

"You got a warrant?"

"I don't want to search your place. Just ask you a few questions. Only take fifteen minutes." Gloria shrugged. "Or, I'll write you a forthwith summons, and you'll have to come back with me to the federal building. By the time we get there, park, and get settled, it would probably take a good part of the day."

Tamika glanced at her Rolex. "I don't believe this. I'm late for my class. OK, might as well get this over."

They walked to the elevator, stepped in, and Tamika pushed the button for the first floor. She looked at Gloria. "We have to get onto the next bank of elevators to get up to my condo."

They got off the elevator, and Lauren approached them from the lobby. "Tamika, this is my partner. She's coming with us."

"Two of you, Jesus Christ. What're you going to do, the good cop, bad cop routine?"

"No, ma'am, it's just procedure," Lauren said.

They entered the next elevator. Lauren was against the back wall. Gloria was against a side wall and Tamika leaned into the opposite wall, facing her. Tamika cocked her head, and Gloria could feel her eyes cutting into her. The elevator pinged to a stop on the twenty-eighth floor, the doors opened, and they walked briskly to keep up with Tamika's long strides down a blue, red, and green oriental runner. She stopped at her door, where 28E was marked in gold. Tamika hit the keypad, opened the door, and stepped into the living room.

Floor-to-ceiling windows looked down onto Grant Park and Monroe Harbor. The remaining leaves on the trees were brown, and white caps roiled beyond the breakers on Lake Michigan.

"Beautiful view," Gloria said.

Tamika sat on a white leather sofa. "You said fifteen minutes and then I've got to be out of here. You already screwed up my day, so make it fast."

Gloria and Lauren sat in white matching chairs across from Tamika. Lauren opened her black-leather folder. Behind them was a six-foot-wide flat-screen television surrounded by massive speakers. They looked at Tamika over a glass coffee table covering a white fur area rug. Behind Tamika, an abstract painting flashing reds, yellows, and blues covered most of the wall. "All right, we'll get right to it. Do you know anyone by the name of Shiquita DuBonnet?"

Tamika shook her head. "I should hope so."

Gloria noticed a tattoo of a semiauto on Tamika's neck. "What do you mean?"

"That was my mother."

"Is she still alive?"

"No, she died a couple of years ago."

"Sorry to hear that. How did she die?"

Tamika crossed her legs. "I don't think that's any of your business."

"The reason I'm asking is that it appears there were some vehicles purchased in her name."

"That asshole told us to do that." Tamika crossed her arms over her chest. "The same asshole that told her he loved her more than anything in the world and then shit all over her."

"What happened?"

"I lived through it once, and now you're going to make me do it again."

"I'm sorry, Tamika, but there's a potential money-laundering violation in question here, and what you're telling me could resolve any questions we might have."

Tamika looked down, exhaled, and slowly raised her head. "A long time ago, my mother got in trouble. She hung around the wrong people and got busted. She was just a hanger-on, not involved in anything."

Gloria glanced at Lauren. *This sounds like bullshit.* "Go on."

"To put it plainly, she got fucked. The attorney that handled the case fucked her good."

"What do you mean?"

"Fucked, like in, fucked her every way he could, and then she still had to go to jail. He said he didn't have a choice, but he would be there for her when she got out. Said it was only a year. You know what? I was born in jail 'cause of the asshole."

"Why didn't she say something?" Gloria asked.

"'Cause she loved him, and he said he loved her. He was going to marry her after she got out."

"What happened after she got out?" Lauren said.

"He kept on fucking her. My mother was his bitch. He was already married, but said he was going to get a divorce and marry my mom, or that's what he told her, anyway. Went on for years, and then he said he wouldn't do it."

Gloria leaned toward Tamika. "That's quite a story."

"Story! You bitch. My mother committed suicide after he told her he wouldn't divorce his wife."

"What about the cars? The Bentleys and the Porsche, they're in your mother's name."

"That's what he told us to do."

Gloria sat back and cocked her head. "That's pretty convenient, putting the blame on someone else."

"Oh, really. Wait here." She rose from the sofa and marched down a hallway. A minute later she returned with an envelope, walked to Gloria, and turned it upside down. A handful of dollar-size documents fell into Gloria's lap.

"He tried to buy me off. But I refused to deposit any of these. He can keep his fucking money. He still calls wanting to see his granddaughter. Ain't gonna happen."

Gloria picked up several of the pieces of paper. They were money orders. The first one was purchased from a currency exchange two blocks from the Dirksen Federal Building. No remitter was listed. The next three were purchased from a currency exchange in Bronzeville. They were all in the amount of five hundred dollars, payable to Tamika Carlton. She looked at the remitter lines; nothing on the first one, nothing on the second one. On the third one she recognized the handwriting. It was his.

Robert Carlton, her husband. Gloria twisted the gold wedding band on her finger.

She gazed at Tamika but had to avoid her eyes. Then she glanced at Lauren. Gloria's hands went limp, dropped to her side, and the money orders fell to the floor. The money orders symbolized a betrayal that had lasted nineteen years.

Gloria went to her knees and scooped up a handful of them.

Tamika got up from the sofa, hurried around the coffee table, knelt, and grabbed the remaining money orders. "These are mine. You can't take them."

Gloria dropped the money orders she held into her satchel and grabbed the ends of those in Tamika's hand. "Let go of these Tamika. As of this moment, they are the property of the government."

Tamika tugged on them.

Gloria held on tight. "I'll write up a summons right now demanding that these money orders be turned over forthwith. Now, damn it, let go. You'll get them back in due time."

"No, these are mine," Tamika said, her teeth clenched.

"Let go, or I'll arrest you for obstruction of justice. You can spend the night in jail at the Metropolitan Correctional Center. Let go, and you can be home tonight with your baby."

Tamika exhaled and let go. "You bitch."

Gloria stuffed the remaining money orders into their envelope. "Lauren, give her a receipt for these. You don't have to individually list them, just write down 'various money orders.'"

"You…you can't do this," Tamika said.

"It's done. I'll mail you copies." Gloria paused, "You know what, I'm sure we'll be meeting again. I'll deliver the copies to you personally. Here's my business card." She laid it on the coffee table.

Tamaki picked it up. "You'll be hearing from my attorney."

Lauren placed the receipt on the coffee table.

Gloria wondered, *Attorney. Will that be Robert Carlton?* She took a good look at Tamika. She could see a resemblance between her and Darius. Both fathered by the same man, Tamika had his long slender body and deep-set eyes. *They could pass for siblings.* She wondered, *How close was he to divorcing me for her mother?*

Gloria and Lauren left the condo. The door slammed behind them. They got onto the elevator, and Lauren said. "This is a grand jury investigation, right?"

"Yeah, so?"

"You know that you can't issue an administrative IRS summons in a grand jury case?"

"Like I said, yeah, so I didn't."

"You threatened her with a summons twice. What you said could bite you in the ass."

"You didn't see who the remitter was on those money orders?"

"See? How could I? You treat them like they're top secret."

"The remitter was my husband. After nineteen years of marriage, I just found out that he has a daughter I didn't know about, a mistress for some period of our marriage, and a granddaughter he inquired about two weeks ago."

Lauren leaned against the back wall of the elevator. "Holy fuck."

"Not to mention that he apparently advised Tamika and McElroy to use a nominee to buy those cars and real estate. A nominee who was his mistress, who committed suicide because he said he wouldn't divorce me to marry her."

"What're you going to do?"

Gloria shook her head. "I…I wish I knew for sure. Right now, I can't do anything. I need a few days to process all this. But I know *you'll* have to handle it."

CHAPTER 24

Dirksen Federal Building-Chicago
Courtroom 2503
Friday, October 8, 2004
11:15 a.m.

JUDGE ROBERT CARLTON STORMED FROM the bench into his chambers, his black robe flowing behind him like a cape. Lead prosecutor Assistant US Attorney Robert Packer and defense attorney Jordan Magil struggled to keep pace with him.

"Listen very closely." The judge clenched his jaw. "If I hear one question I even think is leading to the rape, I'm ruling a mistrial. I'm not putting my record on the bench up for an appeal because of you yokels. That goes for both the defense and the prosecution. We're four weeks into this trial. Magil, I know you don't want to start this trial over again, because I understand your client is out of money, and you don't like to work for free. Packer, if you cause a mistrial it won't be your first…I hear you're on thin ice with the US Attorney. It's tough on the street when you're trolling for a job. Either of you have any questions?"

The attorneys shook their heads. Carlton's cell phone rang. He looked at the caller ID—unknown—and glanced back at the attorneys. Perspiration dripped from Magil's forehead. Packer wrung his hands. Carlton nodded his head toward his chamber's door. "Lunch break. See you gentlemen in an hour." The attorneys limped out of the chambers like two wounded animals.

Carlton hit the answer button. "Judge Carlton."

"It's Tamika."

"Hi, Honey."

"Don't fuckin' honey me. This isn't a social call."

He took a deep breath. "I only want to see my granddaughter—"

"It's not gonna happen."

He glanced at the ten-year-old photo of Gloria, Darius, and Adsila, knowing that his failure to update the picture meant something. "I'm a man who is used to getting his way. Why you persist in taking this position, denying me—"

"The feds were here asking questions about my momma and the cars and buildings you told Spencer to buy under her name."

He closed his left hand and admired his manicured fingernails, thinking Tamika was telling another wild story. "You're just saying that because you think that will make me stop calling you."

"I told the feds everything. How you told my momma to plead guilty while you were fuckin' her. Promised to marry her when she got out, and then backed down 'cause you wouldn't divorce you wife."

He lifted a single brow and cocked his head. "That's quite a story, Tamika. You're forcing me to take unpleasant action if you don't let me see that baby." It was a way he felt he could exert some control over Tamika, to make sure if she did talk to anyone, she would say the right things.

"The only action you'll be taking when I'm done talking to the feds is trying to figure out how to get out of jail. I gave the feds all those money orders you sent me."

He wiggled his forefinger in his ear, cleaning out the wax, and wiped it in a Kleenex. "Yeah, sure, like you'd pass up five hundred a month. I can check with the currency exchanges. I'm sure you cashed them all."

"I would never take your fuckin' money. You killed my momma. I told the agent that."

"Tamika, you aren't really adept at lying." He laughed. "Who was this agent?"

"I've got her card." She paused. "Gloria Nighthawk."

Carlton pushed the button on his phone, killing the call. He felt the pounding of his heart in his chest and throat. He placed his elbows on his desk, laid his face in his hands, and massaged his temples. *I don't fucking believe it.* He pulled his hands down his face. *The only one who was a party to any conversations was Spencer. Anything Tamika knows is hearsay. She can't testify against me.*

He leaned back and slid open his bottom desk drawer. He lifted a stainless-steel Beretta 92FS out of the drawer, ripped off the red evidence tape, and shook his head. *Introduced thirty weapons in the trial and left one behind; only ATF would do that.* He put the semi-auto back in the drawer, closed and locked it.

CHAPTER 25

Offices of Standard Armor
Hyattsville, Maryland
Friday, October 8, 2004
1:00 p.m.

NESTOR GAZED OUT THE WINDOW, feet atop his desk and hands folded behind his neck as he watched the swans gracefully floating across the pond. The future was set. He knew that in the next month he would have another opportunity to grab a couple more million. All he would need to do is take care of Blanton and make arrangements to grease the palms of the right people. The success of Standard Armor would be guaranteed.

His intercom buzzed. "What is it, Joanie?"

"There are two gentlemen from the Department of Defense here to see you."

Nestor huffed, "Bureaucrats looking for an excuse to get out of their office." He looked at his Rolex and laughed. "Ah, extending their lunch break."

Joanie repeated herself.

He glanced at his calendar. "I don't have an appointment with them," he mumbled, pushing the button on the intercom. "I'm booked all week. Make an appointment with them for next week."

"The gentlemen – uh – suggested you see them now, or they will wait here until you have an opening."

He scraped at the cuticle on his thumb. "I hope they brought something to eat. Tell them it'll be a long wait. I'm on a conference call with our senator discussing campaign contributions."

His office door opened and two men in off-the-rack gray suits entered. Joanie stood behind them. "I'm sorry, Mr. Nestor, I told them they couldn't go into your office." She shook her head and her shoulders slumped apologetically.

"Can't beat dumb luck, Sir. You must have just ended your call with the senator," the older of the two men said. He was anemic-looking, wearing horn rimmed glasses complimented by a spot on his tie. He pulled credentials from his inside suit coat pocket and flashed his picture ID. "Auditor John Smikel, Defense Contract and Supply."

Nestor slid his feet off the desk to the floor. "What's the meaning of this? Can't you make an appointment like your other employees? You just can't barge in here."

Smikel ignored Nestor and pointed at his partner. "This is Auditor Richard Thomas." He looked young enough to be Smikel's son. "We have a summons demanding all documents and records relative to the manufacture of all body armor products produced by Standard Armor and any of its subsidiaries. The Marine Corps and other armed services have experienced a high failure rate with your products. I have to advise you that at this point, this is an administrative investigation, but it could lead to criminal charges. Therefore, we ask that you don't leave the country." He placed the summons on Nestor's desk and folded his hands in front of his waist. "Do you have any questions, sir?"

Nestor picked up the summons and read it. His mouth slackened. He tugged at his sleeves, looked at the auditors, and shook his head. "How the hell am I supposed to run this company? Standard Armor is an international operation. If I don't travel, we can't do business."

"In addition to the issue of product quality, we know that there's a lot of cash flying around Iraq, and there's some concern as to where this cash is ending up. So, until there's evidence that payments made to DoD contractors, like Standard Armor, are being properly accounted for, and until a more secure contractual procedure can be initiated, the Secretary of Defense wants to, shall we say, slow things down."

Nestor stood, put his fists on his desk, and leaned toward the auditors. "What do you want me to do, stop making body armor and put our soldiers at risk? This is ridiculous."

Smikel's glasses slipped down his nose as he began his monologue. "The secretary definitely wants the best for our soldiers. There will be two phases to this investigation. Effective in thirty days, the funds for your company and other vendors will be held in escrow and disbursed as soon as a proper accounting can be made. The goal is to expedite this investigation, so vendors do not suffer any financial hardship."

He paused, pushing his glasses with his forefinger back up his nose, and said, "Second, an independent company will inspect the body armor purchased from Standard Armor to determine whether it meets the required standards. So, it is important that the body armor in Iraq stays there until it can be secured by that contractor."

Nestor fell back into his chair. He drummed his fingers on his desk. "Thirty days? So, when exactly will those new procedures go into effect?"

"Sometime near the end of this month, October," Thomas said.

Got to get to the Fed's money before the end of the month, Nestor thought. "Who's the independent company that will do the evaluation?"

"It would be a conflict of interest to disclose that."

"This is disgraceful. For years I've supplied the military with all sorts of equipment. Traveled the world to make sure all the GIs' needs were met, sacrificed time away from my family, and this is the thanks I get? The senator will hear about this."

Smikel sat down in one of the chairs in front of Nestor's desk. "Mr. Nestor, I understand your frustration. Every elected official wants our soldiers to be as safe as possible. I'm sure your senator will agree. So please, don't take this personally. I have to advise you, though, that even though we have not asked you for your passport, your name is now on the No-Fly list, so you will not be allowed to board any international flights. If necessary, the secretary can get a court order demanding you turn over your passport."

Nestor's eyes widened. "I'm not even sure where it is."

Smikel stood and put both hands on Nestor's desk, leaning into him. "That's surprising, Mr. Nestor, for a man who travels as much as you do, not to know where his passport is."

"Well," he hesitated, "I'm not all that well organized, and I rely on my support staff to take care of things like that. I'm more of a big-picture guy." He spread his hands apart.

Smikel placed his business card on Nestor's desk. "If you have any questions, call me. A response on the summons is due in two weeks. You can have the records delivered to my office or call me and I'll pick them up."

"Sure, sure, no problem. Let me see you gentlemen out." Nestor stood.

Smikel raised his hand. "That's all right, sir. We can find our way." They left the office.

Nestor waited a few minutes to make sure they didn't return and to give himself a chance to regain his composure. Then he opened the center drawer of his desk, removed his passport, and placed it in the inside pocket of his suit jacket. He hit the speed dial for Blanton on his cell phone.

"Yes?"

"Something's come up. We need to meet, soon."

"I've a meeting with…never mind. Six o'clock at location five."

"Good."

The sun peeked out on the western horizon beneath gray skies settling across the Vietnam Memorial. Nestor got out of his cab and saw Blanton's familiar silhouette, the wide-brimmed hat and the raised collar of his dark raincoat. He stood before the memorial gazing at, but not seeing, the inscribed name Abraham Jackson. Nestor walked up to him just as an African American woman stopped at the column of names to the right, pulled out a sheet of paper, placed it over a name, and traced it with a pencil. They nodded to her. Nestor grabbed Blanton's arm, pulled him twenty yards away, and told him of his afternoon visitors.

"Shit, you don't have enough money squirreled away, so you had to sell faulty body armor to the DoD?"

"We tried to maximize our profit margins but didn't expect the fiber would deteriorate so quickly. It must be the fucking heat in that goddamn country. But the serial numbers and lot numbers will fade on our vests because the ink is so cheap. They won't be able to tell our vests from those of our competitors."

"Maybe your competitors' vests won't fail. Maybe their ink won't fade."

Nestor's nostrils flared. "What, are you a patriot all of sudden? You didn't have any trouble taking the cash I skimmed from the Fed's shipments."

"That doesn't have anything to do with a GI getting killed or maimed because his vest was made of shit!" Blanton snarled.

Nestor jabbed his finger in Blanton's chest. "Now you're Mister Ethics, but it was okay for you to be fucking some broad from an escort service."

Blanton shoved Nestor's hand away. "Cool it, Nestor. We've got to figure out whether this issue with the vests is going to affect our situation."

"You said there's one more shipment on October tenth. We'll cool it after that. They are putting in some new accounting procedures the end of October. We've got to get the cash before then. They're also putting my name on the federal No Fly list, so I can't fly out. I can't go to Iraq to get the cash. Going to Baghdad to talk to the GIs about the vests was my cover story for being there when the cash was delivered."

"Didn't the soldiers tell you about the problems with the vests?"

"I said that was my cover story. I didn't say I actually talked to them. I need to get another passport. You're the Under Secretary of State for Intelligence. You must have somebody that can make a phony passport."

Blanton shook his head in disbelief, then looked around for anyone who might overhear. "You're getting me in deeper."

"You're already in, so suck it up. There aren't many choices for you at this stage of the game."

"It'll have to be under another name. We'll have to get identification and credit cards under the same name with your picture on it."

"Can you do that before the end of the month, or better yet, get the Fed to make an earlier shipment?"

"Forget contacting the Fed. I never did that before. It would leave a trail a mile wide if they ever suspected anything, and I'd be on the top of the list."

Nestor pulled his hand down his face. *He's right, I've got to think more clearly.*

"We've got about a month to get the false ID. That should be doable. I've still got that problem with my wife. You said you could line up someone to impersonate an FBI agent and contact her attorney. Can you do that before the nineteenth?" Blanton asked.

"I'll make you a deal. You get working on the passport and ID, and I'll take care of your wife's attorney. I've had some former agents who do special assignments for me. This guy, Kane, was canned by the FBI. He'll be happy to impugn their reputation." *And once I get the cash, maybe I'll have him take care of you*

CHAPTER 26

Law Offices of Patricia Elliott and Associates
Washington, D.C.
Friday, October 8, 2004
4:00 p.m.

H E OPENED HIS CREDENTIAL CASE. "Special Agent Frederick Alberts, Mrs. Elliott."

Alberts looked her over. She was portly, dressed in a charcoal-gray suit that surely was not purchased off the rack because of the obvious quality and her hard-to-fit size. He returned his credentials to his inside suitcoat pocket.

Despite approaching fifty, Alberts still had that chiseled Marine Corps look, short salt-and-pepper hair, high cheek bones, and his blue suit jacket tight across his pecs. "Mrs. Elliott," he paused and exhaled. His blue eyes glanced down, and then back up at her pudgy face. "I'm here on a matter of national security." He sat in one of the armchairs in front of her oak desk.

Her green eyes focused on him, and she tented her hands. "And how does this involve me?"

"It appears that Russia's Foreign Intelligence Service is trying, through a series of false pretenses, to blackmail the husband of one of your clients. They intend to force him to spy on our government for them. This man has been courageous enough to contact us. He loves our country, you can be sure, to put his life on the line like this." Alberts shook his head and noticed the family portrait of Mrs. Elliott, her husband, and two college-aged daughters on the credenza behind her.

Four stuffed legal-size files sat in the center of her desk, separating her from Alberts. She lifted them and dropped them to the floor. "Agent Alberts, I'm sure you know my husband was an officer in the army. I would be happy to do my part for our country."

Her eyes were drilling deeper into his.

"I'm so glad to hear you say that. I feel like I can trust you. Why don't we dispense with the preliminaries? You can call me Frederick."

"Call me Patricia, please." She leaned forward and placed her elbows on her desk, forcing her breasts to strain the top of her suit.

"Certainly, Patricia. I feel that I can tell you the whole gruesome story." He took a deep breath in and then exhaled. He could sense her anticipation. "This woman, a rather attractive redhead, was put into situations by her Intelligence Service handlers whereby she would appear in the same places our man was with his wife—a movie theater, a shopping center, among others. She would then behave as though she knew the husband. As you might suspect, this didn't go unnoticed by the wife. And then the coup de grace, the phone call to this gentlemen's home when the Intelligence Service knew he wouldn't be there, a phone call made with expressions of true love and physical intimacy. You can imagine how the wife reacted, what she thought. Who could blame her? But, if you saw the husband and the other woman, you would know in reality it couldn't be."

"Frederick, you know that I have to honor my client's privileged communication. What can I do that would serve my country and protect my client?"

"My friends call me Fred."

"Mine call me Patty."

"Patty, you probably realize I'm referring to John Blanton."

She nodded, "I was pretty sure of that."

"It's my understanding that a tape recording of a message left by this intelligence operative to the Blanton's home phone is in your possession. We would like the original tape so our forensic lab can perform a voice analysis to determine whether the call was made by the woman we suspect. This case is moving fast, so the urgency of my request is high. John is supposed to make contact with the Russian agent by four tomorrow afternoon. We need to set the trap for a sting operation."

"If you don't mind, I prefer to call you Frederick, rather than Fred. You just look more like a Frederick to me."

"That's fine, Patty."

"This is what I can do for the time being to help you and our government. I'll give you the original tape. Of course, I have a copy of the tape, and for the time being I'll hold on to that. If this case is resolved amicably, I will also turn the copy over to you."

Bitch, now I'll have to come back tonight. "That sounds like the perfect remedy. Let's hope that the Blantons can overcome this hurdle in their marriage and we can put these Russian agents away." He watched her push herself away from her desk, waddle to a louvered door, and open it. He could see several black file cabinets. She stopped at the third one, unlocked it, opened the top drawer, and removed a cassette tape. She closed the drawer, locked it, and returned to her seat.

"Here you are." She handed him the tape.

He stood and nodded his head. "Your country thanks you, and let's hope that all ends well for the Blantons."

"Yes, it was good to meet you, Frederick."

"Likewise, I'm sure," and he left the office.

***

At nine that evening, Kane, known to Patty as Frederick Alberts, crept through the dimly lit hallway until he reached the door marked Elliott and Associates, Family Law, Suite 314. Instead of a blue suit he was dressed in black—turtle neck, slacks, shoes, and gloves.

Kane removed a small leather pouch from his pocket, slid out a lock pick, and inserted it into the lock. Thirty seconds later the lock clicked, and he pushed the door open. Stepping into the waiting room, he closed the door and set the deadbolt. He slid the pick into the pouch, returned it to his pocket, and lifted out a penlight, shining his way past the secretary's desk and into Elliott's office.

Kane went to the louvered door, stepped in, and flipped the switch. The file room lit up. He closed the door and went to work with the pick on the third file cabinet. Twenty seconds later he was fingering through the files. First the As and then into the Bs, "Becker, Biggs, Black, and Blanton. She's well organized. Thank you, Patty." The cassette was in the Blanton folder in an envelope marked Tapes.

Kane stuffed the envelope into his back pocket, exhaled, and reached for the door handle just as the office light flashed on. He heard two voices. He flicked the closet light switch, leaving him in total darkness. Manipulating the louvers, he peered into the office and saw Patty and a slender man with thick glasses, protruding Adam's apple, thinning hair, and a drawn face. He wore khaki slacks and a red flannel shirt. The tail of his shirt was sticking out covering his left hip.

"Thank you for seeing me so late. I had to close the library tonight. Anyway, as you know, my mother recommended you. You handled her three divorces. She told me from the beginning that marrying Amy wouldn't work out." The client sighed.

"Sometimes things just aren't meant to be," Patty said. She plopped into her seat, and the springs groaned.

"I should've just stayed with Mom. Now I've got this lease for the apartment for another year. Amy doesn't have a job, but she demands to stay there. How am I going to afford this?" He shook his head and plopped into the armchair in front of her desk.

"How is your mother doing?"

"She married again, three years ago, had better luck this time. Her husband died about a year ago."

"I was wondering why I haven't seen her for a while." She lifted a legal tablet from the credenza, placed it on her desk, and clicked her pen to note his responses. "Is this your first marriage?"

"Yes, who would have dreamed it would end so soon? Less than a year."

"How old are you?

"Forty-two. I'm a Christmas baby. Kind of funny for a Jew."

"Lenny, if I may ask, how much money do you make?"

Twenty-four thousand. I'm due for a review in two months. I should get at least a three percent raise." He smiled.

"Now as I understand, your wife has already contacted an attorney and filed on grounds of irreconcilable differences."

Lenny hung his head, "I might not look it, Mrs. Elliott, but, I'm good, I think." His face turned crimson. "But she has an addiction, wanted it every night, sometimes two or three times. I'd come home after a hard day of stacking books and there she'd be, wrapped in cellophane, waiting." He shook his head.

Mrs. Elliott undid the top button on her blouse. "Lenny, I have to ask you. I mean, I normally get a five-thousand-dollar retainer, and I bill at three hundred dollars an hour. You make twenty-four thousand. Do you have savings to draw on?"

He sat up straight. "I've got seven hundred dollars in a savings account and a couple of hundred in my 401K."

She drummed her fingers on her desk. "I don't see how we could work this out. Is your mother willing to pay your fee?"

"She's really pissed …I'm sorry, I mean angry with me for marrying Amy against her wishes."

"Does it seem warm in here to you?" She unbuttoned another button, revealing the valley between her breasts. She saw his eyes follow her fingers.

He swallowed and smiled. "If you could think of some way, some sort of installment plan, we could work out."

She unbuttoned a third button and bared the lace of her bra. "Why don't you come over here?"

Lenny stood, his hands shaking, and walked over to Mrs. Elliott. She grabbed his head and buried his face between her breasts.

Kane pointed a mini digital camera between the louvers and snapped away for five minutes. *Lenny was quick*, Kane thought, *no wonder his wife is suing for divorce.* He was sure that a photo sent to Patty with the appropriate note would encourage her to urge Mrs. Blanton to reconcile with her patriotic husband.

CHAPTER 27

IRS-CID
Chicago
Tuesday, October 12, 2004

GLORIA AND LAUREN HUDDLED AT Gloria's desk, Lauren sitting in her usual position on the heating vents.

"How did the weekend go?" Lauren asked.

Gloria looked at Lauren, then diverted her eyes from the young agent. "Robert never came home this weekend. No note, no voicemail, nothing. I don't know where he is. Nothing in his closet was touched. Maybe he replaced Shiquita with someone else."

"What did your kids say?"

"What could I tell them? I'm building a case against their father?" She pushed against her desk, her chair slamming into the file cabinet behind her. "I told them he went to a judge's conference in D.C."

Lauren exhaled. "Where do we go from here?"

"I have no choice. We have to tell Stephens what we learned from Tamika. I know this is going to get ugly, rip my family apart But if we don't pursue it, I'll get fired…or prosecuted. I finished the memorandum of interview over the weekend." She handed it to Lauren. "Proofread it and then we'll meet with Stephens."

Lauren corrected a few punctuation errors in the memo. They saw that Stephens was in his office and headed there. Gloria rapped on his doorframe. "Tom, a complex situation has developed. We need to advise you and we'll need to get the chief involved," Gloria said as she and Lauren stepped into his office, closed the door, and sat in the chairs in front of his desk. "Take a look at this memo. It'll give you the details."

Stephens took the three-page memo from Gloria. When he read the last page, he glanced up at Gloria, shook his head, and read the page again. "This Robert Carlton is *your* Robert Carlton? The judge? Your *husband?*" he asked with a slow, disbelieving shake of his head.

Gloria rubbed the back of her neck. "It's his signature on the remitter lines of some of the money orders. According to Treasury Enforcement Communication System, Shiquita Dubonnet was prosecuted and sentenced to a year in jail in 1980 for conspiracy to defraud the government. That sounds to me like a guilty plea to a lesser charge. My husband was an Assistant US Attorney from 1978 to 1987. Then he left the office for private practice for about two years before he was appointed as a judge in 1990. So, the time period fits. To find out for sure, we have two options. We can pull the case file from the Federal Records Center or check with the US Attorney's Office."

"We need to keep this under our hat until we're as sure as we can be that this involves your husband. Go to the records center and pull the files." Stephens flipped the memo back to the first page. His forehead furrowed. "You interviewed Tamika Carlton last Friday, and you're first coming to me with this today. Why the delay?"

"I knew this would be a sensitive matter. Wanted to clear my head and draft the memo so we would have an accurate record of what Tamika said. Lauren proofed the memo this morning and agreed that it correctly reflects what she told us."

Stephens grabbed the memo, rolled it into a cylinder, and slapped the palm of his hand with it. "So, you were home with your husband all weekend and you didn't discuss any of this with him?"

"Robert didn't come home all weekend. I haven't seen him since last Friday morning. I didn't discuss this with him on Wednesday, Thursday, or Friday morning. Since then there's been no telephone call, message, email, or text—nothing. I called his cell late Friday and again Saturday around noon and left voice messages. He hasn't returned my calls."

"Do you think he's been in touch with Tamika? Maybe she told him about your contact."

"That's possible. You'll read it in the memo. He was in touch with her two weeks ago, asking to see his granddaughter. I'm more concerned that Tamika told Spencer McElroy. He was arrested for murder three times, but never convicted."

"I remember that from your summary. Do you think you should file a missing persons report?" Stephens's cell phone buzzed. He picked it up from his desk and read a text message. "That's a text from News Radio. I subscribe to their service. It states that Federal Judge Robert Carlton, from the US District Court for the Northern District of Illinois, has been placed on administrative leave, effective immediately. No further information has been released." He looked at Gloria. "That's some damn coincidence."

Gloria slipped her wedding band off her finger and slid it into her pants pocket.

"He must have talked with Tamika. This changes things. We can't sit on this now while you corroborate that your husband was the prosecutor on Dubonnet's case. I'll go up to the chief and tell him what's going on. He'll want to contact the US Attorney's office, and they'll want to contact the Chief Judge." Stephens tapped the memo on his desk. "You realize that you'll have to be taken off the case."

"I know—"

There was a light knock on the door.

"Come in," Stephens said.

It was his secretary, Margaret Weiss. She was sixtyish, slightly taller than a file cabinet, built like a fireplug, and dressed in red. "Sorry, Mr. Stephens. There's a man on the phone asking for Special Agent Nighthawk. I can hardly understand him, but he said it's very important. He's calling from Baghdad."

Gloria rushed to the phone at her desk. "Transfer the call back here, Margaret."

Gloria picked up the phone. "Agent Nighthawk." She sat and pulled out a yellow legal pad.

"I called you a while ago," the man said with a middle eastern accent.

"I recognize your voice. Thank you for calling back."

"There are many things happening with the money from the Oil-for-Food Program. Our people are starving and a chosen few are stealing millions."

She felt in her gut this could answer her questions about Jim Abbot. "We have to meet. How can I get in touch with you?"

"I can't leave Iraq. Every week I will get a new cell phone and call you about this same time. I will keep the phone for twenty-four hours before I destroy it. If I don't hear from you during that period, I will call you again the following Monday, unless the situation becomes more urgent. Then I will call sooner."

"I'll give you my cell phone number. I'll come to Baghdad and we can meet." She gave him her number.

"That would be best."

"Can you tell me anything now? What's your name? Your position? What records you have? It would be very helpful to have this information to convince my superiors to allow me to go to Iraq."

"Somebody's coming, I have to go. I have records from bank accounts in Syria that reflect millions of dollars in cash deposits from the oil program. Here's my cell number. That is all I can say."

Gloria jotted the number down. "What about the attack? The body armor?" The phone went silent. Gloria slumped back into her chair, arms at her side. *Did Jim Abbott's death have anything to do with the Oil-for-Food Program? With millions of dollars?*

CHAPTER 28

Washington, D.C.
Wednesday, October 13, 2004

It was just after midnight. Nestor leaned toward the cabbie. "Wait here, I'll only be a few minutes." He stepped into the crisp air. The cherry trees along Ohio Drive bore only a few brown leaves. Nestor climbed up the stairs of the Jefferson Memorial, walked past the Ionic columns, and went into the rotunda. A bright circle of lights cascaded down on the nineteen-foot bronze statue of Jefferson. He looked at the inscription on the frieze along the circumference of the dome and read the words from a letter written by Jefferson. *I have sworn upon the altar of God eternal hostility against every form of tyranny over the mind of man.* Nestor mumbled, "That was in another life."

Blanton appeared from behind the columns on the Potomac River side of the memorial. "What'd you say?"

"Nothing. Let's go back to where you came from."

He followed Blanton down the stairs toward the river, out of the light into the darkness. He steadied his eyes on Blanton. "Come to a place like this, on a night like this, and everything seems right with the world. Listen to the sound of the waves racing to Chesapeake Bay." He took a deep breath filling his lungs. "The water and air, so clean."

"Yeah, well, I'm not feeling too touristy. Let's cut with the commercial and get on with this," Blanton said. "Here's your passport, two credit cards, and a

Maryland driver's license. There're all under the name of John Nelson. Same as your initials, in case you're wearing anything that's monogramed."

"Hey, man," a whiskey-and-tobacco-burned voice said.

Blanton dropped everything. The passport fell to the stairs and the credit cards and driver's license cascaded further down. He looked at the man behind him, pushing a shopping cart containing his life's possessions in five plastic bags. He wore coveralls with torn knees, a dirty winter jacket, and a stocking cap, his face grizzled with gray whiskers and a half-smoked cigarette hanging from his lips.

"Hey man, how about a couple of bucks for a coffee?"

Blanton smelled booze on the man's breath, took a step back, and shook his head.

Nestor bent down and scooped up the documents. He pulled a roll of bills from his pocket. Ripped off a twenty and slapped it in the man's palm. "Here, old man. Get yourself something good."

He waved the twenty in Nestor's face. "Hey, I ain't no old man. Betcha you're older than me. I'm just on a run of hard luck." He pushed his cart past them mumbling, "motherfuckers."

Nestor laughed under his breath and opened the passport. He looked at it, the Visa card, the MasterCard, and the driver's license with a nonexistent address, and stuffed them inside the passport. "Looks good, like the real things. What's the credit limit on these? You know, in case I want to have a good time."

Blanton wiped his sweaty palms on his raincoat and stared at the river. "From what I hear, there aren't too many places nowadays that you can have a good time in Baghdad. But I guess if there is, you'd know about them."

Nestor fanned his fingers out across his chest. "John, if someone heard you talking like that, they might think you don't have a very good impression of *moi*."

Blanton ignored him. "Do what you've gotta do, but after you get back from Baghdad, I suggest you run all those through a shredder. Your cover is as a member of a nongovernment organization known as World Vision for Peace. It's a CIA front whose supposed purpose is rescuing Iraqi children from the streets of Baghdad. They actually do some good, but it's mostly a cover for recruiting assets and spreading cash around."

"You mean they use Iraqi kids as a front for bribing Saddam's former associates?" Nestor laughed.

Blanton ran his finger around the collar of his white shirt. "Don't ever say that, anywhere. You never know whose listening. You should realize that after the business with my wife."

"So, what do I tell anyone who asks me what I'm doing?"

"You're looking for abandoned kids. They're all over the streets of Baghdad, orphans selling Chiclets for a nickel, or whatever people will give them. Is there anything I need to know about how you get your hands on the cash?"

"Better that you don't know."

Blanton nodded. "When will you be heading over there?"

Nestor took a step closer, invading Blanton's personal space. "You're asking a lot of questions."

Blanton scraped a hand through his hair. "Just nervous, with that shit with my wife and this being the last trip. Don't want anything to go wrong. I keep thinking we should quit while we're ahead."

"You're the one that wants more money. Just don't blow it on some dumb bitch like last time."

"Don't worry about me. Are you sure we won't have any trouble with my wife's attorney?"

"Hasn't your old lady dropped the divorce case?"

Blanton shook his head. "Yeah, but she seemed pretty reluctant."

"As long as she doesn't switch attorneys, you'll be all right."

"How did your guy convince the attorney to talk my wife out of filing?"

"He used the story you came up with. You know, the Russians trying to recruit you as a spy." Nestor paused. "More questions, John. You're making me uncomfortable. Unbutton your raincoat."

Blanton stammered, "What…what the? Come on."

"You heard me. Do it, or I'll do it for you."

Blanton opened his coat. Nestor reached in, ripped the man's white shirt open, and pulled up his undershirt. There was nothing but a pot belly and hairless chest.

"Hope you're fucking satisfied."

"Not yet." Nestor reached his hands around Blanton's back, slid them around the man's waistline, and up his back. Then he stepped back and grabbed Blanton's crotch.

"Jesus fucking Christ, I don't believe you! How do I know *you're* not wearing a wire?"

Nestor held his coat out to his sides like a flasher. "Go ahead, check me out."

Blanton dragged his hand across his lips. "I guess if you were, you wouldn't say that." He tucked his shirt in, buttoned his raincoat, and slipped his hands into his pockets.

"I'll be in touch when I get back." Nestor did an about face and returned to his waiting cab.

CHAPTER 29

One of Saddam Hussein's Palaces
Baghdad
October 15, 2004

THE COALITION PROVISIONAL AUTHORITY WAS supposed to be staffed with people experienced in foreign service, law, medicine, transportation, agronomy, and other key areas to aid in nation building, the intent being to transform Iraq into a model democracy in the Middle East. The authority would control billions of dollars from American foreign aid, the Oil-for-Food Program, and other sources. However, the first eleven staffers had little or no practical experience, and many were hired because they had strong Republican connections.

Ilene LaDuque and Morris Burnett were two of the first hires. They got the jobs without any interviews or background checks. LaDuque had taught English in Japan. She thought going to Iraq would help her pursue a career in international relations. Burnett had worked at an internet startup and had made a million when the company went public. He wanted to pay it forward.

They were leaving their office, formerly a bedroom in one of Saddam Hussein's palaces, carrying a handful of disbursement vouchers authorizing payment to various contractors. Ilene wore jeans and a T-shirt that read Property of USC Athletic Department. Morris wore Nike sweats and jogging shoes. They entered the foyer. It was circular, forty feet in diameter and height. A gold chandelier nearly the width of the room was suspended from the ceiling, which was magnificently tiled in blue and beige.

At the elevator Morris hit the button and the brushed steel doors opened. They took it to the basement, where an army guard sat in an overstuffed black-leather chair that had been extricated from one of Saddam's offices. The GI's M-16 leaned against the wall. To the soldier's right was a six-foot-tall vault door. It was considered a soft assignment. No risk of incoming rounds.

The soldier stood. "Hi Ilene, you're looking good today."

"What about me, Private Matson? How am I lookin'?" Burnett said, his smile baring pearly white teeth that stood out against his black face.

"Not good enough for me to ask you out to lunch. How about it, Ilene? Want to go to Micky D's and get some falafel?"

She put her hand on her right hip and leaned to her left. "What are you nineteen, Sonny Boy? Hormones raging and everything, I wouldn't be safe with you. How about you do your job and open the safe so we can do ours?"

He turned, hit the keypad on the door, and spun the wheel. "I'll be twenty in three months."

As she walked past him, she gave him a wink. "When you start shaving, look me up." The safe door clanked closed and lying in front of them were two rows of pallets, each four deep. The pallets were stacked shoulder high with bundles of one-hundred-dollar bills in shrink-wrapped plastic stamped New York Federal Reserve. "Morris, grab a handful of gunny sacks and a dolly, please. A mil in each sack will give us the eight we need today."

Morris went to a shelf to the left of the safe door, pulled down eight gunnies, and tossed them onto a dolly. He pushed it to the closest pallet, and they lifted ten bundles into each sack. She prepared an inventory form in duplicate for each sack, and they both scribbled their initials on the forms. Ilene put a copy into each sack and took one for her records. Forty-five minutes later, she put her hands on her hips and leaned back. "That's eleven kilos of cash in each sack. We weigh our cash instead of counting it. The only thing this job is qualifying me for is working for the Cali Cartel. Why did I work so hard to get a master's in philosophy?" she shrugged. "As they say, 'close enough for government work.'"

"Another eight mil for the good of Iraq." Morris pushed the intercom button and said, "Open the safe, Matson."

Morris and Ilene pushed the dolly with eight bundles of cash out the door, where a sergeant and two PFCs in full body armor and shouldering M-16s were waiting. The sergeant signed the receipts for the cash. The privates pushed the dolly into the elevator, off-loaded the gunnies into the back of a pickup truck, and were off to pay the vendors.

CHAPTER 30

Warehouse 23, Green Zone
October 15, 2004
1:00 p.m.

N ESTOR WAITED IN THE EMPTY warehouse, one of the many structures that had been built to justify the cash that was being disbursed. In this case, at least the government received something for the money it paid out. Nestor didn't mind waiting for two hours. He could afford to be patient. He had four million in cash coming for one million worth of faulty product.

In fact, Nestor was in a million-dollar air-conditioned warehouse, sitting in a comfortable chair behind a steel-gray desk, twenty feet away from a waiting shipping container. At this moment, he was feeling like a small-time crook. He knew that there were more than one hundred thirty thousand Department of Defense independent contractors chasing the billions of government cash floating around Iraq, some smaller, some larger, some honest, but many more crooked that he was.

His phony passport and Maryland driver's license were tucked safely inside the desk. The driver's license with his real name on it sat in his wallet, which was in his pocket. A fraudulent Standard Armor invoice justifying the four million sat on the desk, neatly squared off in the center of the polished surface.

At one p.m., Nestor heard the sound of an engine rumbling outside the door, followed by the slamming of the vehicle's doors. There was a loud banging on the warehouse door.

Nestor opened up and met two PFCs, M-16s in hand.

"Sir, we're sent by the Coalition Provisional Authority to make a payment on behalf of the DoD to Standard Armor officer Jack Nestor."

Nestor pulled the driver's license from his wallet and handed it over, along with a copy of the Standard Armor invoice.

The PFC examined the photo in the driver's license and looked at Nestor. The GI reviewed the invoice and handed Nestor a disbursement voucher. "Can you sign this, and we'll bring the cash in?"

Nestor signed the voucher. The PFCs walked back to the jeep and handed it to the sergeant, who looked at it, got out of the jeep, and approached Nestor. "So, you're the son of a bitch that's peddling this crap. How can you have the gall to accept money for the shit you sent here?"

As the PFC's dropped the gunny sacks containing four million dollars in cash on the warehouse cement floor, Nestor, who had been waiting for someone to hassle him, had his lying response prepared for the sergeant. "We meet all the specs the DoD required. They're the ones that are responsible for the performance of the body armor. If they sent us different requirements, we would have met those."

"One fucking bureaucrat blaming another. What a shit excuse if I ever heard one."

After they left, Nestor mounted the stairs to the shipping container. He removed a set of keys from his pocket and opened the two-inch hardened steel lock. Nestor lifted the vertical locking bar, swung the shipping container door open, and loaded the gunny sacks into the shipping container.

CHAPTER 31

Warehouse 23, Green Zone
October 16, 2004
12:00 a.m.

NESTOR WAS DRESSED IN BATTLE fatigues. He slouched down in the driver's seat of a jeep parked between two vacant jeeps, thirty feet from the warehouse where his four million in cash was stashed. Now, he just had to wait for the body armor to be delivered. After that, he could ship the armor and cash back to Standard Armor. He lifted the helmet off his head and wiped the sweat off his brow with his sleeve. He had a thirty-minute window to gain access to the warehouse. The nametag above his pocket read Nelson, and above that, World Vision for Peace.

The midnight moon disappeared behind an inky cloud. He heard a US Army LMTV cargo truck grinding into low gear as it turned the corner of the warehouse. The crushed stones in the parking lot crackled under the weight of the truck, and the wind circled sand in the air like a small tornado. The truck came to a stop, and its red brake lights flashed over the loading dock as it backed up.

Two soldiers jumped out of the cab. A cone of yellow flashed down from a motion detector light as Corporal Jackson dropped the tailgate. Its hinges squealed, and then the tailgate slammed against the undercarriage. "Henson, get that dolly and bring it over here."

Jackson jumped into the back of the truck and lit a cigarette. "Look at these fucking vests. Half of them have bullet holes that went right through."

Henson pushed the dolly to the rear of the truck and stepped into the back end. "It's not the bullet holes that get to me. It's the fuckin' blood stains."

Jackson shook his head. "How could they send this crap over here?"

"Ya wear what's here and hope ya get a good one." Henson grabbed three of the vests, swung them off the truck, and they plopped down onto the dolly. "What're they going to do with this crap?"

"Burn 'em, I hope. Why don't you stop talkin' and get to work, so we can get out of here?" Jackson said.

"Yeah, yeah. Why don't you stop tellin' me what to do?" Henson grabbed a handful of vests and flipped them out of the truck.

Jackson took a drag on his cigarette and sat down on the dock. "I'm tellin' you what to do 'cause I've got two stripes and you've only got one." Jackson finished his smoke and one more, and forty vests later the back of the truck was empty. The GIs hopped out of the back, into the cab, and drove way.

Nestor glanced at his watch as he jumped out of his jeep and sprinted to the loading dock. *Idiots cost me five minutes,* he thought. He jammed the key into the lock on the warehouse door and tried to turn it. It didn't budge. "Motherfucker."

He stepped back and gave the lock a kick with the heel of his boot again and again. The door vibrated on its hinges. Nestor tried the key again, and this time it turned. He pushed the dolly next to the steps leading to the shipping container. He closed and locked the warehouse door, hustled back, climbed the stairs, and opened the shipping container. Four plump gunny sacks lay on the floor.

Nestor slid a Ka-bar US Army knife out of the sheath on his belt. Its seven-inch blade was partially serrated, and he ripped it easily through each gunny sack. *The last time I'll be doing this.* He held each sack up by its end and watched the shrink-wrapped packages of one-hundred-dollar bills sprawl across the floor of the shipping container. Perspiration rolled down his forehead and the back of his neck. He looked at his Rolex. Ten minutes had passed.

He returned to the dolly, ripped the blade through the tops of twenty body armors, and yanked out Standard Armor's top-secret bulletproofing ingredient — Graptonian. "Two million dollars on R & D, and it turns out it wasn't worth shit," Nestor mumbled. He shrugged his shoulders and smiled. "It's worth millions to me."

Nestor flipped the empty body armors into the shipping container, climbed the stairs to the container, and stuffed the cash into the hollowed-out body armor. He found an electric staple gun on a nearby work bench and sealed the body armor. There were still ten bags of cash lying in the container. He snatched five more body armors and heard scuffling at the door.

"Hey, Sarge, you in there? Let me in."

Nestor froze and glanced at his watch. Another ten minutes were gone. *What asshole in the Army comes five minutes early?* He covered the remaining ten bags of cash in the container with body armor.

"Come on, Sarge. I can hear you."

All the cash is in there now. I can have this fool throw the rest of the body armor into the container and get rid of the rest of these vests. "Fuck it." The Graptonian lay loose on the floor. He went to the door, unlocked it, and gave the PFC a look. *Put him on the defensive.* "Where you been, soldier? You were supposed to be here twenty minutes ago."

"I'm sorry, sir. I thought you were my sergeant. I didn't know I supposed to get here earlier. You won't tell him, will you?"

Nestor put his hands on his hips. "Well, you're here now. Buckle down and get this shit cleaned up and we're good." He pointed at the Graptonian.

"Yes, Sir. Thank you, Sir. Jesus, what is that crap?"

"That's all it is soldier, just crap. Sweep that stuff up and make this floor clean enough so you GIs can eat off it. And throw the rest of the body armor into the shipping container." Nestor nodded, *Get rid of all the evidence.*

"Yes, Sir." The soldier's eyes caught the name tag. "Yes, Sir, Mr. Nelson."

Nestor watched the young private clean up the mess better than he would have. Then he locked the container and slipped the young GI a twenty. He was heading to the door when it squealed open and he came face to face with the sergeant, a tall black man, mid-forties, an obvious lifer.

Nestor nodded, "Sergeant." He glanced at the GI's nametag. "Oliver."

He felt the sergeant gaze at his face and the nametag on his shirt. "Mr. Nelson." It came out more like a question than a statement.

Oliver pulled his forefinger and thumb down his chin. "Don't I know you?"

"No, I don't think so." Nestor shook his head, but Oliver's face pushed him back to April 1980, Operation Eagle Claw. Oliver was the surviving brother of one of the eight fatalities.

"I know you from somewhere. You been here before?" Oliver glanced at the nametag again. "I mean as a GI?"

Nestor thought total denial was the best approach. "No, not me. Been here on business, but never in the service."

"You sure look familiar. You got a brother, that's it, you got a brother that looks just like you I bet."

"Nope, only child. You must be thinking of someone else. It's getting late. I better head out and let you guys do your duty."

"Hold on. What's in that shipping container? That wasn't here yesterday when I left."

"That's some materials we're shipping back to the States." Nestor pointed above his nametag at World Vision for Peace. "Non-Government-Organization."

Oliver put his hands on his hips. "Sir, these facilities are limited for military use. You can't have private goods here."

"Sergeant, it's only documents and miscellaneous items."

Oliver pointed at the container. "Open it."

Nestor paused and took a step back. "I don't have a key. My boss has the key. I just snapped it shut."

"Who's your boss?"

"He's no longer in Iraq. He took a plane back today."

"Sounds kind of hokum to me."

Nestor tried to change the direction of the conversation. "Hokum, wow. That's a word I haven't heard in long time. Where you from, Sergeant?"

"Mississippi, Ruleville, to be exact. But asking me silly questions ain't gonna get you outta here. That thing wasn't here yesterday, now it is, but it's locked. You don't have a key. We got ways of opening it. Private, get that bolt cutter."

"Yes, Sir." The PFC went to the workbench and lifted a heavy-duty cutter.

"Son, you really don't want to do that," Nestor said. "Anyway, I doubt that bolt cutter will bite through two inches of hardened steel."

The private frowned. His face tightened. He looked first at Nestor and then at Sergeant Oliver.

"Do it," Oliver said.

Nestor moved in front of the doors of the shipping container. "You better not."

Oliver motioned toward the container. "Do it, I said."

The private moved toward the container.

Nestor stood strong. "Sergeant, you and I better have a talk before there's a serious breach of control over the contents of this container. Dismiss the private."

"I think you're right, 'cause I remember who you are. Private, take the night off."

The PFC looked at Oliver, then at Nelson, gave a hasty salute, and left the warehouse.

"So, who do you think I am?" Nestor asked.

"No, you go first. You say who you are, and tell me what's in the fucking container?"

Nestor pointed at his nametag. "I don't know anyone named Nelson. I'm CIA and we've a shitload of Saddam's records in there." He pointed over his shoulder. "They identify hidden bank accounts, shell holding companies concealing his assets all over the world, and funding for terrorist organizations. We need to get this stuff to Langley ASAP, so our analyst can determine the next step."

"So, what's your name?"

"You know I can't divulge my identity. To you, I'm Nelson. That's all you need to know."

Oliver shook his head. "Maybe I'll just call you James, like in James Bond."

"That's fine, whatever you want."

"But I know you as Colonel Nestor. Right? That's who you are?"

"I'm not going to lie to you about anything. But I'm not going to admit to anything."

"I can't say that I blame you. If I wuz the drunk fuck-up that caused eight GIs to die, I wouldn't admit to anything either. You see, Colonel, it's because of you I saw my brother die. He screamed the most awful sound I ever heard as he was burning to a crisp."

"You've got me confused with someone else—"

Oliver's hands flew in front of him. "Fuck you, dickhead. I know you were drummed out of the army after that clusterfuck. So, I find it had to believe the CIA would take you on as a spook. Now believing that, I don't think there's anything in that container that belonged to Saddam." Oliver lifted a Colt semiauto .45 out of his holster. "Back up real slow, Nestor, and show me what's in that container."

"No problem, you can holster your piece. There's going to be no trouble." Nestor stepped backward fifteen feet and climbed the wooden stairs of the platform until his back hit the doors of the container.

"Now, I suspect you were lying to me about not having a key. Ain't that right?"

"It's right here in my pants pocket, right side."

Oliver's cheeks and forehead were shiny with sweat. "Asshole, don't you feel better telling the truth?"

Nestor reached into his pocket with his right hand.

Oliver wiggled the pistol. "No, no, no. You go for the key with your left hand. Just in case you have something nasty in your pocket."

"Nothing in there but the key." He brought his left hand across his stomach into his pocket and came out with the key." Nestor thought, *There's four million in cash in there. Time to make a deal. Let him have one million, and I'm still left with three.*

"Now turn around real slow, open the door, and step back toward me. Don't turn around, just step backwards. You understand?"

"Got it. Let me tell you something before you get any deeper. You got me, I'm Nestor. But you're wrong about one thing. I am a spook for the company."

"I don't really give a fuck. I'm just gonna pay you back for my brother."

"What would it take to make that go away?"

"You don't get do you? You know what a payback is?"

"I'm sorry for your brother. It wasn't just me calling the shots. But I was the easiest one to take the hit so the big guys could cover their asses."

"What're you saying?"

"Your brother have a wife, any kids?"

"He had a boy that was four and baby girl born a month after he was killed. He's twenty-eight and she's twenty-four now. Shit, they got kids of their own. Grandkids he never saw."

"How would you like to make those kids financially secure for the rest of their lives?"

"So, I got to figure if I want to kill you or set up my brother's kids?"

"You can do whatever you want with the cash, a cool million. Keep half for yourself and give the rest to your brother's kids. It's up to you."

"So where is this money?"

Nestor raised his arm and knocked on the container door. "Right here."

"So, it's right here. How you gonna fix it that I don't take the cash and kill you anyway?"

Nestor stepped to the side. "Sergeant look at the lock. It's heavy-duty steel, with a back-up combination. Only the company would have a lock like this."

"You son of a bitch. Playing me along from the very beginning. You know that bolt cutter is right over there."

"That's no ordinary lock. Didn't you hear me? With that kind of steel, that bolt cutter won't do a thing. You don't think the company is going to go cheap, do you? You can try to shoot it open, but then you'll draw attention. Have to explain my body and split the cash."

"So, how you going to do this?"

"That Colt holds nine rounds. You take out the magazine, empty it, and open the chamber. Show me that it's empty. You've got a million in cash."

"Sounds like a plan."

Nestor turned around, facing Oliver.

Oliver ejected the magazine. With his thumb, he ejected eight rounds. They hit the floor and bounced in different directions. Then he pulled the slide back on the Colt, and the chambered bullet flew into the air and came to rest with its sisters. "A deal's a deal. Open it up."

Nestor nodded, spun the dial to the left three times to forty-eight, to the right two times, stopping at twenty-one, and then to the left at zero. *Click* and the lock released. He inserted the key and yanked it open, holding the heavy-duty locking mechanism in his hand. Then he lifted the vertical locking bar, opening the shipping container door. "Do you want me to go first?"

"Good idea."

Nestor stepped in and lifted the body armor that covered the ten shrink-wrapped bundles. "Here you go. A hundred grand in each bundle, ten bundles, and there're all yours."

Oliver slipped behind Nestor, keeping an arm on him, then side-stepped around Nestor and knelt next to the bundles. "Holy shit, never saw—"

Nestor gripped the lock mechanism tightly and crashed it into Oliver's head again, and again. Blood flowed from the back of his head and he collapsed to the floor on his stomach.

Nestor walked out of the container, knelt, and scooped up the ammo. He loaded the magazine, cycled the action to chamber a round, then topped off the magazine.

"You motherfucker," Oliver said, steadying himself, gripping the door of the container ten feet behind Nestor.

Nestor spun, facing the sergeant, extended his arm, and fired one round. It hit Oliver in the kill zone, dead center, and he fell back into the container. "To bad you didn't have any body armor. Stupid son of a bitch," he laughed.

CHAPTER 32

Baghdad, Iraq
Wednesday, October 13, 2004

G LORIA WAS ALREADY IN BAGHDAD when Blanton delivered the fake credentials to Nestor. As the handoff was occurring in the dead of night in Washington, Gloria was already at her desk in the IRS-CID office at Baghdad International Airport. Three stacks of incident reports from Army Intelligence were on it, each pile six inches high, documenting the deaths of men on the day she received the initial phone call alleging Jim Abbott's death was a murder.

Lauren took a deep breath, exhaled loudly, and looked at Gloria. "We busted our asses to get to Baghdad on Sunday, because the source said he would call you on Mondays. It's Wednesday, and we haven't heard a word. How many days are we going to give this guy?"

"As long as it takes," Gloria said. Her desk was one of eight. IRS special agents manned four, their desks covered with reams of financial records as they looked for leads to Saddam's missing billions. The remaining four were for anyone who wanted to rest his or her tired body. The hours were so long that personnel often slept at their desks or in the hallways rather than return to their sleeping quarters.

Gloria returned her attention to the incident reports.

Lauren pushed against her desk, sliding back. "As long as it takes to do what?"

Gloria grabbed a handful of the reports. "Here, go through these. If there's anything that makes you think the victim in one of these reports is the original caller, pull it out and put it to the side."

"Haven't you gone through these?"

"I did, but four eyes are better than two."

Lauren cleared her throat, "What are we doing here if this guy doesn't call? Sooner or later, someone other than me is going to ask you the same question."

Gloria banged her fist on her desk. "Don't worry about it! I'm the senior agent; it's my responsibility."

Lauren grasped the incident reports. "What should I look for?"

"I don't know. If something seems unusual or stands out for some reason, pull it."

An hour later, Lauren flipped over the last report in the stack. "Nothing unusual in these. I'm going to get a tea. Do you want anything?"

"No." Gloria's cell phone rang. The caller ID was blocked. She picked it up. "Hello."

"Agent Nighthawk?" The Arabic sounding voice said.

"Yes, I've been waiting for your call. You said you would call on Mondays."

"I couldn't call earlier. They were watching me. We can't meet in Iraq. Too dangerous for you and me. Go to the airport to the private jet hanger. There'll be a Lear jet there to take you to Amman. You have a reservation under the name Azizi. Be there eight thirty Friday morning."

"What about passports?

"You won't need any passports, but you will need burkas. When you land in Amman, you won't have to go through Jordan's immigration or get a visa. I've cleared you all the way through. A limousine will take you to the Sheraton Amman Al-Nabil Hotel. A suite is reserved for you under the name Ghatiya Azizi."

"I have an associate who will be coming with me. What about her?"

"She can come as your sister. Pick a name?"

"How will we get in touch with you?"

"You won't. I'll call you. Remember, make sure you wear burkas. It is important to keep your identity confidential."

The line went dead. "Hello? Hello? Who is this? Shit, he hung up." Gloria slammed her phone down.

"Finally, he called?" Lauren leaned toward Gloria. "What'd he say?"

Gloria slid her chair next to Lauren. "Keep your voice down. He said it was too dangerous for us to meet him in Iraq." She gave Lauren the travel information

"Who is he?"

Gloria shook her head. "I don't know. He hung up before I could get his name." She gave Lauren a quick account of the conversation.

"Don't we have to get the travel approved? Will our passports work?"

"No passports. He's cleared us all the way though. I'm going as Ghatiya Azizi." Gloria gazed at an incident report on her desk documenting the bludgeoning murder of an Iraqi man. She glanced at the name of the dead man's wife. You're going as my sister Lubanah. We have to wear burkas."

Lauren's eyes narrowed. "You sure it was the same guy who called you before?"

"Sounded like him. We have no choice. We have to go."

"We do? I mean, we're going to travel to another country to meet someone we don't know. You sure we don't have to get approval from someone?"

"Don't worry about it. I'll take care of everything. We go, and if afterwards someone doesn't like it, we ask for forgiveness."

Lauren exhaled. "If it's too dangerous to meet him here, why is it safer in Jordan?"

Gloria's frustration showed on her face, "I said, don't worry about it. I'll tell Musgrove where we're going. He'll cover for us. We have to take advantage of this situation." *I'm sure Musgrove will back me, even if I tell him after the fact. I need to know if Jim came to Iraq to be with me, or to get one hundred thousand.*

"I don't like this. What if it's a setup? What if he's an insurgent?"

"If you don't want to go, that's all right. I'll go alone."

Lauren shook her head. She spoke in a low tone. "I'm beginning to think you enjoy putting me in situations like this, like before with the abortion. I didn't like it then and I don't like it now, but I'll be damned if you're going alone."

"Wait a second. Give me those reports." Gloria took them from Lauren and paged through the stack. She stopped half-way through. "Look at this. Abdul Azizi. His body was found in an alley in Baghdad a couple of hours after I received the call." She leaned back in her chair. "There's got to be a connection."

Lauren crossed her arms. "What's so important that we have to do this? What is it? What are you not telling me?"

CHAPTER 33

Amman, Jordan
Friday, October 15, 2004
Morning,

FIFTY MINUTES AFTER DEPARTURE FROM Baghdad the Lear was lowering its landing gear, preparing for arrival at Queen Alia International Airport in the outskirts of Amman. Its two passengers, wearing matching black burqas, rested in the white leather recliners in the passenger section.

Gloria pulled the scarf away from her face and pointed her cell phone at Lauren. "I know how fashion-conscious you are. Want me to take a picture?"

"Sure, go ahead. No one will ever be able to tell it's me," Lauren laughed.

Gloria tapped the button and the camera flashed. She looked out the window and saw the massive white terminal that looked like a hundred Bedouin tents. The Lear glided past it to a hangar marked 'private jets.' The hangar doors slid open. Two more Lear jets and a white Rolls Royce limousine sat inside. Their jet stopped in front of the open doors, and a tractor pulled it inside. The door opened and Gloria fastened her veil.

A man entered, wearing a black suit and an open-collared white shirt. His skin was bronze, and he had black hair combed back, a trimmed mustache, and a beard. "Good morning, ladies. My name is Adar. I will transport you to the hotel. Your luggage will be taken care of. Follow me, please."

They left the plane and followed him to the Rolls. Adar held the rear door open and they entered.

"Adar, we appreciate the first-class treatment. To whom do we owe our gratitude?" Gloria asked.

"The gentleman will be contacting you in your suite approximately an hour after you arrive. He wants to make sure that you have adequate time to rest after your trip. He said that you should feel free to utilize room service for anything you need."

Lauren leaned forward. "We appreciate your hospitality and generosity."

"You're welcome. We should be at the hotel in thirty minutes. There is chilled water and iced tea in the compartments. Enjoy." A darkened window slid up, separating the rear compartment from the driver's.

They entered a four-lane highway and sped through a desolate desert terrain before entering Amman. The city was a combination of ancient buildings, high rises, construction cranes, and bustling traffic.

The limo approached the hotel. It was a ten-story, semi-circular building of white concrete, with towers extending another two stories on each end. The Rolls stopped at the front entrance. Adar jumped out and opened the door for his passengers. A hotel porter in white, short-sleeved jersey and gray slacks took their bags. He exchanged words in a hushed tone with Adar.

Adar approached Gloria and Lauren. "You don't have to check in. Follow the porter to the elevator. He will take you to your suite." He bowed his head, retreated to the Rolls, and drove away.

They rode the elevator to the tenth floor. The porter slid the key card into the door and opened it, bowing to Gloria and Lauren, allowing them to enter. He placed two key cards on the coffee table separating a beige sofa and matching armchairs. Floor to ceiling windows gave a view of the city. Lauren slipped out of her shoes and caressed a thick blue and green oriental carpet with her feet. He showed them to their separate bedrooms with en-suite baths. "If you have any questions, please call the front desk. We will be glad to be of service."

Gloria reached into her pocket and pulled out five dollars to tip him.

"Not necessary, Madam. Your gratuities have been taken care of." He backed out of the room, closing the door behind him.

"This is a few steps above sleeping quarters in the Green Zone." Lauren looked around and laughed.

"Not too shabby. We can get out of these burkas for a while." Gloria pulled hers off, laid it over the sofa, and stood there in camouflage shorts and a matching tee-shirt.

Lauren did the same and was left standing in a white Nike tennis outfit.

Gloria looked at her. "Did you forget your racket?"

"Hey, at least I don't look like GI Jane." She laughed again. "Did you pack your AR-15?" Lauren took a military stance, pretending to brace a weapon against her hip. "Bang, bang, bang."

"You're funny. Truth be told, I'd feel more comfortable if I had."

Lauren put her hand behind her back and whipped out her Sig Sauer. "One of us did."

"What the…do you realize the trouble that could cause? We're not authorized to take a weapon out of Iraq." *We're not even authorized to be here.*

Lauren slipped the pistol back into her waistband. "Rather be judged by twelve than carried by six."

Gloria shook her head. *Somehow, I've got to get that out of her hands.* "Keep that out of sight. Let's hang up our stuff. Hopefully, we won't be here long."

"A few days of R & R would be fine. See you in a bit." Lauren headed to her room.

Gloria sat on the sofa, pulled her laptop out of her bag, and rested it on the coffee table. She turned it on to check her emails. *She's in vacation mode, and I want to find out if Jim's murder was a setup.* Her desktop appeared, she clicked on internet explorer, and ran down the list of emails. "Here's one from Stephens with subject, The Judge," she mumbled.

> Gloria, sorry to break this to you. I know you have a lot on your plate over there. After the US Attorney received the information you gathered on your husband, somehow it got to the FBI. They arrested him today. I'll monitor the situation closely and keep you informed. I'll try to find out how this happened. I know this was a difficult situation to begin with, now only made worse. Good luck to you and Lauren. I'll make sure your kids are doing the best they can.

She slammed the top of her computer down "Motherfuckers."

Lauren rushed out of the bedroom. "What's wrong?"

Gloria rested her elbows on her knees and held her head in her hands. "The fucking FBI is taking over my husband's case. My kids, I should be with them. The last time I returned from Iraq I told them I wouldn't leave them again.

What the fuck do I do? What're they going to think?" She stood, closed the laptop, and stuffed it into the bag. "I've got to get back. Go pack up. We're going home."

"Even if you were able to get a plane non-stop from Amman to Chicago, it would be, what, at least 24 hours before you'd be there, given airport time and all, if there even is a non-stop flight. At best, even if you managed only one layover, you're looking at 48 hours, give or take, before you get home. Your husband will make bond right away, and he'll be out before you set foot in Chicago, in either case."

"My kids need me." Her eyes welled.

"They lasted the whole summer without you."

"Goddamn it, Lauren, you sound like my husband." Tears rolled down her cheeks.

"Your kids are young adults. They understand that you and your husband have responsible jobs—"

"Yeah, and now their father got charged with, who knows what, probably conspiracy, money laundering, whatever... and we have no control over anything. The FBI is going to use all their press contacts to show how great they are. They'll make sure the press covers this nationwide: FBI Busts Federal Judge. It should have been our case."

"Maybe this is better. It won't look like you're responsible—to your kids, I mean—for putting him away."

"If this case goes to trial, who do you think the government witnesses are going to be? Me, first of all, and his illegitimate daughter."

"Maybe that will motivate him to plead out, so she won't have to testify."

"Maybe that will motivate him to go to trial so I *will* have to testify. That would be just like him. Then he gets the satisfaction of his kids' knowing that I put him in this situation."

Gloria's cell phone rang. She looked at the phone and leaned back against the sofa.

Lauren picked up the phone.

"Is Agent Nighthawk there?"

"She's not available right now. Can I take a message?"

"What name is she traveling under?"

Lauren looked at Gloria and mouthed the question. Gloria whispered, "Ghatiya."

"Ghatiya," Lauren said.

"What is your relationship to her?"

"Sister."

"Very well. The gentleman who was going to contact you must stay in Beirut overnight. He will come to your room tomorrow morning, approximately nine-thirty. He apologizes for any inconvenience." The line went dead.

Lauren cradled the phone, gave Gloria the message, and looked her in the eyes. "It's time to tell me, Gloria. I know the company line for why we're here. But what's the real reason?"

CHAPTER 34

Amman, Jordan
Saturday, October 16, 2004
10:00 a.m.

G LORIA SAT ON THE SOFA, STARING at the monitor on her laptop. There had been no update from Stephens about her husband's arrest or the wellbeing of her kids. There had been no telephone call from the anonymous source. It had been a sleepless night. She took a sip of her coffee, her fifth cup since seven thirty.

"Well, nine thirty has come and gone, and no sign of our man," Lauren said.

"Lauren, can you make a fresh pot?" Gloria said.

"Don't you want something to eat? I'll call room service."

"I'm not hungry. With everything that's happening, my stomach's doing a nervous gurgle. Just make a fresh pot from what's in the room."

Gloria stretched and closed her eyes for a second. The laptop chimed its 'new mail' notification. The 'From' line was Tom Stephens, and the 'Subject' line was simply JUDGE. She hunched over the keys and opened it.

> Gloria,
>
> Sorry for not being in touch. Had to take one of my kids to the ER. Turned out she needed an emergency appendectomy. Anyway, because your husband was arrested Friday, his bond hearing won't be until Monday. So, he has to spend the weekend in the Metropolitan

Correctional Center. I visited your kids Friday afternoon, and despite what I know about the case, I tried to reassure them that their father is innocent until proven guilty. Both of them told me that they know that, and they are sure this is some kind of mistake. I played dumb and didn't tell them any details. I offered for them to stay with me and my wife until their dad is released. They preferred to stay in your house, but I decided it was best for them to stay with us. I told them because of the time difference, it's difficult for you to call them. Keep in touch and I'll do the same.

"I'm going to call my kids again," Gloria said.

Lauren topped off Gloria's coffee. "Good idea."

She glanced at her watch, 10:15. *It's 6:15 in the morning back home.* She pulled up Adsila's number on speed dial. "If I call Adsila's cell, Darius will be angry, and if I call Darius, Adsila will be angry," she mumbled.

The phone rang four times and went to voicemail.

"Kids, its Mom. Just checking in and—". There was an incoming call from a blocked number. "I'll call you back in a little while."

She took the incoming call. "Hello."

"Agent Nighthawk?"

"Yes."

"I just landed and will be at the hotel in thirty minutes. I'll come to your room in an hour. It's been a long twenty-four hours, but I have some worthwhile information for you. I am sorry for the delay."

"It's been a long night for me, too. It's time you tell me who you are."

"It is better not to mention any names until we see each other in person. What I have for you is very valuable, and therefore also very dangerous. You are safer not knowing anything until it's absolutely necessary. I will introduce myself when we meet. The wait is not long now." The call terminated.

Gloria looked at Lauren, standing in the doorway to her suite in jeans and a T-shirt, sipping an orange juice. "He'll be here in a half-hour. I'm going to shower."

"I'll believe it when he steps through the door. Shower's a good idea. You need to freshen up and put on a clean GI Jane outfit if you have one," Lauren kiddingly said.

"I'm going to send an email to my kids." She sent it to both of their email addresses.

> Hi Kids,
>
> I hope you are both doing all right. I know this must be rough for you guys. I'll be home as soon as possible. Not exactly sure when, but as soon as possible. Please stay at Mr. Stephens's house. I'm sure your father is retaining a very good attorney to resolve this issue. I love you.
>
> Mom

CHAPTER 35

Amman, Jordan
October 16, 2004
11:00 a.m.

A LOUD RAP SOUNDED AT the door. Lauren, in jeans and a crimson long sleeve T-shirt with HARVARD printed across the front, looked through the peephole and saw Adar, wearing a black suitcoat, and another man. The other man was dressed in a bisht, the traditional Iraqi black ankle-length robe. On his head was a keffiyeh, a shoulder-length white cloth. It was held on his head by black goat hair cords that circled his head.

Lauren looked over her shoulder at Gloria, raised two fingers, and whispered, "Two men. One of them is Adar."

"Let them in," Gloria said, firming the Sig in the back waistband of her black slacks and covering it under the tail of her white, long-sleeved shirt.

Lauren opened the door. Adar stepped to the side as the Iraqi man entered, then Adar followed. The man looked to be in his fifties. He wore black-framed glasses and was clean shaven.

Adar stood with his hands folded in front of him and stayed behind the Iraqi man. "Allow me to introduce. This is Mr. Zayad Azizi. Mr. Azizi, these are American agents Gloria Nighthawk and her protégé, Lauren Ashberry." Adar nodded, and Azizi took a seat in one of the armchairs across from the sofa. Gloria and Lauren sat on the sofa. Lauren held a yellow legal pad. Adar stood with his back braced against the wall.

"I apologize once more for the delay in getting here from Beirut, but I assure you, it was time well spent," Azizi said, pointing a forefinger at Gloria. His eyes shifted to Lauren and he raised his eyebrows, "Are you an Ivy Leaguer? I attended Wharton at Penn."

Lauren shook her head. She pointed at her T-shirt. "No, this was a gift from a friend. I went to DePaul University in Chicago."

Azizi shrugged his shoulders.

"Mr. Azizi, would you like a cup of tea?" Gloria asked. "There's a good selection."

"No, thank you. I had a cup in my suite. Please call me Zayad."

Gloria crossed one ankle over the other. "I'm anxious to hear what you have to tell us. What—"

Azizi held up his hand. "Let me tell you what I know and what I recently learned. I believe that may answer most of your questions. You see, I was the first aide to Iraq's Minister of Defense. He was a corrupt man and escaped the country before he could be prosecuted. He is living lavishly in Switzerland, enjoying the largesse of his numbered account. Hundreds of millions of dollars, I'm told. I'm afraid Switzerland has become a very common residence for the former associates of Saddam and many others who have enjoyed the chaos since the American invasion."

Gloria nodded again. *Controlling SOB. Probably be worse if I was wearing the burka. I'll have to wait him out.* "Certainly. Please go ahead, Zayad."

"Because of the confusion of all the American dollars floating around, Iraq trucks full of cash made regular trips to Syria to take advantage of their banking system. So much, in fact, that the Syrian banks were overflowing with dollars." Zayad waved his hands in the air. "More than they could ever absorb. Commoners rented out their houses to store millions that the banks couldn't handle, and needless to say, it was not unusual for there to be shortages of hundreds of thousands of dollars. In fact, the criminals involved, more or less, considered it a cost of doing business."

Azizi took a breath of air, and Gloria took the opportunity to ask a question. "What was the source of this cash?"

"The Oil-for-Food Program, of course. That's what brought me here. Because of my position, I had knowledge of what was going on. I told my brother about it. He was a foolish young man. He wanted to get involved because he thought he could make money transporting the cash. I warned him that it was a dangerous proposition." Azizi exhaled, slumped forward, and stared into his open hands.

Gloria waited, knowing that he would fill the silence. She felt the tension thicken.

"They killed him. The word on the street was that they tortured him into confessing, accused him of stealing a million dollars. I don't think he did, but what does it matter now? What is a million dollars when those whores were stealing billions from their people?"

Gloria leaned forward and folded her hands. "I'm sorry for your loss, Zayad. Who killed him?"

Azizi shook his head. "I do not know. I suspect it was someone who stole much more than my brother was accused of taking. Someone who was afraid my brother would tell the authorities of his knowledge of the theft."

"What was your brother's name?"

"Why do you ask?"

"We may have some information on his murder. Something that might help identify the murderers."

"His name was Abdul Hazim Azizi."

That was the answer she expected, but she decided to play dumb. "When we return to Baghdad, I'll check our case files and see if we have any information that could help."

"I would appreciate that. Shall we move on? I prefer to focus on avenging my brother's death rather than thinking about his murder."

"Of course."

"I'm sure the most important thing to you is finding Saddam's assets."

Gloria glanced at Lauren. That was the official reason for being there, but the real reason was more personal: finding out whether Azizi's brother passed the information about Jim Abbott's murderers. "Yes, that is the priority."

"To do that, it would be to your benefit to understand how those funds were generated. Let me give a hypothetical explanation. The sale price of Iraqi oil was generally around twenty-five dollars a barrel. Saddam would skim—shall we use an American term—two dollars of each barrel's price. Another two dollars went to the firm brokering the sales, and the balance went to the Oil-for-Food Program. Saddam had several different entities set up to receive his share. You have to, as your famous Deep Throat said, 'follow the money'."

"Two dollars a barrel doesn't sound like much. What would that come to in dollars?" Lauren asked.

"From the production reports I have seen for 2000 through 2003, we have produced more than twenty million barrels of oil. Simple multiplication yields forty million dollars. But I believe the production was much higher, because substantial quantities of oil sold directly to Syria would have been purposely omitted from the production reports so the Oil-for-Food Program could be circumvented. We could be talking about one billion dollars."

Both Gloria and Lauren struggled not to look stunned. "Who could do that? And where would Saddam hide that?"

Azizi appeared very relaxed. He spread his legs wide and braced his right arm over the back of the armchair. "We'll get to 'who' and 'how' in a minute. Saddam wasn't stupid. He wouldn't put it all in one place. I suspect that there's some deposited in Switzerland and probably in all the other places people hide dirty money, like investments in real estate and companies through various trusts. Wouldn't surprise me to find out he owns exclusive properties in the United States and shares of major companies listed on the New York Stock Exchange."

Gloria thought, *He knows a lot, a lot more than he's telling us. Lear jet, Rolls limo. I wonder how much he pocketed.* She leaned back on the sofa. "Zayad, I'm confident that the amount of money you mentioned is probably accurate, but the leads as to the disposition of those funds are merely speculative. Unless you have more solid information, there's not much we can do."

"Because of my position and my family's history, many doors are open to me. I was told by the former defense minister that individuals with strong ties to President Assad brokered the sale of Iraq's oil. I was also told by a relative of Assad's that these individuals set up what they called bridge accounts in Jordan and Lebanon under individual Iraqi names, false names and numbers, to avoid detection. Now you see why this knowledge can be very dangerous to possess. With all this money passing through Syria, it's not hard to imagine some of it getting in the hands of Hamas or Hezbollah and being used to finance the purchase of weapons, explosives, and who knows what else." His eyes shifted from Gloria to Lauren. "Can you get me a glass of water?"

Gloria nodded at Lauren. Lauren opened her mouth as if to say something, then put her pad down, went to the kitchen, and returned with a glass of water half-filled with ice cubes.

Azizi took a sip and rested the glass on the coffee table. "It's my understanding there were substantial sales of oil outside of the UN Oil-for-Food Program. The funds from these transactions were deposited in an account at the Commercial Bank of Syria. Those funds were transferred to the Syrian Lebanese Commercial Bank in Beirut, and subsequently, ninety million dollars in cash was withdrawn. That cash was used to buy military goods and other items that were shipped back to Iraq. Some of the goods were used by the Republican Guard, and some eventually ended up in the hands of insurgents. There is probably more than one account, and those other accounts are most likely numbered accounts."

Gloria extended her hands palm open, "That's very interesting, but again without documentation—"

Azizi slipped his hand inside his bisht and pulled out a thumb drive. "Here are copies of some of the bank records reflecting the ninety-million cash withdrawals, as well as the signature card containing the authorized signatures required to move the money, and documentation of weapons purchased and shipped to Iraq."

Gloria took a deep breath and maintained the poker face of an experienced agent. She took the thumb drive and calmly slipped it into her pants pocket, although she could feel her blood rushing with the adrenaline spike that comes with closing a case and with the knowledge that they may have found Saddam's stash. "This should be very helpful." *Does he know anything about Jim Abbott?* She glanced at Lauren again. "Is there anything else?"

Lauren finished the notes she was writing on the legal pad and leaned forward. Her blond hair fell across her face. "Would there be additional sources of funds that Saddam may have had access to?"

"As I said, much of the money was used to purchase military goods and other merchandise in Syria. I was told that the bills for those items were marked up ten percent and that markup was forwarded to Saddam through various nominee bank accounts. I don't know how that was handled, but that's what I was told by a Syrian businessman who brokered millions of dollars of sales to Iraq. He is identified on the documents on the thumb drive."

Lauren looked up from her notepad. "From what you're telling us, these schemes generated a lot of cash in US dollars. You said that sometimes cash would be stored in homes in Syria. I can't imagine that anyone would leave substantial amounts of cash in those places for an extended period. It seems like the risks would be too great."

Azizi shrugged, "I can't think of—"

Adar cut in. "Tell them about the bunker."

Azizi's eyes drilled into Adar. Adar dropped his head and closed his eyes.

"How could I forget?" Azizi's face reddened. "I was blindfolded by the Syrian official and taken to a bunker outside Beirut. I'm guessing a thirty to forty-five-minute ride. He took me into this bunker, and I saw many pallets of US currency, much of it shrink-wrapped. I would guess, easily a billion dollars. There were also gold bars lined up against the wall. As you can imagine, there were several armed guards."

Azizi stood. "That is all I can tell you. Adar and I must go. If I learn anything else, I will call you."

"One more question," Gloria said.

Azizi turned, showing some frustration.

"Why did they take you there?"

"Because I was the top aide to the Minister of Defense. They believed he took a large amount of cash out of Iraq to Switzerland and I must have known how he did it. They offered me a million dollars to facilitate the movement of the cash from the bunker. But I had no knowledge of how that was done."

Gloria nodded. *If you did, we wouldn't be sitting here today.*

Azizi turned toward the door once again. "We must go."

"There's nothing else you can tell us?" Gloria asked.

He glanced at Adar. "Did I forget anything, my friend?" he said sarcastically.

"No, Mr. Azizi, that is all," Adar said, his voice low.

Gloria raised her hand, forefinger pointing at Azizi—

"One more question," Lauren said. She looked at Gloria, then back at Azizi, and asked, "What about the murder of Jim Abbott?"

CHAPTER 36

AZIZI SAT DOWN. HIS EYES went from Gloria to Lauren, to Adar, and back to Gloria. "James Abbott, I've never heard of him."

Gloria swallowed. "Are you sure? He was an IRS agent like me. Late forties, white male. He was killed on the way to Baghdad International last September—an insurgent attack." She opened her briefcase, removed a copy of Jim's ID photo, and laid it on the coffee table

Azizi stretched across that table, put his finger on the photo, and pulled it toward him. "Looks like a nice man. Did he have any family?"

Gloria swallowed again and said, "Yes, a wife and three children. Two boys and a girl."

"That's terrible. I'm sorry for their loss."

"Have you ever met him?"

"No, I've never even heard his name until just now. Why do you ask me?"

"You're sure you have never met him? Or maybe your brother mentioned him to you? He was in the army in Iraq back in 1980. Is it possible you might have met him in some capacity back then?" Gloria felt Azizi's black eyes trained on hers.

"Why are you so insistent? I'm telling you that I did not know him or know of him. Do you think I'm lying to you? Why would I do that? I've answered all your questions and have given you information that you would otherwise have had no access to, at considerable risk to my own well-being. I haven't asked for any reward. I'm doing this in the memory of my brother."

Azizi stood. "We must go. No more of your cross examination." He went toward the door, his bisht flowing behind him.

"Zayad, wait. Your brother told me he had information about Jim's murder, in addition to the things you've told us. That is why I'm struggling with your saying you don't know anything about him, or about what happened to him."

Zayad stopped and turned to face them. "I promise on my brother's soul that I do not know, nor have I ever heard of, this man. My brother did not mention him to me. Abdul and I did not share all our secrets. I'm sorry to disappoint you. We must go. Enjoy the suite and all the hotel has to offer. Adar will pick you up tomorrow morning at ten. Is that satisfactory?"

Gloria stood and sighed. "Yes, thank you, Zayad, for your cooperation."

"I will call you on Monday if I obtain any additional information on Saddam's assets." He marched toward the door. Adar hurried to get in front of Azizi and held the door open. Then the door clicked closed, and they were gone.

"Do you think he's telling the truth?" Lauren asked.

Gloria slumped back onto the sofa. "Who knows? He didn't seem to falter in his denial. He looked me right in the eye, but I have a feeling he would be capable of looking you in the eye and still lie." She leaned forward and put her face in her hands.

Lauren sat next to her and put her arm around Gloria's shoulder.

"All I want to know is, did he come to Iraq to be with me, or to get that money?" Gloria sniffled.

"There's wine in the liquor cabinet. It's probably damn expensive, but it'll be on the sheik. Should I open it?"

"That seems entirely appropriate. After today, some politician who didn't do anything will be able to take credit for finding Saddam's money," Gloria said.

"Maybe we'll get bonuses. What the hell, the G gets a couple of billion, and we get fifteen hundred. I'll take it." Lauren laughed and popped the cork from the wine bottle. She glanced at the label. "Mouton Rothschild, 2010. Take a look at the wine list. What're they asking for this stuff, anyway?"

Lauren filled two wine glasses and took a sip. "Not bad. Reminds me of Blue Nun."

Gloria's eyes bulged. "Holy shit, thirteen ninety-five a bottle."

"What do you usually drink, five-buck wine?" Lauren laughed. "Thirteen ninety-five isn't too much."

"Not thirteen ninety-five as in thirteen dollars and ninety-five cents. Thirteen ninety-five as in one thousand, three hundred, and ninety-five dollars."

Lauren's eyes bulged. "Well, the sheik said to help ourselves. Drink up, baby, there's another bottle." She drained her glass and filled it again.

An hour later they opened the second bottle, just in time for lunch. They ordered from the American menu: two filet mignons, broccoli, baked potatoes, and crème brûlée for dessert. An hour later, Gloria was sacked out on the sofa. Lauren had made it to the bed in her suite.

Someone rapped on the door of their hotel suite. Gloria rolled off the couch onto the oriental carpet. She looked at the window. The cityscape was black, except for the lights dotting the night from the high-rises. She glanced at her watch; it was eleven thirty. She leaned on the sofa and pushed herself up.

The Sig lay on the sofa's cushion. She picked it up and stashed it in her waistband. She pushed her fingers through her hair trying to bring it back to life. There was a knock on the door again. Gloria went to the door and looked through the peephole. "Adar," she mumbled.

She opened the door. Adar rushed in, closed the door behind him, and locked it. "I know about Mr. Abbott, but we must go. Mr. Azizi is dead. I think he was poisoned. Whoever is responsible might be coming after you and Miss Lauren next. Get whatever you must take and leave anything else behind. Put your burkas on. Go! Go!"

Gloria rushed into Lauren's bedroom, turned on the light, and shook her partner.

Lauren covered her eyes with one hand and pushed Gloria away with the other. "What the hell—"

"Get up, put your burka on. Adar is here. Azizi's dead and whoever killed him might be after us next. We've got to leave. Meet you at the door." Gloria ran to her room and put her burka on, and then it hit her. *Do I believe him? How do I know he didn't kill Azizi?* She slipped the Sig into her pants pocket, so it was readily available and met Lauren and Adar at the door.

CHAPTER 37

Saturday, October 16, 2004

THE TWO BURKA-CLAD WOMEN AND Adar rushed out of the hotel suite. Adar jabbed the button and they waited for what seemed an eternity. He hit it again and again as his head swiveled, looking up and down the hallway until the elevator doors slid open. A man wearing a black bisht and dark frame glasses was in the elevator. Gloria and Lauren's eyes opened wide and Adar jumped back. A second look revealed it wasn't Azizi.

"Expecting someone?" the man asked.

Gloria watched the man's eyes move to Lauren. A strand of blond hair stuck out from her burka. Gloria thought, *Three steps out of the hotel room and we fucked up already.* She grimaced and pointed her chin at it. Lauren tucked it in.

Adar shook his head. "No, sir." He stepped into the elevator and the two women followed and stood behind him.

It was a silent ride down to the lobby. The doors opened and the threesome waited for the man to exit first, then Adar led them out. A few late check-ins were among the people in the sparsely populated space. A small group of people headed from the lounge to the elevators. A man in desert camouflage stood near the reception desk. He was in his thirties, well built, and looked like a Special Forces soldier.

Adar turned to Gloria and Lauren and whispered, "Wait here." He walked toward the man in camouflage.

Gloria watched Adar. He nodded at the man and exchanged words. Then Adar and the man looked at their watches. Adar pulled an envelope out of the inside pocket of his black sport coat and handed it to him.

She watched the man open the envelope and brush his thumb over the contents. He shook his head and handed the envelope back to Adar. Adar pushed the man's hand back, turned and pointed at Gloria and Lauren. The man shook his head again and took a step away. Adar reached into his pocket and Gloria saw a roll of cash in his hand. Adar peeled off some bills and dropped the greenbacks into the man's palm. The man smiled and left the hotel.

Adar waved at Gloria and Lauren, directing them to three white leather chairs in a secluded corner of the lobby. They joined him there.

"The only safe way to travel on the roads from here to Baghdad is in a convoy. The man I was talking to is a mercenary. He's made the trip on numerous occasions."

Gloria gave Adar a pained stare. "He looked like he didn't want to take us. How much is this going to cost?"

"It's the way things are done. You have to negotiate so he feels he's the victor. A thousand dollars for each of us."

Gloria shook her head and extended her hands palms up. "We don't have that kind of money."

"It's paid for."

"We'll get money when we get back to the Green Zone and pay you back," Lauren said.

Adar waved his hands palms down. "Not necessary."

"I insist. It's not fair that you have to spend your money."

"It is not mine. It's a loan that does not require repayment."

Lauren leaned forward. "You took it from Azizi!"

"He liked to carry a lot of cash for his impulse purchases, like a Lamborghini on a visit to Italy. He won't need it anymore, and besides his family has much to inherit from him."

"I hope there was more than enough to reward his loyal employee," Lauren said.

"His employee received an adequate bonus. It will be a good year for my family." He glanced at his watch. "We will be joining Flash's convoy in twenty minutes. It's a ten-hour ride—five hundred-fifty miles over rough roads, through desolate country, filled with thieves. Flash's men will be well armed."

Gloria leaned forward. "What about crossing the border? We have our passports, but they aren't stamped showing we exited Iraq or entered Jordan."

"Just hope for a safe trip. Everything else is secondary." Adar tapped the chest pocket of his sport coat. "There are ways and there are ways. We will be safe, *Inshallah.*"

Gloria's eyes narrowed. *We have time before we leave, now's the time to get some information.* "What happened to Mr. Azizi?"

He shook his head, appearing annoyed by her question. "I'm not sure exactly. He ordered something from room service. I went to my room in our suite. He preferred to eat alone, so I always brought my own food. I was watching television, and ten or fifteen minutes later I heard a thud and then my name. I went to the sitting room of the suite and found him on the floor. There was vomit on his mouth and shirt. I felt for a pulse and there was none."

"Shouldn't you advise his family?" Lauren said.

"Under normal circumstances I would, and at some point, someone will, but I felt that it was urgent to get you both out of here as soon as possible. If Azizi was in danger, it's pretty certain we are, too. He was in good health, so I do not believe his death was from a natural cause. When room service comes, they will recognize him, and the hotel will deal with it appropriately."

Gloria thought of Jim Abbott's death, and that Azizi's brother alleged Abbott was murdered. What if Azizi had been lying about knowing anything about Jim's death? What if there really was a connection? How would she ever find out now? "Who would want to kill him?"

"Mr. Azizi had contacts with people from all walks of life. Working for the defense minister I knew that he had been solicited by arms dealers, the CIA, Syrian officials, American corporations, and, I believe, even insurgents."

That reduces the suspects to a few thousand, Gloria thought.

Flash entered the hotel, and minutes later four sand-colored Chevy Suburbans rolled away from the front of the hotel. In the first truck Flash, with a nickel-plated Beretta strapped on his hip, was behind the wheel, and one of his men, armed with an AK-47 and a side arm, was in the passenger seat. A radio journalist and the man in the bisht, they had seen earlier, were their passengers. Another armed mercenary called Vulcan was at the wheel of the second vehicle. Adar was in the shotgun seat, and Gloria and Lauren in the back. The third truck had an armed driver called Ming. Two English journalists and a freelance photographer were in that car. A man named Zarkov drove the fourth car. His wife, Princess Aura, took the passenger seat with an M-16 between her legs. Their passengers were four western journalists.

They cruised through the empty streets of Amman. Once on the narrow two-lane highway, they hit ninety miles per hour. In slightly over an hour, the Suburbans pulled into a truck stop in the town of Safawi, Jordan. The lot was filled with trucks. Even at this hour, men were kneading dough in an open storefront, baking it in brick ovens, and pulling out flatbreads. The passengers in the Suburbans were instructed to stay in the trucks. Two of the drivers went to the storefront and returned with bags full of kebobs and cold soft drinks.

They passed the bags to the passengers. The drivers ate and drank while cruising the desolate highway at a respectable seventy. When they finished their meal, they immediately boosted the speed back to ninety.

After five hours of driving through what looked like a moonscape, the little caravan came to the double arches known as the Karameh border crossing, marking the Jordan-Iraqi border. In between the giant arches was a large blank slate that once featured a picture of Saddam Hussein.

At the checkpoints, officials for both countries examined the passports of the caravan's occupants.

Gloria leaned forward and nudged Adar's shoulder. "They're looking at everyone's passports. What should we do?"

"Let me talk to them. I should be able to resolve the situation." He opened the passenger door and stepped out of the Suburban. Adar met with the Jordanian guards. He made another withdrawal from his pocket and they sailed past the Jordanian border guards.

Next was the Iraqi border stop. Two officials went to the first truck and Adar already had a roll of cash in his hand waiting for them. The two guards approached the second truck and started a conversation with Vulcan. The jabbering in Arabic reached a frenzied pace.

Lauren looked to Gloria. "That doesn't sound good."

"Let him handle it, there's nothing we can do," Gloria said, beads of sweat rolling down the sides of her face.

The guards were waving their hands, pointing at Adar.

Adar's forehead wrinkled. His head swiveled as though he were looking for a path of escape. He said something to the officials, waving his hands and pointing at Gloria and Lauren. One of border guards rushed to the passenger door, opened it, and yanked Adar to the ground. He pulled Adar up, pushed his chest against the Suburban's front fender, and slapped handcuffs onto his wrists. A guard pushed him toward a small building. Another opened the rear door of the suburban and shouted at Gloria and Lauren.

Gloria didn't understand Arabic but was sure the translation was something like 'get the fuck out of the truck.'

The wind swirled the sand around them as their feet hit the ground. The guard pushed them toward the same building Adar had entered, shouting at them in Arabic. They nodded, not understanding a word, but knowing full well that saying anything in English could only bring disaster.

They entered the small cement building. Adar sat on a wooden bench. One of his handcuffs was locked on a metal ring extended from the wall the other tight around his wrist. One of the guards stood inches from his face screaming, spittle flying. It was the Iraqi version of the third degree.

A guard escorted Gloria and Lauren down a narrow aisle between the bench Adar was sitting on and a worn wooden desk. Adar raised his head, glanced at them and then lowered it. Tears rushed down his face. Gloria hesitated and the guard pushed her back. She felt the Sig in her waistband press against her skin. The guard screamed something in Arabic and everyone's attention focused on her.

The guard lifted her burka off and yanked the pistol from her waistband, slamming her against the desk. He felt her pockets and found her credentials and official passport. He screamed, but the only words she could understand was 'American spy.' He snapped handcuffs onto her wrists. Gloria knew that whatever trouble Adar was in, they were now coconspirators.

Seconds later, another guard ripped Lauren's burka off, revealing her fair skin and blonde hair. Her official passport and credentials brought great delight to their captors, and she was handcuffed behind her back. The women stood there in jeans and T-shirts. The guards grabbed them by their arms and escorted them into a windowless room with a dirt floor, no bigger than a closet. Stale air filled their nostrils. The door slammed shut. The metal knick of a key turning in the door's lock meant they were prisoners.

A light bulb hung from a wire in the ceiling. The glare stung Lauren's eyes. "What the hell is happening?"

"Damned if I know. They know we're Americans. They're acting like they're Saddam loyalists. Adar, what's his story…?" She shook her head. "We have to be ready for anything." Gloria tightened her fist. "If they try to rape us, kick 'em in the balls, bite them, hurt them any way you can."

Lauren bit her lips. "Not a hell of lot we can do with our hands cuffed behind our back."

"Fight 'em. Scream and yell," Gloria said, trying hard not to show how terrified she was.

An hour later they heard the footfalls of what sounded like a brigade of soldiers advancing on their makeshift cell. The door creaked open, and a flashlight blinded their vision.

"You two trying to cause an international incident?" someone asked in perfect English.

Gloria's eyes adjusted. The image in the doorway gradually changed from a blurred silhouette to a stout man in an Army uniform. Behind him stood Flash and the man from his shotgun seat, carrying the AK-47.

Gloria exhaled. "Thank God." The relief that flooded her body brought her to her knees. "We have no idea what's going on. Maybe you can tell us." Gloria raised herself from the floor, turned, and extended her handcuffed wrists to the soldier. Lauren, who had been leaning against the wall, refusing to sit on the dirt floor, held her wrists out from her back.

The GI unlocked the cuffs and slid them in his belt. "I'm Sergeant Gene Hickson with the Rangers. You guys came with that man, Adar?"

This is no time for bullshit. "Yes," Gloria said. "We were in a convoy that Adar let us join so we could get back to Baghdad. We're IRS special agents in Amman on a special assignment."

"Before we get out of here, this is the story. Your friend is being held on suspicion of murder. Apparently, he worked in some capacity for this guy Azizi who was a real muckity-muck in the Iraqi Defense Department. Azizi's wife tried to reach him on his cell and he never responded. She called the hotel he was staying at. Security went to his room and found him dead, and his right-hand man, your Adar here, missing. They contacted the Jordanian and Iraqi authorities who put an APB out on him. Then who shows up at the border trying to leave Jordan? Your man, Adar, with you two in tow."

"We know Azizi's dead. Lauren and I met with Azizi earlier in the day. That's why we were all in the convoy trying to get the hell out of here. Adar said he thought someone poisoned Azizi, and that we should leave because it was dangerous to stay after our meeting." Gloria said.

"Poisoned? Azizi's throat was cut, and they found thirty thousand in greenbacks in a money belt Adar was wearing. Sounds to me like they've got their man."

CHAPTER 38

Karameh Border Crossing
October 17, 2004
2:30 a.m.

G LORIA LOOKED AT THE RED marks on her wrist and rubbed them to ease the ache. It didn't make sense that Adar would murder Azizi. If he did kill him by slitting his throat, there'd have been blood on his shoes or his shirt. He's hiding something that scared him. Is it about Jim's murder? Fear that Adar was lost to her strangled her intestines. Without Adar, she would never learn whether it had been love or greed that had motivated Jim Abbott go to Iraq.

Gloria and Lauren followed Hickson, Flash, and his bodyguard, still gripping the AK-47, down the short hallway. Gloria knew she had to act now because in seconds they would be rolling down the highway to Baghdad and would never see Adar again. She grabbed the sergeant's wrist. "Sergeant Hickson, can I have a word with you?"

"I'd think you'd want to get out of here before the Iraqis decide to hold you, too."

"Can you come with me back in the ..." She pointed to the holding cell. "Lauren, you stay out here with Flash and his friend." *I've got to protect her from whatever comes of this.*

Gloria and Hickson returned to the cell. The stench filled her nostrils once again. The single lightbulb was an inch above the soldier's head.

Hickson put his hands on his hips accentuating his powerful forearms. He towered over Gloria. "OK, what's up?"

Gloria took a deep breath to deal with her uncertainty. "We were on a highly confidential mission." *True and untrue, no one knew about it except us,* she thought. "In fact, there's no record of us leaving Iraq and entering Jordan. What I'm going to tell you must stay between us. We were following leads to billions of dollars of Saddam's money. Adar had accompanied Azizi to a bunker in Syria where billions of US currency was stored. They saw it, just sitting there. Without Adar, we don't have a chance of taking the final steps to locate and seize it. We need to take him with us."

Hickson exhaled and laughed. "Ma'am, what you're asking me to do is ten levels above my pay grade."

"Look," Gloria said desperately, "if we leave Adar here, and the Iraqis lock him up, I'm pretty sure he won't last a day, given what happened to Azizi. Remember, he saw the money, too. Or he'll be jail for years, and there's a good chance some of Saddam's people can get to him there, too, especially if they find out he's locked up for murdering Azizi. Best case, he'll disappear into some prison for years. In any case, his information will be lost to us."

Hickson pulled his hand across his lips. "Look, ma'am, I'm a lifer, and if I walk him out of here, I'll be court martialed. I can't do that, ma'am."

"Think about all the GIs, your friends, that have gone down because of that asshole Saddam. Do it for them."

"Don't put that on me. I'm a month from finishing my tour. I've got a wife and two little girls in Charlotte waiting on me to come home."

"I'm not trying to put a guilt trip on you. I think getting Adar out of here is the right thing to do. Actually, I know it's the right thing to do. I'd do it myself, but we both know that's impossible. They think I'm a spy."

Hickson scratched the back of his neck. His tone more formal. "Why, Agent? Why would that be the right thing to do?"

Gloria realized the sergeant was growing impatient and she needed to give him a better reason. "I'll tell you the whole story. It's about more than a couple of billion dollars. It's about the life of another agent. He was in the army and was part of the mission in 1980 in Iran to rescue the hostages—"

Hickson shook his head. "What's your friend's name?"

"His name was Jim Abbott."

"Was? Don't tell me..."

"We were here on a three-month assignment starting last June. When we finished, we left for the airport and we were attacked by insurgents. Jim was killed. Shot right through his body armor."

"I'm sorry about that. I didn't know your friend, but that body armor is what my two buddies where wearing when they went down. They ought to indict the son of a bitch who sold that shit to the Army."

Gloria hoped Hickson would make the connection to his personal losses and hers. She had to push that idea in case he wasn't there yet. "Jim and I were…we were in love. We took the assignment to see if this time away from our regular lives would tell us if we had a future."

"What does that have to do with Adar?" His eyes narrowed and he folded his arms across his chest.

I've got to run with it now. "Last September, out of the blue, Azizi's brother calls me in Chicago from Iraq. I had never heard of him before. He tells me that Jim Abbott gave him one of my business cards while we were in Iraq. I have no idea how Jim met this guy."

Flash came to the door of the cell. "Are we almost done here? These border guards need the cell for the prisoner."

Hickson pushed his fingers through his hair. "I'm just a simple farm boy from North Carolina. Why me? Why do I have to get involved in this? Thirty days, and I'm homeward bound."

Gloria hoped, for her own selfish reasons, that her story would bring the desired result, one that would benefit her. "Azizi's brother was killed while he was talking to me. He said the attack was a set-up. Now Azizi's dead, too. Adar is the only person that can help us find Jim's murderers and the two billion dollars. That money he and Azizi saw in the bunker was in shrink-wrapped plastic from the New York Federal Reserve." Gloria gazed down at the dirt floor. "Just like the cash that Jim's wife showed me after his funeral."

Hickson did an about face, marched out of the cell, walked toward Lauren. and stopped. "Let's get our prisoner and get out of here."

Gloria saw Lauren give him a blank stare, and then her eyes went to Gloria, who nodded to her. Lauren fell in step behind them, and they marched forward to take custody of Adar.

CHAPTER 39

Iraqi Border Patrol Office
Saturday, October 17, 2004

HICKSON LED THE WAY. GLORIA, Lauren, Flash, and his bodyguard followed. The man sitting behind the desk had been Adar's interrogator. He wore desert camouflage and was taking a bite from a lamb kabob. Adar was sitting on the bench opposite the desk still handcuffed to the wall. Sitting next to him was one of the other border patrol guards and a second sat in a chair next to the interrogator.

Hickson said something in Arabic to the interrogator.

Gloria and Lauren exchanged glances. Their eyes widened in surprise at Hickson's language skills.

The interrogator put the kabob down on a tin plate and pushed it away. He looked at Hickson, then pointed at his two associates and flicked his finger at the door. The two guards got up and without a word, scuffled out of the building, closing the door behind them.

Hickson placed his hands on the desk and leaned into the interrogator. They stared into each other's face without saying a word. The Iraqi's eyes narrowed. His lips pursed.

Hickson's knuckle's whitened as his grip on the edge of the desk tightened. A stream of words in Arabic shot from his mouth. The only understandable words were, 'thirty thousand dollars.'

The Iraqi waved his arms and shook his head in response.

Hickson came on stronger. He straightened up, puffed out his chest, and folded his arms, looming threateningly over the Iraqi. Again, they heard the words 'thirty thousand dollars' followed by 'bribe,' a word Gloria understood.

The Iraqi jumped out of seat, knocking his chair to the floor. He violently shook his head in denial. Perspiration flew from his forehead. He pointed at Adar, said something derogatory, and spat on the ground.

Hickson banged his fist on the desk and pointed his finger at the interrogator.

The Iraqi pushed Hickson's hand away and bumped his shoulder into Hickson's rudely as he marched past him to where Adar was sitting.

Gloria braced herself, getting ready to yank Adar away, if necessary, to prevent him from being thrown into that cell and lost to them for good.

The Iraqi reached into his pants pocket and pulled out the handcuff key. He unlocked Adar's hand and pointed to the door. Gloria held her breath.

Hickson held out his hand and gave another command to the interrogator.

The man pulled the Sig he had seized from Gloria from the back of his waist and slapped it into Hickson's palm. Then he produced the confiscated passports, which Hickson grabbed and handed to Gloria.

Hickson stuffed the semi-auto in his waist band, grabbed Adar by the elbow, and dragged him out of building. Gloria and Lauren followed them to an Army Humvee. Corporal Hobson was waiting in the driver's seat. Flash and his bodyguard got into the Suburban. The Humvee and Suburban squealed away from the border checkpoint and convoyed toward Baghdad.

Gloria sat in the back with Lauren and Adar. "Sarge, whatever you said, nice job. I was sweating it. Thought we'd never get out of there with Adar."

Adar sat there silent, cold sweat dripping down his ashen face.

"These border guards are as corrupt as they come but they can't readily admit it, especially in front of an audience, so the jerk has to make a scene and act like he's insulted that I would think I could bribe him. That cash was never going to see the light of day. They've already divvied it up."

"All I have to say is, thank God for the US Army," Lauren said. "Sarge, when you get back home, you ought to go to law school. I don't know what the hell you said, but that was one hell of an argument you put up. I can just picture you in front of a jury." She smiled at him.

"Lawyer, no thank you. I'm a carpenter, and when I get home, all I want to do is cut wood and pound nails."

Gloria looked out the window as they sped across Saddam's highways. The roads were wide and well-marked, a definite improvement over Jordan's. Guardrails ran the length of the roadway. There were rest areas with concrete picnic tables and metal umbrellas. The only signs that there had been some people in the rest areas were a few stranded cars riddled with bullet holes. The wind blew sand across the highway.

During the long night Gloria, Lauren and Adar drifted in and out of sleep. By the time they approached the exit for Fallujah, four hours and three hundred miles had passed. Explosions from bombs and sustained small arms fire coming from the city jolted them awake. Gloria glanced at her watch. It was six twenty-five in the morning. An orange glow was breaking through the gray cast at the horizon. Gloria shook her head. *How insane is this? I should be home with my kids. But I'm here now, hopefully, only for a few more days. I have to act now or all this is wasted.*

Hickson noticed the movement in the back seat. "The military action is the second battle for Fallujah. It's a joint American, Iraqi, and British offensive to retake the city. The first battle was only seven months ago when insurgents mutilated and killed four members from Blackwater security. You know Blackwater—one of our big military contractors."

He could hardly be heard over the roar of the Humvee. Lauren grabbed the back of his seat and leaned forward. "How much longer before we get to Baghdad?"

"It's about fifty miles. The traffic will pick up as we get closer, so it'll take an hour or so."

Lauren closed her eyes again and leaned against the window.

Adar's head bobbed as he floated in and out of sleep. Gloria elbowed him lightly in his ribs. His eyelids lifted and he looked at her.

She slid closer to him and said in a low tone. "Adar, now is the time for you to tell me what happened. If you don't, we'll have to turn you over to the Iraqi authorities. They will lock you up and you'll die in Abu Ghraib."

"If I tell you, I'll die anyway."

Gloria gave an exaggerated sigh. "Why do you say that?"

"The man that killed Azizi will see that I die, if not by his hand, by those he hires."

"Why do you believe that? The Army will put you in protective custody. You won't have to worry about the insurgents or the Baathists. No one will harm you."

"It is not the insurgents or Saddam's loyalist that will kill me." His voice trailed off.

"Who are you so scared of?"

He locked his elbows to his sides and his knuckles whitened. "It's the American. It's the Army." Adar's voice was shaky and halting. His eyes flitted at Hickson, then the corporal in the front seat, and then down.

Gloria had a confused look on her face. She hesitated, trying to sort out what she had heard. She whispered. "The Army? American? I don't understand."

"Azizi lied to you about everything. He wasn't blindfolded when they took him to the bunker. I was with him. I know what they were going to do."

"Why would he lie? What was going on?"

"He lied to make his presence to you important, and to learn what you were going to do."

That son of a bitch, Gloria thought. "Start from the beginning, Adar, please."

Adar's chin trembled, but he went on. "Azizi was involved in getting the defense minister's money to Switzerland. That's how he learned to do it and how to make the contacts he needed. Because of his relationship with the defense minister, defense contractors came to Azizi to move cash they received out of Iraq."

"How did they do it?"

"The defense minister was diverting some of the military equipment purchased by Iraq to Syria, for a handsome profit. Assad's people made it easy for him by letting Azizi open an account at the Bank of Syria, and they paid the minister and Azizi by crediting the account. The minister liked it because his name was not on the account. I'm sure Assad sold the things Syria purchased to Al Qaeda, Boko Haram, and Hezbollah."

"That makes perfect sense. That's why Azizi would want to know what our plans were. What kind of equipment was sold to Syria?"

"Everything: weapons, body armor, medical supplies. They stayed away from heavy equipment like tanks and trucks because it would be too hard to transport without detection and too easy for people to recognize such things."

"How did Azizi get the defense minister's cash to Switzerland?"

"They only deposited a fraction of the cash to Azizi's account in Syria. The remaining cash was stored in the bank vaults. They would take truckloads of cash from the bank and store it in the bunker we visited. We went to the bunker so Azizi could see how much there was, negotiate a fee for his services, and arrange transportation of the cash to the Swiss banks."

"How much did Azizi take to Switzerland?"

Adar shook his head. "None."

Gloria rubbed her chin. "None? What happened?"

"When Bush signed the act imposing tighter restrictions on Syria, Assad became very angry. He knew some of the cash in the bunker belonged to American businesses, so he decided to claim all of it as Syrian assets. That's his revenge. All of that cash from the Food-for-Oil-Program, and cash held for American businesses was now Syria's. Or, more exactly, it was now Assad's."

"What does this have to do Azizi's murder?"

"I was asleep in my room. I heard Azizi arguing with someone. They started yelling at each other. The other man was screaming, 'You took millions from me and I want my money.'"

"Azizi told him that he had to be patient, but the truth was that he may never get it back."

"The man was very angry. Saying things like 'I trusted you. You told me this would be the safest way to get my cash out of Iraq. That I could make even more money when I sold equipment to Syria, and now you're telling me it's all lost. You motherfucker.'"

"Then I heard them fighting. I went to my door and I saw the man standing behind Azizi. He grabbed Azizi's hair, yanked his head back, and cut his throat. The man stared at Azizi lying on the floor, his hands covering his throat, and said 'You'll never get any of your money, either.' Then he ran out of the room."

Gloria flinched. "Do you know who he was?"

"No, I saw him several times waiting to meet with Azizi, but they always kept their meetings private."

Gloria shook her head. "Can you describe him?"

"He was a white American man, short, and well dressed in expensive suits. He looked like a military man, short haircut, but never wore a uniform."

Gloria nodded, thinking that cut it down to a few thousand. "You lied about Azizi's murder because you think that an American, maybe even a military man, killed him?"

Adar hunched his shoulders, nodded, and stared at his hands folded in his lap.

Quiet filled the air. Adar raised his hand, his forefinger extended. "One more thing. I remember he had a scar on his left cheek. I heard Azizi refer to him when he was talking to one of Assad's generals. The general was telling Azizi about complaints from the insurgents about faulty body armor Syria had sold to them."

Lauren leaned forward. "Sounds like the guy at the medal ceremony."

Gloria's emotions ran the gamut. She pushed her shoulders back and put her hand on Adar's forearm. "Adar, I will personally guarantee your safety." Then she pictured Jim Abbott lying in the back seat of the Humvee, the black stain of his blood coloring the bullet hole in his body armor. She had one more question she had to ask but was almost too frightened to hear the answer. She closed her eyes and felt like a spike was driven into her heart.

"Adar, back in September, late at night, an agent like me was killed when we were being transferred from the Green Zone to the airport. We were attacked by a group of insurgents. There were so many of them, they never stopped coming. It was an ambush. What do you know about that?"

Adar glanced at Hickson and the corporal. "Talk later."

Gloria leaned back in her seat, and then toward Adar. "I have to know everything. Tell me now."

"I tell you now, and when we get to Baghdad, you will leave me with the soldiers." He nodded toward Hickson.

"That soldier saved your life getting you out of the checkpoint. What do you think those Iraqis were going to do? They were going to keep the cash they found in your money belt and kill you as soon as we left. Anyone asked about you, they would have said they'd never seen you."

Adar swallowed. "Maybe, but what do you think the soldiers will do to me if I tell you about the Army man?"

"They won't do anything to you. They're here risking their lives in your country for your people. If someone is compromising their safety with bad equipment or selling it to people that put weapons in the hands of insurgents, they'll want that person arrested and prosecuted. You'll be an important witness in the case. They'll need you. They wouldn't let anyone harm you, especially if that person is hurting their brother soldiers."

Adar wet his lips. His shoulders tensed. He glanced around uneasily and rubbed his neck. "Can we talk when we get to Baghdad? Some place private."

Gloria nodded.

Adar slid back in his seat and closed his eyes. A heavy sigh escaped him.

CHAPTER 40

Baghdad
The Green Zone
October 17, 2004
7:45 a.m.

CORPORAL HOBSON DROVE THE HUMVEE past tall cement walls topped with barbed wire that circled the five square kilometers of the Green Zone. Everything from Vespa scooters to tanks rolled down the street. The road's shoulders were littered with chunks of cement from roadside bombs. Hobson pulled the Humvee up to the checkpoint. A host of well-armed GIs manned the post. They checked the personnel in the vehicle and did an under-carriage inspection, gliding mirrors beneath the chassis. After passing through the checkpoint, the Humvee wove through a series of cement blast walls and fell in line behind five vehicles waiting before steel gates. They opened, and the Humvee followed the other vehicles into the Green Zone.

"Sarge, where do we go from here?" Gloria asked.

Hickson turned in his seat to face her. "I've got to check in with my lieutenant. After that, I can take you anywhere in the zone." He lifted Gloria's Sig from his belt and handed it to her. "You might want this."

Gloria took the pistol and watched Adar's concerned brown eyes follow the weapon from Hickson to her. She ejected the magazine, saw that it was full, press checked for a round in the chamber, then stashed it in her waistband.

The corporal drove through the busy streets, filled with Iraqis buying wares from street merchants and soldiers marching on security patrols. Some of the merchants' storefronts showed damage from insurgents' mortars and rockets. He parked the Humvee in front of a nondescript building.

Hickson glanced at the backseat passengers. "Be back in five." The corporal followed Hickson into the building.

Adar glanced at the pistol's butt sticking out from Gloria's waistband. "Why did he give that to you?"

"It's assigned to me. It's my responsibility."

Gloria caught Lauren eyeing the Sig and waited for her to comment that it was hers, but she didn't say anything.

"Where do we go now?" Adar asked.

"I'm not sure. We'll ask the sergeant to take us some place that will be secure, some place where there won't be many people and we can talk some more," Gloria said, hoping Adar could answer the one question she had not asked; *Who killed Jim Abbott?*

Ten minutes later, Sergeant Hickson and the corporal approached the Humvee. Gloria got out and met them in front of the vehicle. "Sarge, thanks for everything you've done. Can I talk with you in private?"

Hickson nodded at Hobson, who saluted. "I'll go back inside. See you in ten." He headed back into the building.

Gloria took a deep breath. "Sarge, we need to take Adar some place where he'll be secure. He's concerned that Azizi's murderer is a threat to him."

"Who's the killer?"

"He doesn't know his name, but by the physical description he gave us, we think we know who he might be. If it's who we think he is, he's a former Army officer who now runs the business that sells body armor to the military."

"Body armor. There have been a lot of problems with that stuff. What's his name?"

"I'm reluctant to say his name, because I'm not one hundred percent sure it's him."

"You're the investigator. What do you want to do?"

"First, I've got to find a place to take Adar. He's afraid this guy will want to kill him. Second, he gave us a lead to a substantial amount of Saddam's cash. I need to get in touch with our lead agent to start the procedure for seizing the money. It's a hell of a lot of money—in the billions."

"Holy shit. Let me think. Some place quiet and safe, huh? Okay, there's an old warehouse that we used that was emptied when the Army built a new facility. Too much money floating around, and they had to figure out something to do with it. I still have a key for the old place. If no one's using it, that might work for you. Telephone lines and computer hook-ups were still functioning the last time I was there."

"That sounds perfect. If you don't mind, can you take us there by yourself? With everything that's happened, Adar is rattled, and I have to confess, I feel safer with you. As far as Adar is concerned, the fewer people that know where we are, the more comfortable he'll be."

"Sure." Hickson pulled out a card from his shirt pocket. "Here's my cell number. You need anything, give me a call. I'll tell Corporal Hobson to wait for me here, and then we can head out."

Fifteen minutes later Hickson drove the Humvee to a secluded back alley on the south side of the Green Zone. A truck was parked fifty feet from the front entrance of the warehouse. The black warehouse door had a large number 23 painted on it in white numerals. Hickson gave her the key. Gloria unlocked the door and she, Lauren, and Adar entered.

The hair on Gloria's neck stood up, and her instincts for danger kicked in immediately. She locked the door and pocketed the key. Gloria pulled out her pistol and did a sweep of the warehouse. It appeared to be clear, but Gloria still couldn't shake the feeling of danger.

<hr />

Eyes peered over the dashboard of the truck, watching the personnel from the Humvee entering the warehouse, and then the sergeant driving the Humvee away. *What the fuck! It's that agent from Chicago, her protégé and Adar, and what's left of my cash is inside. Jesus Christ.*

His smile gleamed like a glistening knife blade, and his laugh crackled as he realized that an unexpected opportunity had presented itself. *Soon, I'll be rid of this interference and have my cash.*

CHAPTER 41

Warehouse 23
Green Zone
Saturday, October 18, 2004
9:00 a.m.

A TYPICAL, STEEL-GRAY, US Army-issued desk sat thirty feet from the warehouse door, with the usual paraphernalia sitting on it: a black phone, a tablet of paper, and an empty glass ashtray with *US Army* scripted on the bottom. A scattering of chairs was in front of the desk, a larger chair behind it. Stashed in the corner twenty feet away was a shipping container with wooden stairs leading to its doors.

"Lauren, check the trailer. Adar, sit here." Gloria pointed to one of the chairs in front of the desk." She sat in the chair behind the desk, picked up the telephone receiver, and put it to her ear. "What do you know, we've got a dial tone."

Lauren inspected the shipping container and sat next to Adar. "The trailer's locked."

"I'm going to call Bill Musgrove. He'll be in a pissy mood since we've been missing for a couple of days, but when he hears about the two billion in cash, that should pacify him." Gloria checked the contact list on her cell for Musgrove's number and dialed it on the desk phone.

She decided her best approach would be to keep it light. "Bill, it's Gloria. How's my favorite senior special agent?" It didn't work quite as planned. She held the receiver away from her ear toward Lauren, as Musgrove went through a series of four-letter words, throwing in a couple of five-letter expletives for emphasis.

There was a moment of silence, and she returned the receiver to her ear. "I'm sorry, Bill. I know we fucked up big time. Everyone is okay." She nodded and put her hand over the mouthpiece until he stopped yelling. "I've got Lauren here with me. She's fine." Gloria went through the same routine with the mouthpiece again. "I know we should have checked in with you, but something big came up and we had to run with it."

Musgrove asked, "What is it?"

"We've got a witness who has identified the location of two billion dollars of Saddam's cash. We're going to debrief him further, but you need to start the process of doing whatever you have to do to seize the cash. There's a lot of gold, apparently, too.

"It's in Syria. We'll tie down the location as best we can. You can reach me on my cell or on the landline at Army warehouse 23. It's in the south side of the Green Zone. I've got to go."

As anticipated, Gloria heard the change in Musgrove's tone of voice as he harrumphed and gruffly ended the call.

CHAPTER 42

Warehouse 23
Green Zone
Saturday, October 17, 2004
11:00 a.m.

"ADAR, WE NEED TO KNOW everything you know before the Iraqi authorities want to take you into custody. It's the only way we can justify keeping you in our custody. Do you understand?" Gloria looked across the desk and hoped the threat of being locked up in an Iraqi prison would pry anything Adar knew about Jim Abbott's death out of him.

"Yes, but I have told you everything I know."

Time is short. I'll try the direct approach, she thought. "Early last September, a group of us was being transported from the Green Zone to Baghdad International. After the third bridge, we were attacked by a group of insurgents. My partner was killed, and several soldiers were shot."

Adar nodded and shrugged. "I'm sorry for your loss."

Gloria folded her hands, placed her forearms on the desk, and leaned forward. "What do you know about the incident?"

Adar held his hands out, palms up, and shook his head. "Nothing, why would I know anything about that? You think I was involved in the attack?"

"I'm not suggesting you were, but I have strong feelings that you must know something about it."

Adar tilted his head. "Why do you say that?"

"After I returned home, I received a call from a man I didn't know who would not give me his name. He told me that the attack was planned, and that he had knowledge of bribes and cash dealings. I later learned that it was Azizi's brother. Unfortunately, he was killed before he could give me any additional information."

"I remember Azizi telling me his brother was killed. Did Azizi have any more information from his brother?"

Gloria unfolded her hands and leaned back into the chair, her left hand at her side and right elbow on the armrest. "You were there when we talked to him in our hotel suite. You know what he said." She pointed her index finger at Adar. "I want to know what he told you before our meeting, and anything he said to you after the meeting."

"He told me after the meeting that he was angry with me initially because I mentioned the cash in the bunker. He wasn't going to tell you about it but then he realized it was probably wise to mention it, because he could find out what you planned to do. That would give him an idea of how much time he had to move the cash and make a multi-million-dollar fee."

"Tell me more about the man you saw kill Azizi."

"I know nothing about him. Don't know his name, where he's from, what business he's in, nothing."

"You said Azizi put his money in the bunker. How did Azizi get his money?"

"I never saw the man give any money to Azizi. You saw how he treated me. I was his servant, not his confidant. He never discussed that with me."

"You said you saw them meet. When and where did they meet? How often?"

Adar wrung his hands. "I don't know. I saw them meet two, maybe three, times."

Gloria was growing impatient. She banged her fist on the desk. "Where, Adar? Where?"

Adar sat back in his chair. His posture stiffened. He squinted, making the wrinkles around his eyes more pronounced. "The first time was in Azizi's limousine."

Gloria calmed herself, waited, and focused on his eyes. She knew that sometimes silence was more effective at getting information than a question.

"I don't know what they said. I was in the back seat with Azizi. He told the driver to stop and then told me to get out. I did, and that man got out of a jeep and took my place in the limo."

"Did he give anything to Azizi?"

Adar looked down at his shoes. "He carried a duffel bag into the limo."

"What was in the duffel?"

Adar rubbed the back of his neck. "I don't know. I never saw the contents."

"Did the bag look heavy? I mean, the way the man carried it, did it look heavy?"

Adar nodded.

"What do you think was in it?"

He shook his head. "I said that I never saw the contents, and Azizi never told me."

"When the man left the limo, did the duffel stay with Azizi?"

"Yes."

"Where did he take the duffel bag?"

"We went to his house and I carried it into his office."

"What do you think the duffel weighed?"

"I don't know, twenty kilos, more or less."

"Describe the duffel."

"It looked like a typical Army duffel bag, an olive drab color, two shoulder straps and one handle."

"And you never saw the contents?"

"No, never."

"Did you ever see the duffel again?"

"No, I never saw it after I carried it into his office."

"Was there another man in the jeep?"

Adar nodded.

"Describe him."

"I didn't get a good look at him. A white man in army khakis."

"And when did the meeting in the limo take place?"

"I don't know the exact date. I would guess around the middle of June."

"What about the other times you saw the man with the scar on his cheek?"

"Like I said, maybe another two times."

"When and where?"

"It would have been after the meeting in the limo at one of Azizi's houses in Baghdad. Probably would have been the middle of July, and then the last time late July or early August."

"What did you see?"

"The same two men. The man with the scar and the man in khakis. The man in the khakis carried the duffel bag those times. They met in private with Azizi in his office and left without the duffel."

"Did you get a better look at the other man on those occasions?"

"Yes, much better. The first time I just glanced in the direction of the jeep. In the house, I saw him for several minutes."

The muscles in Gloria's neck corded. *Why hadn't he said that before?* She reached into her pocket and took a photograph out. It was creased and folded. She ripped it in half and shoved the piece containing her own image back into her pocket. She placed the other half face up on the desk and pushed it toward Adar. "Was this the other man you saw with the man with the scar? The man that carried the duffel bag the last two times."

Adar picked the photo up, placed it back on the desk, and nodded, "Yes."

Gloria's eyes welled. She grabbed the photo, the only picture she had of Jim Abbott and herself. She crumbled it in her hand and returned it to her pocket. All at once she felt like stone, as though her heart had stopped. *I'm certain he came to Iraq for me, for our love, but this fucking war corrupted that. It was the war that killed him, not me.* In her heart, she knew she was rationalizing.

CHAPTER 43

Warehouse 23
Green Zone
Saturday, October 17, 2004
1:00 p.m.

G LORIA HEARD THE WAREHOUSE DOOR scrape against the cement floor. She dragged her forearm across her face, clearing the tears. In front of her, Lauren and Adar looked over their shoulders at the open doorway. Standing there was the man with the burn scar on his cheek, brandishing an M-4 rifle, with an M-9 semi-auto pistol strapped at his hip.

"Well, well, now, look who we have here. My friend Adar, the medal winner, and," he pointed the barrel of the rifle at Lauren, "you, sweetheart, must be the medal winner's note taker."

Gloria looked through her blurry eyes. "You're Nestor. You run Standard Armor, making all that shit body armor."

Nestor kept his right hand on the rifle's pistol grip and held the stock at his hip. He jutted his chin up and puffed out his chest. "Ah, you remember me. You ran off the stage so fast I didn't think you knew who I was." He leaned his back against the door, jammed it closed, locked it, and swaggered toward the trio, stopping behind Lauren. He pushed the barrel of the M-4 against the back of her head. "I suspect that you ladies are armed. So, one at a time, slowly pull your weapons out and place them on the desk. Young lady, since you and I are so close, you go first."

"I'm not armed," Lauren said.

"Not that I don't trust you, but I think it would be wise for me to check." He moved to his left, rested the barrel of the rifle on Lauren's shoulder, and pointed it at Gloria. He bent his knees and patted Lauren's left side from under her arm down to her hip, and then moved to her right side and did the same. He pushed her forward, checking her back around her waist, and slid his hand around the front. "Good girl, you were telling the truth. Now, you sit still while I check out Adar."

He went through the same procedure and found nothing.

"Now, leader of the pack, it's your turn. You stay right where you are." He kept the M-4 pointed at Gloria as he side-stepped, circling the desk, and stopped behind her. "I'll ask you first. Hope you've enough sense to answer me honestly. Are you armed?"

Gloria turned her head facing Nestor. She felt his eyes probing hers in an attempt to measure his opponent. She nodded, "Of course."

"And where's your weapon?"

"A Sig Sauer, tucked in my waistband behind my back."

"Smart lady." Nestor rested the rifle's barrel on Gloria's shoulder, pointed at Lauren. He yanked the pistol from Gloria's waist and stuffed it into his own waistband. "Not that I don't trust you, but I think I better pat you down too." He checked her right side, then her left and front. "Now the question is, what do we do from here?" He twisted his mouth to the side with malicious delight.

"You see, the problem is that I have some cash in this shipping container behind us, among other cargo, and I need to get it out of here tonight to send it home."

"Why don't you send it to Syria, so all of your cash is in one place?" Adar said.

"Adar, you talk too much." A burst of three shots blasted into Adar's abdomen, and a second volley went into his chest. He torpedoed backwards, knocking the chair over. The report of the gunshots echoed through the warehouse. Adar's body quivered as it lay on the floor. Blood pooled around him.

Gloria covered her ears. The shots deafened her. She felt sick with another death on her conscience. Fear consumed her as she contemplated what lay ahead for her and Lauren.

Lauren jumped from her chair, trembling, shaking her head in denial, "No, no, no," as the acrid smell of gun powder filled the air.

Nestor laughed arrogantly. "Yes, yes, yes, my dear. Now sit your ass down." He waved the M-4 at her. "The problem is, what do I do with you two ladies? I know, I'll send you for a little ride with my cash. Both of you come over here and lie on your stomachs on the floor." He pointed to the front of the shipping container, where wooden stairs were leading up to the door. "That's it, lie down right there."

Gloria and Lauren got up from their chairs and laid down on the floor, ten feet from the stairs.

"Not that I don't trust you ladies, but lock your hands behind your back. That's it."

Nestor climbed the stairs, removed the lock, opened the doors, and stepped back down to the floor. "When I tell you, I want you to get up, pick up Adar's body, and put him into the container. But before you do, Nighthawk, I'll tell you a little tale about your friend Jim Abbott. I don't want you to be disillusioned about the type of man he was.

"You see, Jim and I went way back to 1980 and the attempted rescue of the hostages in Iran. I was going to make a name for myself, but the whole thing got fucked up because of some bullshit sandstorm and the fact that a few GIs bit the dust. Abbott told me to postpone the rescue attempt, but it was my chance for fame and glory, so I went ahead. Then he fucked me over and reported me to the generals, and I got fucked.

"So here I am, twenty years later, and who do I run into while I'm receiving a duffel bag full of cash, but my old adversary, Jim Abbott. He tries to fuck me over again by demanding—no that's too kind—*extorting* my hard-earned cash. So, I give him a packet, but I know it's just the beginning, and he'll be back for more.

"My friend Azizi, he'll sell anything to line his pockets. I tell him about this mutual threat to our steady stream of cash. The day you're leaving the country, Abbott calls me to let me know he's in Iraq, telling me he'll be in touch. Obviously, that means one thing—he's going to hit me for more money. Time was running short. I had to take advantage of the opportunity. For a price, not more than what Abbott demanded, Azizi paid off a bunch of sand niggers to attack you guys. That's the story of your friend, or should I say, your shagger, Jim Abbott. After all, I'm sure you were fucking him, right?"

Gloria turned her head and stared at Nestor, pain in her heart and fury and vengeance in her eyes.

"I just thought you were entitled to know about your friend. Okay, ladies, get up and put our buddy there into the container. Oh, by the way, don't be shocked. There's already someone in there waiting for him."

Gloria and Lauren stood and walked to the opposite side of the desk.

Nestor kept the rifle pointed at them. "Come on now, don't be wusses, you're big-shot agents, and it's only blood. Just step over there and pick him up."

They walked into the growing pool of blood to get close enough for Gloria to be at Adar's feet and Lauren at his hands. The blood squished disgustingly under their shoes and they both gagged. They bent over, grabbed his feet and hands, and lifted him.

Adar's bloody hand slipped out of Lauren's grasp, and his body fell to the floor with a thud and a splat. She screamed and wiped her hand on the side of her jeans.

"Hurry up, don't be girly. Lift him up. We've got stuff to do."

Lauren's face was ashen. She mouthed, "He's going to kill us."

"Let's go note taker, grab his hand, and the two of you get him in there, right now."

The pulse in Gloria's neck throbbed. She mouthed something back.

Lauren's forehead furrowed.

They were thirty feet away from the container. Lauren reached down and grabbed Adar's lifeless hand again. The tendons in their arms strained as they lifted his body. They shuffled around the desk, leaving a trail of bloody footprints and more blood seeping from the body.

Nestor moved the rifle in a circular motion. "Come on, come on. Let's get this done, for Christ sake."

Gloria and Lauren approached the first step and turned sideways, each going up one step at a time. They reached the fifth step, and then the platform at the level of the container's floor.

Nestor walked up to the first step. "Just drop him right in there. You don't need to carry him all the way in."

Gloria give a hard look into the container and saw a pile of shrink-wrapped packets of US currency, body armor, and a dead man with three stripes on his sleeve and a cracked skull. "Who's that?"

Nestor looked up at them. "Nobody you know, just another fool left over from 1980."

Gloria nodded to Lauren, and they heaved Adar's body at Nestor.

He raised the M-4 and shots tore into the body as Gloria and Lauren jumped from the top of the platform. Gloria hit Nestor high, and Lauren came in low. The rifle flew from Nestor's grip and bounced across the floor, fifteen feet behind them. Lauren straddled Nestor. Gloria landed next to his right side and locked two hands onto the grips of the pistol.

Nestor went for the holstered semi-auto. He grabbed Gloria's hands and twisted the pistol's grips, trying to pry it from her grasp.

Lauren jammed the base of her palm into his nose, again and again. His cartilage crunched on the third and fourth thrust, as his nose flattened into his face and blood spurted over him. She pulled the Sig out of his waistband.

Nestor screamed and let go of the M-9.

Gloria jerked it out of the holster.

Nestor grabbed his nose and then flicked his hand back, only to find an empty holster.

Gloria jabbed the barrel against his temple. "Don't move, Nestor. Lauren, get the rifle."

Lauren stood and retrieved the weapon.

Gloria took Lauren's old position straddling Nestor. She had a score to settle. "All right, you son of a bitch." She gripped the M-9 tighter with her sweaty hand and screwed the barrel into his forehead.

"Do me a favor. Do it! Get this over with," Nestor screamed.

"What's your hurry, Nestor? I'm sure Jim suffered after he was shot. Why shouldn't you? You'll be dead soon enough."

"No, Gloria don't!" Lauren said.

Gloria pressed the barrel of the pistol harder into Nestor's forehead. The skin around the barrel whitened, and she locked onto his eyes. She could see and feel his fear. *Where do I find peace?*

Lauren shook her head. "Come on, Gloria. You've got enough on him to put him away for a long time."

"Lauren, why don't you go for a walk while I finish my business? We can say you went to get help, and he tried to go for my gun. It'll be a good shoot."

"I'm not going anywhere. You don't want to do this, Gloria. Haven't you had enough shit with everything that's happened back home and with Jim?"

Gloria put a little more pressure on the trigger. She could see the hammer inch farther back. Her heart was pounding, the throbbing in her ears drowning all the outside noise.

She knew the first shot would be double action, a harder trigger pull. She was almost there. There couldn't be much farther for the trigger to travel. Gloria was doubtful that another shot would be necessary. They'd be easy single action pulls on the trigger, and she felt a real need to empty the magazine into this motherfucker.

Lauren eased the M-4 to the floor and stepped slowly toward Gloria. "Don't sacrifice yourself for this asshole. You've got your kids. If you do this, can you live with yourself?"

Gloria eased off the trigger a fraction.

"What's wrong, Nighthawk, losing your nerve?" Nestor smirked.

Gloria's arm fell to her side. Lauren was right. What good would evening the score do?

Some long-ignored moral sense stirred in Gloria, but most of all, her love for her children gripped her. Gloria realized, at that moment, that holding onto her guilt over all the deaths in her past was killing her. She had more than enough reason to survive—she had a life to live with Adsila and Darius. She took a deep breath and lashed the M-9 across Nestor's face. He screamed. She stood, straddling him, and dropped the hand holding the semi-auto to her side. She gazed at the red ring on his forehead and realized that was better for her by far than a bullet hole. Sweat dripped down her face onto Nestor's bloody one. "You're not worth it, asshole."

"Lauren, call Hickson."

CHAPTER 44

FIFTEEN MINUTES LATER, THE THREE inside the warehouse heard the sound of blaring sirens and vehicles screeching to a halt in front of the warehouse. Hickson charged through the door with six MPs and two special agents from Army CID, all of them bearing M-9s.

Gloria, strapped with Nestor's semi-auto, sat in the chair behind the desk. The M-4 laid on top of it. Lauren sat in one of the chairs in front of the desk, the Sig stashed in her waistline. Nestor was spread-eagled on his stomach under the chair.

"We didn't have any handcuffs. It's the only way we could secure him," Lauren said.

Hickson stepped up to Gloria. An African American, who towered over Hickson, stood next to him, his shirt tight around his chest, and a black armband bearing the letters MP in white around his sleeve.

"This is Lieutenant Maxwell. Max, these are IRS Special Agents Gloria Nighthawk and Lauren Ashberry. Max will want a statement from you guys."

Maxwell nodded. "Hickson filled me in, ladies. Good work. Agent Ashberry, if you don't mind getting up, we'll take custody of Nestor."

"Gladly." Lauren got up from the chair, and with one hand Maxwell tossed it to the side. "Get up, scumbag."

Nestor covered his nose with one hand and pushed himself up with the other.

"Cuff him and search him." Maxwell ordered.

Two MPs stepped toward Nestor. The first one, Paulson, cuffed him, and the second, Rogers, patted him down.

Paulson, hands on his hips, stood in front of his prisoner. "Nestor, as of this time you're being charged with the murder of Adar Mustafa. I'm sure before long, they'll be other charges pending. As I understand, you were a colonel in the Army. I'm sure you were schooled in military justice at West Point. You understand that you have the right to remain silent?"

Nestor nodded.

"Verbalize your response so it can be witnessed." Paulson ordered.

Nestor hung his head. "Yes."

Jensen laughed. "By the look of your nose, I have to ask if you would like medical attention?"

Nestor nodded, raised his head, and stared at Lauren.

She smirked and gestured, extending her open palm toward Nestor. "Defensive Tactics 101."

Maxwell looked at the Army special agents. "Jensen and Gillespie, I assume you guys want to do the search of the shipping container. I'll have my guys take Nestor to the lockup."

They slipped on latex gloves and headed to the container.

"You can do that without a warrant?" Gloria asked.

"Under military law, all we need is authorization from the CO. I filled him in on the way over." Jensen said.

"There's cash in there, body armor, and a dead sergeant," Gloria said.

Maxwell shook his head. "Probably another murder count against Nestor." He looked at the Army CID agents approaching the container. "Be careful in there guys. Don't destroy any evidence."

"It's not the first time we've done this," Jensen said somewhat testily, as the two men climbed the stairs and entered the container.

Jensen leaned back out almost immediately. "Lieutenant, it's Sergeant Oliver. Looks like he's been dead for at least a day. Have one of your guys bring us a body bag." Gillespie took photos of Oliver, the loose shrink-wrapped bags containing cash, and the body armor.

"Oliver was a good man." Maxwell narrowed his eyes and stared at Nestor. "Get him the fuck out of my sight."

Two of the MPs took Nestor out of the warehouse.

Gillespie joined Jensen on the platform with a vest in one hand and a shrink-wrapped package of currency in the other. "The vests have bullet holes and are stuffed with cash."

Gillespie went back into the container and stepped out a minute later. "There's a copy of a bill of lading. This container was supposed to be delivered to Baltimore, to Standard Armor."

Gloria nodded. "That's Nestor's company. I bet he was planning on destroying the vests." She looked at Hickson. "You said that the GIs were having a lot of issues with them, and my friend was killed when his vest failed. We'll give you the whole story later in our statement."

"Nestor must have had a plan to hide Sergeant Oliver's body and the cash," Lauren said. "What happens to the container now?"

"We contacted the medical facility to take the sergeant's body. They should be here any minute, and then we'll take the cash over to the Coalition Provisional Authority – that's the CPA to you, I'm sure. They have money counting machines there," Gillespie told her.

A few minutes later the medics came for the bodies of Adar and Sergeant Oliver. Gloria heard the bags unfold and the zippers open. The medics placed their bodies into the bags, closed them, and carried them to their vehicle. The night from last September flashed in her mind when she saw Jim Abbott's body dropped into a bag. That was the beginning of this nightmare but not the end of her pain.

"It won't be hard to count unless there's broken packets. Each packet should contain a hundred thousand," Gloria added.

"We'll get a rough count on the cash here. You ladies mind witnessing the count? I mean, IRS and all, you're probably good at that." Jensen smiled at Lauren and Gloria.

"Not a problem," Gloria said.

They dumped the packets of cash out of the body armor and stacked them against the wall inside the shipping container. "Eight across and five high, forty packets times a hundred thousand. Four million bucks, gentlemen." Lauren looked at the piles, sighed, and went silent.

Jensen prepared the evidence receipt, and all four of them signed it. Gillespie took several photos, initialed and dated them, and put two of the photos in an evidence bag with the receipt. "Let's put twenty packets in each duffel bag and take them to the CPA for verification."

"Leave the body armor in the container and secure the doors with our locks and evidence tape. The container and all the contents are evidence," Jensen said. The men wrapped the place with crime scene tape and posted a DO NOT REMOVE sign with ARMY CID and their names and contact information.

On the ride to the CPA, Lauren and Gloria sat in the back of the Hummer. Lauren leaned toward Gloria. "What about the money in the bunker in Syria?"

"I haven't forgot about it. We have to give our statements regarding Nestor's murder of Adar. Then we'll have to see Bill Musgrove. He's the senior IRS special agent in Baghdad."

Hickson waited for them at the CPA so that he could give Gloria and Lauren a ride back to their quarters.

CHAPTER 45

Saturday, October 17, 2004
4:00 p.m.

IT WAS GLORIA'S IDEA TO run all four million through the money-counting machines three times. She was delaying meeting with Bill Musgrove as long as she could. Gloria, Lauren, and the Army CID agents entered a large vault in one of Hussein's presidential palaces, where the cash was to be counted. Lauren gazed at the interior. "Holy shit, this is three times the size of my college dorm."

They put on surgical gloves before cutting open the plastic packets. They placed the packets into evidence envelopes and Army CID agents, Lauren, and Gloria all initialed and dated them. Then they secured the cash and evidence envelopes in a locker in the safe.

Gillespie closed the safe and locked it. They took an elevator to the main floor and went to the Army-CID office, where Gloria and Lauren gave their statements.

It was approaching six p.m., and Gloria could no longer avoid meeting with Musgrove. She knew he had every right to throw the book at her for leaving for Iraq without authority. It was blatant insubordination, among numerous other violations, should he choose to list them. The thought came to her that she may have to look for another job. She would be entitled to a check for the annual leave she had earned but that would only last for a couple of months, and then what? Federal law enforcement would be out of the questions. Once the Feds canned you, there is no looking back. OK, OK, maybe she was overreacting. Maybe, just maybe, there was nothing to worry about.

Gloria and Lauren signed their statements and handed them to Jensen. He dropped them into a file. "Where can we take you two?"

"The IRS office is located at the military base at the airport." Gloria stood and swallowed. "They want to talk to us."

Gillespie pulled Lauren's chair back as she stood. "It'll be six thirty by the time we get you there." He gave her a head-to-foot once-over. "We could stop at the club for a cold one. You two deserve a break after the last couple of days."

Gloria felt less apprehensive about meeting Musgrove alone. His foreboding words lurked in her mind. If she could isolate Lauren from this confrontation, she might be able to save Lauren's career. Gloria had a sinking feeling that hers was over. "Musgrove will wait for me until I come in. Lauren, if you want a break, go with them," Gloria said.

Lauren stepped close to Gloria. "Not a chance in hell. I'm going to see this through to the end. I'm your partner, remember? You are not doing this alone."

Gloria shifted from one foot to another. "Listen, I really think you—"

"No, you listen. A few months ago, you told me that partners watch each other's back. If it weren't for you, I'd be in Chicago working a case involving fraud by a dentist or funeral parlor director or some other dopey shit. I'll never forget what you've done for me. You've given me experiences that most agents wouldn't even dream about—wouldn't have in a lifetime. I've seen how tenacious you are, and I want to be just like that. It's the only way to do this job right. No, I'm sticking with you all the way, partner. I've got your back."

Gloria pressed her lips together. *This kind of loyalty, in spite of the shambles I've made of my personal life.* She smiled at Lauren.

Gillespie put his arm around Lauren's shoulder. "C'mon on, have a little fun."

She grasped his hand and gently lifted it off her shoulder. "Thanks, my friend, but I'm going with my partner." She looked at Gloria and nodded. "Let's go."

In spite of her concern for Lauren, Gloria felt that Lauren was the one person in her life right now upon whom she could rely completely. "Sorry guys. Could you give us a lift?"

The foursome left the palace and climbed into the CID Humvee. Gloria and Lauren sat in the back seat.

Gloria leaned toward Lauren and said in a low tone. "I don't know what to expect from Musgrove, but he was really pissed when we talked on the phone.

I have to tell you what the last thing was that he said to me. 'I've got some not-so-good news for you.' Then he hung up."

"What can they do to you? With the faulty vests that were seized, you've got the evidence to prove Nestor was running a huge scam on the Army. Nestor's been charged with Adar's murder, and you developed the lead to billions of dollars and gold in Syria."

"What can they do? That's easy to answer, anything they want. You put one spin on what happened. They can put their own spin on it. They could say they knew about the vests, state Adar was murdered as a result of my unauthorized investigation, and deny the allegation of billions in Syria as false intelligence or unprovable. Who can testify to it?"

"Come on, you can't be serious? Besides, who's 'they?'" Lauren threw her hands up.

"Don't be naïve. There are so many government agency power brokers, NGOs, and Iraqis playing the game that anything is possible. That cash didn't get to Syria on its own. It had to be a joint effort by several people from who-knows-what organizations. Who knows who's protecting whom? Someone besides Nestor is involved here, you can be sure of that, someone high up, and my sense is that we aren't out of the woods yet."

"Gloria, you're a hero. They can't touch you," Lauren said, a hint of doubt creeping into her voice in spite of herself.

The Humvee exited the Green Zone and thirty minutes later cleared the checkpoint at Baghdad International Airport. They stopped in front of the building housing the IRS-CID office.

Gillespie turned in his seat and faced the IRS agents. "One last chance, report for duty or go have some fun."

"Sorry, I tried to talk Lauren into going with you guys, but…." Gloria looked at Lauren. "She's a good partner, one of a kind. I'm sure you can appreciate that. Good luck, and get home safely," Gloria said, and stepped out of the vehicle.

Lauren gave each of them a nod and a wink. "See you guys." Then she followed Gloria.

They stood in front of the single-story beige building and watched the Humvee pull away.

"Last chance, Lauren. Go to the Officer's Club on base, and I'll call you when I'm through getting my ass chewed."

"Drop it already. You know where I'm headed."

Gloria nodded. "I appreciate that. I hope you won't be sorry."

They climbed three stairs and flashed their IDs to the sentry on the door. He hit the keys on the security pad and held the door open as they entered. The interior was bland government beige and the floors creaked. The walls were decorated with photos of aircraft in black picture frames. They stopped in front of a door marked CID.

Gloria looked at Lauren. "Last chance."

Lauren pushed the door open, stepped inside, and held it for Gloria.

Inside were six desks, piled high with documents. Only the last two desks were occupied. The agents looked up from their laptops. Musgrove and another man sat behind the agents in a glass enclosed office. They both looked at Gloria and Lauren, and their eyes told the agents they had been waiting for them far too long.

"We're Special Agents Nighthawk and Ashberry from Chicago," Gloria said.

One of the men at the desks stood. "I'm Dennis Johnson from Buffalo." He approached them, shook their hands and pointed at the other agent. "That's Jose Hernandez from Miami." Hernandez nodded at them from his desk.

Johnson looked over his shoulder at Musgrove and the other man in the office. "You better get in there. They've been waiting a while. Good luck."

"Who's the other guy with Musgrove?" Gloria whispered.

"Don't know," Johnson said as he stepped aside.

Gloria led the way and Lauren followed. Musgrove and his associate stayed seated as the two agents entered the office. Musgrove had gray hair. He wore black-framed glasses, a blue short-sleeved shirt, and black cargo pants. The man seated at the side of his desk wore beige Dockers and a green polo shirt. He looked like he was ten years out of Harvard. He gestured with his hand at two chairs in front of the desk, and the agents sat down.

Musgrove stood up from behind his desk, went to his office door, and opened it. "Hernandez and Johnson, why don't you two call it a night?"

Hernandez looked up from his laptop. "Bill, I'm only a couple of pages from completing the analysis of the docs the rangers seized."

"Hernandez, that wasn't a question, it was an order. Call it a night."

The two men shut down their laptops. Musgrove closed the door, returned to his chair, and silence filled his office until Johnson and Hernandez were gone.

Musgrove slid his chair forward and rested his forearms on his desk. "What, may I ask, were you thinking?"

Gloria looked at Musgrove. A thought came to her mind, A famous saying by some thoughtful soul: *Their place shall never be with those cold and timid souls who know neither victory or defeat.* She glanced at the other man and she knew she couldn't give an inch. "Who's this gentleman?"

"That's on a need-to-know basis, and you don't need to know." Musgrove said.

"Oh, yes I do. Is he a prosecutor or an investigator? If he is, I'm entitled to know that." Gloria glanced at Lauren. "We're entitled to know if we're under investigation."

"Why would you be under investigation?" Musgrove asked.

Gloria crossed her arms. "I can't think of any reason, but before we make any additional statements, we are entitled to know what's going on and who this man is. If the statements we gave to Army-CID were secured under false pretenses, we'll withdraw them."

"As of this point in time, neither of you is under investigation." The man in the Dockers said, with a tone in his voice that let them know that he, not Musgrove, was in charge.

Gloria shifted her gaze from Musgrove to Dockers. "Who are you? What's your role here? Whose interest do you represent?" She rested her forearms on the armrests of her chair and sat erect.

Lauren swallowed. She shifted her weight from one side to the other, growing uneasy at Gloria's aggressive inquiries.

"Like Agent Musgrove said, that's on a need-to-know basis."

"Well then, I can't really talk about what happened. If anyone needs to know what's going on, I'd say it's me and Lauren."

"Maybe you'll find out. Maybe I'll tell you. But not yet."

"You've got to be a spook from the company," said Gloria with a smile, as the truth dawned on her.

Lauren's forehead furrowed, and she glanced at Gloria.

"The company's CIA. He's CIA." Gloria said to Lauren, hoping that she was taking the right approach. She felt she needed to come on strong, let them know she wasn't going to be pushed around. If their minds were made up, she was gone anyway. She had nothing to lose.

Dockers glanced at Musgrove, then back at Gloria, coming to some internal decision. He sighed. "OK, no bullshit. You're right." He tossed his ID on the desk.

Gloria picked it up. "Henry Mason," she read aloud, suspecting that wasn't his real name anyway.

Mason reached into a briefcase sitting at his side. He pulled out two documents and placed them on the desk. "Go ahead. There's one for each of you."

Gloria and Lauren picked them up.

Lauren scratched her temple. "These are the statements we gave to Army CID."

"What about these? They're accurate and we're not going to change them." Gloria tossed it on the desk.

"We don't want you to change them." Mason said.

"Look, mystery man. Why don't you stop playing games—"?

Mason stood and pointed at Gloria. "You look, lady. This is what's going to happen. Your statements are going to disappear, because there's material and allegations in there that go beyond the scope of your little IRS careers. Do you understand?"

Gloria felt the first ember of anger starting to burn in her chest. She exhaled, trying to cool down. She looked at Mason. "Or what?"

"Or you and your little protégé will be bounced from CID, lose your pensions, and have a hard time finding a good job. I might be kind enough to get you a job pushing a broom for Streets and Sanitation in Chicago. You'd be cleaning up horse shit behind one of those parades down State Street."

Gloria looked at Lauren. "What did I tell you?"

"Yes, Lauren, tell us what your mentor told you."

Lauren turned to Gloria and then back to Mason.

"Tell him, Lauren." Gloria said.

Lauren looked Mason straight in the eye. "She said something like, 'Don't be naïve. There're so many power brokers playing the game. There's no telling who was behind getting the money to Syria, or even if it's there, or who's protecting whom.'"

Mason nodded. "That's why she's your mentor. You're lucky you can benefit from the wisdom of her experience… if she makes the right decision now."

Gloria tapped her fingers on the armrest. She waited a moment, regaining her composure. "We're entitled to know what's going on. We put our lives on the line trying to do the right thing."

Musgrove shook his head. "Don't push it, Gloria."

"That's okay, Bill. She's entitled to know something. You see, there are certain negotiations going on between unnamed countries that could resolve issues in the Middle East for a long time. This would be a significant accomplishment, worth far more than a couple of billion dollars. Obviously, you never heard this from us."

Gloria and Lauren looked at each other.

Mason picked up their statements and walked to the corner of Musgrove's office. He held the statements over the shredder, looked at them, and nodded.

Gloria raised her hand. "Wait."

"For what? Don't you understand? You're putting everything on the line," Musgrove said.

She edged forward in her seat. "What about Nestor? Is he going to be prosecuted for the vests, for killing Adar and Azizi?"

"That's really none of your business," Mason said.

Gloria forehead furrowed. "I have to know."

"All right, but this is it," Mason said. "In exchange for getting a life sentence instead of the death sentence, he signed an agreement pleading guilty to all the charges, testifying against a guy from the State Department, John Blanton, and one more thing."

"What's that?" Gloria asked.

"Bribery of a federal agent and conspiracy to murder a federal agent—namely one James Abbott." Mason said.

Gloria held back her tears. She swallowed hard and then wiped her sleeve across her face.

"There's an unrelated manner we need to fill you in on," Musgrove said.

Gloria looked up as her thoughts swirled, *she would never know if Jim Abbott came with her to Iraq to explore their relationship or for Nestor's money. At least his murder was vindicated, with the knowledge that Nestor would have to pay the price.*

"You know your husband was arrested by the FBI for money laundering and conspiracy to defraud the government," Musgrove said. "Go home. Your kids need you and they'll appreciate that you'll be there for them. It's going to be tough on them."

"I know, Stephens emailed me." She nodded and fell back into her chair, realizing how tough this had to be on Adsila and Darius. She was determined to be a better mother. "I've got to get home to my kids…."

"Are we in agreement?" Mason asked.

Gloria stood. "I don't really care. Just get me out of here. I want to go home"

"That's fine. I can get you on a plane to Germany within the hour." He pulled two documents out of his briefcase. "First, I need you and Lauren to sign these."

"What am I signing?" Gloria asked.

"An agreement that you will never disclose your knowledge in writing, verbally, or in any other form, of the facts and circumstances surrounding the funds in Syria and any related information," Mason said.

Gloria started reading the first page of the four-page document, leafed through the last three pages, and stared at Mason. "If I don't sign it?"

"I never considered that possibility," Mason said.

She initialed each page, scribbled her signature on the last page, and handed the pen to Lauren. "You want to get out of here, don't you? Please sign it. We have to go."

"We need both of you to sign it before we can release either of you," Mason said.

"Yeah, sure," Lauren leaned over the desk and signed.

"Where do we catch the plane?" Gloria asked.

"It'll be on the runway in twenty-five minutes. It'll be one of my company's planes. There will be a satellite phone on board that you can use to call your kids." He glanced at his watch. "It's Saturday, eleven a.m. in Chicago. They should be home."

"Let's go," Gloria said.

"Do you need to get your things?" Musgrove asked.

"No, there's nothing we need." Gloria stood and glanced at Lauren. "Let's go home."

"One last thing. You can't take any weapons with you on a contract flight."

"We don't have any. The MPs took them as evidence for ballistic tests."

"Okay. Why don't you two wait out there?" Mason gestured to the exterior office. "I have to make a few calls to get everything lined up for your flight to Munich."

Gloria and Lauren moved into the outer office space and closed Musgrove's door.

Lauren bit her cheek. "Why do I feel like they're going to fly us around for hours and land us in the middle of nowhere, never to be heard from again?"

"You've watched too many TV shows. We've left a trail of witnesses—Army CID, Musgrove, the MPs, Sergeant Hickson, and more," Gloria said.

Lauren exhaled. "I guess so, but I won't be comfortable until my feet are on the ground in Munich."

◇

They boarded a Lear Jet and taxied down the runway. Ten minutes into their flight, Gloria knocked on the cockpit door. The door opened. The copilot took off his headset and turned in his seat, looking at her. Gloria noticed a Smith and Wesson 9mm strapped on the right hip of the pilot.

"What can I do for you?"

"I was told you would have a satellite phone that I could use to call home, to call Chicago," Gloria said.

"Sorry, ma'am. We aren't authorized to let passengers use the phone. And in case you're thirsty, we're not allowed to serve alcoholic beverages on a contract flight for the government. But I can get you a coke if you'd like?"

"Look, I know who contracted this flight and I want to use your satellite phone."

The copilot glanced at the itinerary. "It says here that Capital Transportation is the company that made your travel arrangements."

Gloria glanced at the name tag on the copilot's shirt. "Look, Zabrosky, I'm not supposed to know who or what Capital Transportation is, but if I have to, I'll go public with what I know and who my crew was. It won't bother me at all. I'm sure the vendor does not want his identity disclosed. I assume you know what I'm getting at."

The pilot leaned forward and handed the phone to Gloria.

"Thank you." She marched back to her seat. "Not to make you anymore uncomfortable, but the copilot is carrying a .45 and the pilot is packing a 9 mm." She turned her attention to the phone and dialed Tom Stephens's number.

In two rings, he picked it up.

"Tom Stephens."

"Tom, it's Gloria. Long story here. I'm on the way home. Do you still have my kids?"

"They're here with my family. They can stay as long as you need them to. I tried calling, but your cell wasn't working."

"Thank God. Let me talk to them. Oh, and Tom, I'll be eternally grateful to you and your wife for all this."

"Don't mention it. I took Darius to basketball practice, and I'm picking him up in couple of hours. I thought it would be best to keep their lives as normal as possible. Adsila's here. I'll get her."

In a moment Adsila was on the phone. "Mom, I can't believe what happened. A bunch of FBI agents came to the house. There must have been ten of them. They arrested dad and searched the house. The put him in handcuffs like he was a drug dealer. It must be a mistake. How could they do that?"

What do I tell my daughter? I'm the reason he was arrested, Gloria thought.

"We'll find out more later, honey. I'm sure your father has hired a good attorney, and he will be able to resolve this. Right now, just try not to be too upset. Mr. Stephens said that you can stay with him until I get home. That should be late Sunday or early Monday morning. I'm on the way already. As soon as I can confirm my flight to Chicago, I'll let you know. We'll be landing in Germany in about eight hours. I'll call you back then. I love you, honey, and tell Darius that I love him, too. Can you put Mr. Stephens back on the phone?"

"Tom, thanks again for taking care of my kids. I'll explain everything that happened to us once we get home. There are restrictions about what we can discuss. Just know that Lauren and I are okay. What's going on? Why did the FBI arrest my husband? It's our case."

"I'm sorry. The US Attorney's office didn't want to risk his hearing any cases, knowing he was going to be indicted. The decision came at the highest level. We'll take care of your kids in the meantime."

"Tom, thank you so much. I was so worried about them. We'll call when we land. Goodbye."

CHAPTER 46

Munich, Germany

THE LEAR LANDED IN MUNICH AT four-thirty in the morning on Sunday. By five, they were entering the Hilton Munich. Its giant glass façade encased four stories of the hotel. Located between Terminals One and Two, it was an obvious choice.

Gloria, wearing Army cammies, approached the front desk. Lauren wore jeans, a T-shirt, and a warm-up jacket. Both outfits were wrinkled from two days of wear. Their lack of luggage drew an uneasy look from the sole hotel clerk on the overnight skeleton crew.

They presented their government credit cards, CID credentials, and passports. Gloria glanced at Lauren and laughed. "We look like we're from the homeless division."

They made their reservations for the next leg of their journey. The best flight available was a 1:00 p.m. departure Sunday on Icelandair, arriving in Chicago at 5:15 p.m. on Sunday. Gloria texted their flight itinerary to Stephens with a note. Please bring my kids. Thanks, Gloria.

They stepped into the elevator and hit the button for the third floor. "First things first. A long hot bath and a drink from the mini-bar for me," Gloria said.

"One? You must be kidding," Lauren said. "I'm lining the bottles up. Our plane doesn't leave until one o'clock. That means I can get a solid six hours of sleep for the first time in how many days?"

"I'm not sure how many days it's been," Gloria said. "Don't forget to leave some time to shop for some clean clothes. I wouldn't want to be the passenger that has to sit next to either of us in this condition."

"That won't take me more than fifteen minutes. Express shopping is my specialty." Lauren stopped at room 308. She looked at Gloria and gave her a hug. "Goodnight, hope you get a good night's rest. If you need to talk anything through, you know where I'll be."

"I'm going to crash in that tub. See you in the morning."

Lauren slid the pass key into the door and entered her room. Gloria headed two rooms down and kept her word. She was done for the night.

At ten the next morning, they headed down to breakfast and a shopping spree. They left their old clothes in the changing rooms. Lauren came out with pink skinny jeans, a matching jacket, tennis shoes, and a white sweater. Gloria wore a blue Nike warm-up suit, matching jogging shoes, and a red pullover sweatshirt imprinted 'Ich Liebe Berlin.'

They went through security and boarded the plane, sharing three seats between them. Somewhere over the Atlantic, Gloria took a sip from a glass of chardonnay and rested it on the tray. She wrung her hands and looked at Lauren.

"I don't know what I'm going to tell the kids."

"At some point in time, you have to tell them the truth."

"How do I ease into, 'your father helped a drug dealer launder his money?' It's a conversation I have to delay at least until we get home."

"What about his relationship with Shiquita?"

Gloria shook her head. "At least that was before we were married, I think."

"Is he going to be arraigned Monday?" Lauren asked.

"He's going to be in one hell of a mood after spending the weekend in Metropolitan Correction Center. I'm sure they'll have him in isolation. Can't have a federal judge in a cell with all the other criminals," Gloria said.

"Your kids are going to want to be at the arraignment."

"No way. I don't want them hearing what the prosecutor will be saying — betraying public trust, selling his position."

"He didn't actually sell his position. I mean, there's no evidence he profited in any way," Lauren said.

"That might be his best defense. Deny he received any benefit and attack the credibility of McElroy and Tamika. But sooner or later, the prosecutor will put as much dirt on him as possible. The unwritten rule of the US Attorney's office is 'we will not lose.' I'm going to shelter my kids as long as I can."

"What about discovery? When will the prosecution turn over our memos to his attorney?"

"The defense attorney will demand the discovery at the arraignment because of the sensitive nature of this case. Once that's done, the cat is out of the bag. They'll know about our contact with Tamika. I'm hoping they'll start plea negotiations before discovery. The prosecutor will probably disclose that Tamika will be a witness against him. Maybe he'll be reluctant to have his daughter testify against him." Gloria licked her lips with cautious hope.

Lauren tilted her head. "Is that likely?"

Gloria shook her head. "I don't know. I said I'm hoping. I doubt that Robert would enter a plea before he received the government's discovery. It would look bad to have his wife testify against him. The prosecutor will want you to testify."

"I had a feeling it would work out that way."

The hours inched by. Lauren closed her eyes and fell asleep. For Gloria, it wasn't so easy. She spent hours flicking through pages of flight magazines without reading a page. What, and how much, to tell Adsila and Darius dominated her thoughts.

CHAPTER 47

O'Hare Airport
Sunday, October 17, 2004

THE PLANE LANDED AT O'HARE and taxied to their gate at the international terminal. Gloria and Lauren went through customs. Only a few months ago, Gloria had met her husband here after returning from Iraq.

They went downstairs to ground service for arrivals. Darius and Adsila were waiting for them.

The kids rushed Gloria and piled onto her. The three of them locked in a group hug. Tears cascaded down Adsila's face. Darius held his in, but his eyes welled. Lauren stood aside, her hands folded in front her, concealing her emotions.

"Mom, I'm so glad you're home," Adsila said. "This has been such a nightmare. I've hardly slept since they arrested dad."

Gloria kissed her daughter on the cheek, and then Darius. "Honey, things will get better. We'll just have to work our way through this."

Gloria walked sandwiched between her kids, and Lauren followed. Gloria glanced over her shoulder. She cocked her head and Lauren scooted up to the threesome. "Kids, you remember Lauren from the medals presentation?" They nodded. A smile broke across Gloria's face and for one moment, everything was perfect. She was home and more importantly with her kids. But the fury of a firestorm was approaching, and she feared it would cause a lifetime of pain and anger for her children.

The group met Stephens at the arrival pick-up area. He gave his two agents hugs, and they all jumped into his family van.

"It's good to have you both back on home turf," Stephens said.

"It's good to be home," Gloria said.

"I second that," Lauren said.

They all avoided the main topic of conversation, but it loomed over everyone like a heavy cloud. There was an understanding that this was an issue that would have to be dealt with in the privacy of the Nighthawk/Carlton home.

At six p.m., Stephens dropped Lauren off at her parents' home. One look from Gloria as she climbed out of the car confirmed for Lauren how much she was dreading the upcoming conversation. At six forty-five, Gloria and her children thanked Stephens for watching over them and went up the front steps to their home.

They sat in the living room, Gloria on the sofa next to Adsila, and Darius in his father's recliner. Darius filled the embedded impressions and shallows left in the chair, as though he were trying to replace his father's essence.

"Whatever happens, the most important thing to remember is that your father loves both of you," Gloria said.

Darius leaned forward, "What do you mean 'whatever happens?' This has got to be a mistake. The charges will have to be dropped. Or if not, Dad's going to be acquitted. I'm sure that between the two of you, you can straighten this mess out."

"Honey, in my position it would be considered a conflict of interest to—"

Darius snarled, "What? You can't help your husband defend himself? Dad always said that trials are slanted in favor of the government. We know he's innocent, but if he's convicted, he could go to jail. You better quit that little job of yours and do what's right." His voice went up an octave.

Gloria leaned forward rubbing the back of her neck. "I'm sorry, this is so hard to explain." She reached for Adsila's hand, but her daughter pulled it away.

Gloria's eyes shifted from Adsila to Darius and she realized there was no way she could explain the circumstances to her children's satisfaction. "Kids, the truth is that we stumbled upon the evidence in this case through an informant and a witness before we knew it involved your father."

"What do you mean, we?" Darius's brow furrowed.

"Lauren and I."

"Jesus Christ, you believe a snitch over dad, a federal judge?"

"Honey, I didn't make the decision to arrest your father. That was made by the US Attorney. I can't control what they do."

Darius jumped to his feet, his arms flailing around. "You're ruining Dad's life and mine! I don't believe you. What's going to happen Monday?"

"He'll be arraigned and then released on bond."

"He'll come home?"

"I'm not sure. He could, unless…unless he plans to live elsewhere in the meantime."

"I think you're the one who should go somewhere else. You're the reason this happened. If you're going to live here, I'm moving in with Dad." Darius stormed out of the room.

CHAPTER 48

GLORIA ARRIVED IN THE OFFICE at seven thirty, after seeing her kids off to school with a stern warning for Darius, "Don't you show your face in court, and don't you dare miss school!" With her husband's arraignment scheduled for this morning, she was feeling a growing sense of turmoil, and her heart was filled with dread.

Stephens arrived a few minutes after Gloria. "When you get settled, come to my office, would you?" he said. "Lauren can join us when she gets in."

"Let me get a cup of coffee and I'll be right there." A few minutes later she joined Stephens.

He pointed at the door. "Close it."

Gloria sat in the chair closest to the door. She rested her coffee on his desk, leaned over, and pushed the door closed.

"How are you?" Stephens asked.

"Stressed, not looking forward to this morning."

"And the kids? How were they?"

"Everyone is upset. No, it's much worse than that. Darius is beside himself with rage. Adsila is standing by me, I think largely because Darius is so angry with me. I tried to explain how this case unfolded, how we backed into it through the informant and Tamika, that we didn't even know who the attorney was that she kept referring to. I didn't tell them yet that she is their stepsister."

"I wish I had some good advice to give you. But I can't think of any."

Gloria shook her head and exhaled. "I appreciate the thought, but I don't think anyone could come up with any words of wisdom."

"What I'm going to ask you is none of my business, and if you don't want to discuss it, I understand. I'm only asking you to get a better picture of the circumstances." Stephens hesitated, "Were there any signs of this going on? Issues that came up?" He shrugged.

Gloria narrowed her eyes, confused at the sudden interest in her personal life. "I understand why you're asking me, I think." She turned away to gather her thoughts, thinking Stephens was sincere. "We've been struggling through some rough patches the last few years. I don't know if it was directly related to the case. Everything is more difficult when you keep secrets from each other." Gloria paused and lowered her head, realizing that she was as guilty as her husband. She looked up and saw that Stephens was waiting for more information. "We are both independent people. Maybe we just grew apart and reached the point of no return."

It was as much as she could reveal. She leaned back in the chair and opened the door. Lauren was draping her trench coat over the back of her chair. She looked ready for court, with a double-breasted navy suit, matching pumps, and a white blouse.

"Look at you. I'm impressed," Gloria called through the open doorway. "Join us when you get a chance." Lauren quickly entered and sat in the free chair. Gloria closed the door again.

Stephens looked at Gloria. "Not surprisingly, the US Attorney wants you recused from any activity on this case." He glanced in Lauren's direction. "That means Lauren will be doing whatever is required from our office."

Gloria nodded. "I understand. Who's prosecuting the case?"

"The US Attorney himself, Todd Jeffreys. I guess he sees a lot of press, prosecuting a sitting federal judge. Could make him the next senator, or a partner at a major law firm."

"Which FBI agents are working the case?" Gloria asked.

"Jeffreys's personal entourage, Axelrod and Fanelli."

"Old school FBI. They'll try to keep Lauren arms-length from the case," Gloria said.

"I'll talk to the chief, make sure he understands that this was our case, and they stole it from us only because you two were in Iraq. Speaking of Iraq."

Stephens held out his hands, palms open. "Are we ever going to get any kind of explanation?"

"Tom, the only thing we can say is that the CIA had us sign confidentiality agreements that we wouldn't make any statements. So, I guess we'll have to wait for them to make a statement for us." She shrugged. "Until then...."

Stephens took a deep breath and exhaled loudly. "The arraignment is at ten. Lauren and I will go to the US Attorney's office at nine thirty. We'll make our introductions. Gloria, you stay glued to your seat. I'm sure Jeffreys and the FBI will want to talk to both of you sooner rather than later."

Lauren's long strides led the short walk from the Kluczynski Federal Building past the Calder orange flamingo, across Dearborn Street to the Dirksen Federal Building. She felt emboldened thinking that she could do this job for her partner.

It was rush hour for all the attorneys, witnesses, reporters, and others with an interest in the federal courts. The lines waiting to clear security were long, accompanied by the usual annoyed mumblings as people removed winter coats and suit jackets, pulled computers from their briefcases, and stuffed everything into trays at the metal detectors.

Lauren and Stephens waited patiently. Once they had cleared security, they took the north bank of elevators to the fifth floor. They showed their IDs through the bulletproof glass, signed in at the front desk, and waited for someone to meet them and escort them to the inner sanctum of the US Attorney's office.

In a few minutes, FBI Agent Wayne Axelrod opened the door and nodded for them to follow him. He was a burly man, well over six feet tall, with curly salt and pepper hair and meaty hands. Axelrod wore a brown off-the-rack suit. He greeted them with an understated handshake. "Nice to meet you. Come this way."

They followed him to the corner office, where Agent Anthony Fanelli sat in a chair, waiting while the US Attorney was on the phone. Fanelli stood and introduced himself. He looked more like a mobster than an FBI agent, and his demeanor told them he would remain distant. He was barely five foot seven, slender, with a bald spot surrounded by short-cropped gray hair. He wore a tailor-made, black pinstripe suit and a silver tie.

Jeffreys hung up the phone and came around his desk to meet Lauren and Stephens. He shook Lauren's hand like a practiced politician. "I understand you just returned from Iraq. You're a busy lady."

"I just tried to keep up with my partner, Gloria Nighthawk. She's the one that led the way," Lauren said.

"I feel for her. We realize she's in a difficult position. We felt we had to act on the case because of its sensitive nature. We weren't trying to do an end run around you."

But you did, Lauren thought.

Stephens extended his hand. "We understand. Lauren's here to assist in the investigation in any way she can."

"We appreciate your cooperation. Let's head upstairs for the arraignment. Judge Petersen has the case right now. It's entirely possible, though, that there will be a motion filed to have an out-of-district judge hear the case, assuming there will be a trial. The local judges probably feel it would be appropriate to recuse themselves. We hope that Petersen keeps the case. He's a former prosecutor and leans in our direction."

They headed up to the courtrooms on the twenty-fifth floor, joined by Assistant US Attorney Phillip Tunney, who was the second chair assigned to the case. He was a Harvard-educated lawyer who had played on his college basketball team, an African American still in good enough shape to dunk the ball. He wore a grey suit, shiny black shoes, and a red and black striped tie.

There was a buzz in the courtroom. The benches were loaded with reporters from the newspapers and TV stations, along with the usual collection of courtroom buffs.

The court clerk announced, "All rise. Court is now in session. The Honorable Judge James T. Petersen presiding." Everyone in the courtroom stood as the judge took his seat.

A quiet fell across the courtroom as case number 04-CR-1803 was called, *US vs Robert Carlton.*

Two US marshals escorted Judge Carlton from the holding cell to the lectern, where Jeffreys and Tunney stood. Carlton was wearing the standard-issue prisoner's orange jumpsuit.

"Good morning, gentlemen," Judge Petersen said.

The prosecutors acknowledged the judge's greeting.

"It's hasn't been very good for me. I found the accommodations lacking," Carlton said.

"Let's get on with it, shall we?" Petersen said.

"Mr. Carlton, you have been charged with conspiracy to defraud the US government in violation of Title 18, Section 371 and Section 1956, the Laundering of Monetary Instruments, in violation of the US Criminal Code. Would you like a reading of the indictment?"

"No, Your Honor. I obviously have a thorough understanding of these ridiculous charges. I'll waive," Carlton said.

"How do you plead?"

"Absolutely not guilty," Carlton said.

"You realize that if convicted, you could receive a maximum sentence of twenty-five years in jail and a fine of five hundred thousand dollars."

"Not going to happen."

"Mr. Carlton, you stand here today without the benefit of counsel. If you wish, I'll grant you the time to seek an attorney, and provide an opportunity to review the charges."

Carlton folded his arms. "No, Your Honor. I intend to represent myself. So, if you could set my bond, I can get out of this jumpsuit and start my defense against these scurrilous charges."

"Your bond is set at two hundred fifty thousand. As you are aware, ten percent of the value of the bond is required for your release."

"No problem. I've got the cash."

"I had a trial canceled last Friday, and that leaves an opening for the first week in December. I realize that is not far off. Can both parties be prepared to start that soon?"

"The government can be ready," Jeffreys said.

"Your Honor, I'm anxious to exonerate myself as soon as possible, but I haven't received any discovery from the government—"

"We can send the discovery to Mr. Carlton this afternoon. We just need an address—"

"You locked me up the entire weekend, knowing that I would not be available to receive your discovery," Carlton said.

"Gentlemen, I anticipate that the government will argue its case aggressively, and the defense will contest the evidence in the same manner, but let's allow each other to finish our sentences. We are then set to begin trial the first week of December. Call the next case," Petersen said.

The marshals escorted Carlton toward the holding cell. He stopped halfway and nodded at someone in the back row of the benches.

Lauren was seated in the first row. She stood, looked over her shoulder to see who it was, and saw Darius, glaring at the judge and prosecutors.

CHAPTER 49

IRS-CID
Chicago
October 18, 2004

G LORIA WAITED AT HER DESK. The arraignment was taking an unusual amount of time. *What could be taking so long? Is he pleading guilty?* She saw Lauren enter Stephens's office and followed her in.

She slid into the chair next to Lauren. "What happened?"

"He pled not guilty and is representing himself," Lauren said. "You would think with all the defense attorneys he deals with he would have retained one."

Gloria shook her head. "He's got the arrogance to think he can represent himself better than anyone else."

"His bond was set at two hundred fifty thousand. He said that he had the cash to pay it."

"Where's that money?" Gloria said, her hands locked onto the chair's arms. "Any other surprises?"

Lauren put her hand on Gloria's and braced her for the next bit of information. "Darius was there."

"What? After I specifically told him not to miss school and not to go to court." She yanked her cell phone out of her pocket, hit Darius's number on her speed dial, and rushed out of the office. She didn't want to make a scene in front of Stephens.

Lauren followed Gloria to her desk.

Gloria got his voicemail, "Darius, I told you not to miss school. Call me as soon as you get my message." She slammed the phone down on her desk. "I don't believe it. I tried to be calm. I told him don't miss school and specifically not to go to the court. I'll give him a half-hour to call back." She glanced at her watch: 11:00 a.m.

The minutes crept by. Lauren filled Gloria in on Carlton's attitude. "He seemed extremely confident that he'll beat the charges."

Gloria looked at her watch again. She wanted to call Darius. "Robert doesn't know anything about the case yet. Of course, we don't know much about it either. The prosecutors almost have to give immunity to McElroy, but if they do, they'll want him to plead guilty to something."

At eleven thirty, Gloria called again and left another message. "Darius, if you don't call me back in the next fifteen minutes, I'm going to start looking for you. I'll pull you out of school if I have to." She closed her eyes, realizing that was not very threatening because he's wasn't in school.

At eleven forty-five, she went to Stephens. "Tom, I need to take the afternoon off. I have to find Darius."

"No problem. Let me know how that goes and if I can help in any way, call," Stephens said.

"Thanks." Gloria turned and saw Lauren standing in the doorway. "Put me on leave, too. I'm going with her."

Gloria twisted her wedding band. She pictured Robert moving in with some woman she knew nothing about. A new Shaquita, and even worse, Darius living with them. She was grateful to Stephens for being understanding, and to Lauren for being supportive.

It was a short ride from the federal building to Bronzeville. "My husband breaks the law and my son hates me. Try to make sense out of that. Even Adsila is hardly talking to me. It feels like she's staying with me out of some sense of misplaced loyalty."

"It will take time. They love you and they know you love them."

Five minutes later, Lauren parked the Blazer in front of Gloria's house.

"Do you want me to come in with you?" Lauren asked.

"Probably a good idea. I might need a witness if Robert is home."

"You don't think he was released already?" Lauren said.

"Probably not, but he might have some influence because of his position," Gloria opened the front door. There was stone silence in the house.

"Darius, are you here?" Gloria said loudly.

There was no response.

"Come with me. Let's check the closets." Gloria marched up the stairs to the second floor and Lauren followed. They went to her son's bedroom first. His dresser was covered with basketball trophies. A poster of Michael Jordan hung over his headboard. Clothes were thrown over the bed. Gloria opened the closet. "His closet is half empty. Took what he needed and left in a hurry."

"His father has to get processed out of MCC. That would take a few hours, so Darius must be waiting somewhere for him in his car. Do you want to try calling him again?" Lauren asked.

"He didn't return my other calls." Gloria shook her head and hit Darius's number again. "Darius, I understand you're upset with me. I just want you to call so I know that you're all right. Please." She ended the call. "Let's check Robert's closet."

They walked down the hall to the master bedroom suite. It looked like a replay of Darius's room. Clothes had been picked out of the closet, and the ones that were not packed were tossed onto the king-sized bed. Two suitcases were missing.

Gloria pushed the clothes to the side and sat down. "Looks like Darius got instructions from his father on what to pack and where to meet him when he's released. So, he's cruising around in the Lexus, waiting for the word."

"I'm going to put some coffee on. I think this will be a long night," Lauren said.

At three in the afternoon, Judge Robert Carlton was released from the Metropolitan Correctional Center. He headed south on Clark Street across Congress Parkway. A block further was a cop bar, a hangout populated largely by those who fell prey to the feds—cops facing another internal affairs investigation, some already indicted, and local politicians subjected to another grand jury investigation. Even an indicted federal judge could find allies there.

Carlton stepped to the front door and looked into a small diamond-shaped window, only to see his reflection. He pulled the door open and was hit by the aroma of stale beer. The bar that ran the length of the room was to his left, and to his right a scattering of tables already occupied by cops who had just finished their shift. Against the wall, the juke box blared 'I can't get no satisfaction...'. With each footfall, the wooden floor creaked as though a thousand secrets were being revealed. He found a stool at the bar and got comfortable.

The bartender gave him a sidelong glance. He wore a white T-shirt that had yellow stains under the armpits. "Is you that judge that got busted?"

"That's me." Carlton put a twenty on the bar.

"First one's on the house, Your Honor. We the guys that got screwed by the feds. Put me away for a year on some dreamed up tax charge. We stick together. Just call me Otto. Whadda ya have?"

"A Bud would be great. I've been locked up the entire weekend."

The barkeep put an ice-cold bottle on the bar. Carlton watched the beads of sweat drip down the label. He picked it up and took a long draw.

"Hits the spot, thanks." He pulled out his cell and called Darius. "Hey son, I'm about a block south of Congress on Clark at a place called Stebbins. Park the car and come in."

In a few minutes, Darius stepped into the bar, into a world he had never been exposed to. He cautiously slid onto the stool next to his father.

Carlton put his arm around Darius's shoulder, "Son, today we're going to do something we've never done before. You and your old man are going to get drunk together. It's a rite of passage for a father and son." Carlton pulled out his money clip and put a Ben Franklin next to his beer. He turned in his seat. "Drinks are on me, to celebrate my son's and my special day. Barkeep, get my boy a beer and a shot of your best whiskey."

Otto looked at Darius. "Not that it matters to anyone here, but I got to ask, is your boy over twenty-one?"

"Otto, you got my word that my son is legal," Robert winked. "Now set us up."

The barkeep set a bottle of Crown Royal and two shot glasses on the bar. He filled the shot glasses and set up two more Buds for the judge and his son.

A crowd formed around the bar. Cops slapped the judge on the back. "You'll beat them SOBs," they said, as they tossed back the judge's booze.

Darius grabbed a shot glass and took a sip.

"Son, that's not how you do it." Robert held the shot glass between his forefinger and thumb. Brought it to his lips, jerked his head back, chugged it, and slammed it down on the bar.

Darius tried the same approach. He coughed as the whiskey burned down his gullet. "Whoa."

His father handed him the beer. "Take a swallow. It will cool the burn."

Darius followed the instructions again. Beads of sweat popped on his forehead. He set the Bud on the bar. "Dad, what's going to happen now? I mean, with your case? With mom?"

"Tomorrow, son, I'll explain everything to you tomorrow. It's a bunch of lying sons of bitches that're trying to set me up. But tonight is our night. It's a night for a father and son. It's the beginning of a new relationship for you and me." He wrapped his hand around Darius' neck and pulled him close. "You good with that, son?"

Darius nodded.

At eight o'clock, Carlton was still surrounded by hangers-on mooching free drinks. He glanced at Darius, saw him push the bottle of Bud away and bury his face onto his forearms resting on the bar. Carlton was sure he had planted enough seeds to win his son over.

CHAPTER 50

Chicago
Tuesday, October 19, 2004

TUESDAY MORNING, JUDGE CARLTON WOKE up in a cold sweat. For a terrifying moment, he thought he was still in an eight by twelve cell. The fear hit him that this could be his life for the next ten years or more. He pictured a line of gangbangers waiting to rape him, then he glanced at his Rolex. It was eight o'clock in the morning, and he realized he was in a king-sized bed on soft sheets. He took a deep breath and exhaled.

Carlton cast his long legs over the side of the bed, stood in his boxer shorts, and stretched his arms overhead. He left the bedroom and went into the living room, feeling a mild hangover from the evening at Stebbins. He wondered how Darius was feeling. He opened the curtains and gazed through the large window of the presidential suite. The pale sun attempted to break through gray October skies. The wind blew the last brown leaves from the naked trees.

The owner of the hotel had welcomed him with open arms when he inquired about a vacancy. It was payback for ruling in favor of the hotel owner in the civil lawsuit filed against the man. Carlton had thought the lawsuit was frivolous anyway.

Carlton walked across the suite to Darius's bedroom. He opened the door. The room was dark, and he stumbled on his way to the bed. He bent over and picked up a Bible. Sitting on the corner of the bed with the Bible in one hand, he reached out to his son with the other hand. Darius's flesh was warm to the touch.

"Darius, how are you feeling?"

His son groaned. "Like shit. My head is pounding. I puked my guts out. Can we find another way to celebrate next time?"

Carlton set the Bible on the nightstand. He thought that his son must be looking for a ray of light for his family to survive this unraveling. "You're a good young man. Maybe next time, we'll just take in a Bulls' game. You're late for school, but I guess you can take the day off. I'll let you sleep in, but when you wake up, call your mother to let her know you're all right. I'm sure your phone is full of voicemails. In the meantime, I've got work to do. If you feel like eating, call room service."

"Room service?" Darius pulled the cover over his head and rolled over. "Where are we?" he mumbled.

"We're in the Wilton Hotel; don't tell your mother. I'll fill you in later. Go back to sleep." He left the bedroom and closed the door.

———◆———

Gloria and Lauren had a nine fifteen meeting with second chair Phillip Tunney and Agent Axelrod. They headed across the street to the attorney's office.

"I have a feeling that Tunney is going to do most of the grunt work," Gloria said. "Jeffreys will want to keep the action in the courtroom for himself." As they crossed Dearborn Street, Gloria received a text message from Darius. *I'm going to be staying with Dad.*

She frantically hit Darius's number, almost pressing through the keyboard. "Where are you?" she asked when he picked up.

"Dad doesn't want me to say."

"Why can't I…" She paused. "Never mind. I'm not going to get into an argument with you or your father. Are you in school?"

"No, I didn't feel well, so I stayed home…I mean, I didn't go. I will tomorrow."

"Honey, I just want to know that you're all right. I'm not trying to get between you and your father. If you don't want to tell me where you're staying, that's up to you, but I want to talk with you every day. I have to go into a meeting. I love you."

Gloria looked at Lauren and shook her head. "I don't believe it. He hung up."

———◆———

The judge sat in a rent-a-wreck 2000 gray Honda Accord parked a half block west of McElroy's condo. At eleven a.m., the gangbanger exited the building's garage, driving the Bentley. Carlton followed him south on Lake Shore Drive, westbound on Congress Parkway, and then to the Eisenhower Expressway where he exited north on Central Avenue.

"This isn't so hard," Carlton mumbled to himself as he adjusted the 9mm Beretta in his waistband. He lagged a block behind his subject and watched him turn east on Madison. The judge punched the accelerator and caught the light at Madison. He saw his man head east a block then north on Lotus Avenue.

The judge checked the traffic. It was light. He turned right on the red light, accelerated, and turned on to Lotus. He caught the tail end of the Bentley turning east into an alley. He stepped on the gas. He checked the alley and saw the big car pull into a garage on the north side. The judge put his car into reverse, backed down the alley on the south side, and parked behind a couple of garbage cans.

A few minutes later, a 2002 green Chevy Cavalier backed out of the garage. McElroy was driving.

Can't follow this guy all day, Carlton thought. *Break it off now.* He wrote the license plate down in a spiral notebook. *Can't risk doing him in the daylight. I've got a month until the trial starts. There must be a better way.* He returned the rental car.

<hr />

Later that evening, the judge returned to the hotel. Darius was watching TV.

"How are you feeling?" Carlton asked.

"My stomach feels better. I'd like something to eat."

"Take a look at the room service menu. We'll order up."

Darius perused the menu. "I could get used to this."

A half hour later, they sat side by side on the couch, watching *The Bourne Supremacy* on cable. Darius was chomping on a cheeseburger and fries and sipping on a Coke. His father was dining on a T-bone, baked potato, and asparagus, chasing it down with a Heineken.

"Did you call your mother?"

"I texted her and she called me back."

"What did she say?"

Darius shook his head. "She said that she loved me and didn't want to come between us. As usual, she couldn't talk because she was going into a meeting. I hung up on her."

Carlton thought, *Nice, Son. No doubt she's prepping for my trial.*

Darius salted his fries. "Where did you go today?"

His father took a sip of his beer. "I was doing some research on my case."

"Anything I can help you with?"

"Not yet, but maybe soon."

Darius turned to his father. "Yesterday you told me that you would let me know what's going on."

His father picked up the remote and froze the movie. "Son, as you can imagine, this is going to be a very difficult period for your mother and I. We've been struggling the last couple of years. I'll be totally straight with you. I can't see how we can survive this together."

"Adsila and I know that you and mom have been having problems. She found the marriage counselor's business card on the kitchen counter."

"That's true. I confess that I never had much confidence in them. We saw more than one."

"What happened, Dad? You used to be happy."

Carlton turned his head looking away from his son and gazed silently at the TV. "Sometimes people just grow apart."

"But why? How?"

He looked back at Darius. "When married people lie to each other, they learn that they can't trust their spouse."

Darius put his cheeseburger down, sat back, and gave his father a pained stare. "Who lied?"

"Your mother." Carlton put down his knife and fork. He hoped this was getting the desired effect—convincing the boy that his son owed his loyalty to him. "I'm sure she had her reasons, but it really hurt me."

Darius raised his voice. "What did she lie about?"

Carlton shook his head. "This is hard for me to even talk about." He looked down, swallowed, and raised his head, gazing into Darius' eyes. "I feel terrible, like I'm trying to hurt your relationship with your mother. I can't do it."

A tear rolled down Darius's cheek. "Dad, this is tearing me apart. I need to know the truth. To try and understand what's going on."

Carlton bit his lips. "You remember when your mother told us she was going to San Francisco to interview witnesses?"

"Yeah, that was after she came back from Iraq. I remember because she told us she wasn't going to leave us again, and a short while later she left for California."

"That was a lie. I got confused about exactly when she was leaving, so I called her office. Mr. Stephens told me she was going to Oklahoma City on personal business and taking a couple of days of leave."

"Did you ask her about the trip? Maybe Mr. Stephens was confused."

"I did. I tried to bring it up a couple of times, and she refused to answer my questions." Carlton thought, *This has got to move him to my side. Hopefully, Darius will never ask her.*

"There's got to be an explanation, Dad." Darius's eyes welled.

"Then why wouldn't she tell me, Son?" He put his hand on Darius' knee. "It's probably best that you don't mention this to your mother. It'll make your relationship with her more difficult."

"Is there anything else?"

"Probably, but some things I'm not sure of, so I don't want to mention them. But there is one other thing I must tell you. I don't want to hide anything from you, because I want to be totally honest with you."

Darius pressed his lips together in a grimace.

Carlton took another slug from his beer. "There was a woman that I had a relationship with before I met your mother. Her name was Shiquita Dubonnet. She had a baby, a daughter, my daughter."

Darius swallowed in a gulp of air and blew it out.

"I wasn't aware of that until many years later. The daughter's name is Tamika Carlton, and she had a baby girl not long ago."

Darius leaned away from his father in disbelief.

"When I learned about the baby, I sent her money orders every month."

"Dad, I…I don't know what to say."

"I was trying to help. As it turned out, this entire case revolves around allegations that I told Tamika's boyfriend how to launder money. Can you imagine me, a federal judge, telling a dope dealer how to launder money?"

Darius straightened his back. "Her boyfriend's a dope dealer? Geez, Dad. You would never tell a dope dealer how to launder his money."

"I know that, and you know that. The prosecutor is the US Attorney for this district, Todd Jeffreys. He sees my case as a chance to make a name for himself by prosecuting a federal judge, and he's jumped at the opportunity.

They're going to give this dope dealer immunity so he doesn't have to worry about being prosecuted, so he can testify against me."

"That's not right."

"He's going to get on that witness stand and lie about what I allegedly told him. Then they're going to use the money orders I was sending Tamika, to show I was paying her off, to make it look like I was buying her silence."

"That doesn't prove anything."

"It will give that dope dealer credibility, and a reason why I would advise him how to launder his money. Jeffreys will use it to show how close our relationship was."

Carlton paused. He took a deep breath and exhaled. "If those lies convict me, they'll lock me up for a long time. Jeffreys will pound it into the jury that Robert Carlton, a sitting federal judge, violated the public trust at the highest level." Carlton rested his elbows on his knees, held his face in his hands, and sniffled. "Darius, I'm scared."

Darius slid next to him and put his arm around his father.

CHAPTER 51

US Attorney's Office
October 20, 2004

ON WEDNESDAY, THE SECRETARY AT the US Attorney's office dropped the discovery for Judge Carlton's case into the mail. It was addressed to the Carlton residence in Bronzeville. On Friday, US Attorney Jeffreys was getting ready to spend the weekend prepping for the trial. It was four thirty, and he saw his secretary slipping on her coat, ready to leave for the day. "Judy, did you send out the discovery to Carlton?"

"Mr. Jeffreys, you've asked me that at least ten times in the last couple of days. Here's the return request for a signed receipt." She placed it on his desk and turned to leave the office.

Jeffreys picked it up and checked the address it was sent to. "Judy, this is the wrong address. This is his residence—"

"Well, where else would I send it?"

Jeffreys took a deep breath and blew it out. "He wants all mailings sent to his post office box. Here it is." He slid it across his desk to her. "You better send this by messenger right now. If Carlton doesn't receive the discovery in time for the weekend, he'll file a motion with the judge claiming that we're not meeting our obligations."

"Oh, sorry," she said, thinking, *It would have been a good idea to tell me about the address in the first place.* Judy returned to her desk, took off her coat, and called a messenger service.

October 22, 2004

On Friday evening, Gloria Nighthawk arrived at her home in Bronzeville. Adsila had gotten home earlier, collected and signed for an envelope in the mail, and left it on the kitchen counter.

"Hi, Honey. How was school today?" Gloria asked.

"I got an A on my French test."

Gloria gave her a hug. "You're my star."

Adsila pulled the stool away from the kitchen island and sat down. "Mom, how long is this going to go on, Dad and Darius not living at home?"

Gloria sat next to her. "I don't know, Honey. I wish I had an answer for you."

"This is so messed up."

"Let's just stay focused on the fact that we are a family. We all love each other, and we will get through this."

Adsila's eyes welled, and a single tear slipped down her cheek. She brushed her forearm across her face. "Do you think you and Dad will stay married?"

Gloria wrapped her arms around Adsila, "We'll just take this one day at a time and hope for the best. We can't predict the future. Just know that nothing in the world is more important to me than you and Darius." But Gloria knew the chance of her marriage surviving this was as close to zero as it could get.

They settled in for the night. Gloria ordered egg foo young and chop suey from the local Chinese carryout and rented two comedy movies, *The Seagull's Laughter* and *Fifty First Dates.* She made a large bowl of popcorn and set it between them on the couch. Gloria wanted to keep the mood light.

By the end of the night, their heads were nestled on each other's, eyes shut, in front of a white screen on the television.

Gloria woke and gave Adsila a nudge. "Honey, let's go to bed."

"What time is it?" Adsila asked.

"Eleven, come on." Gloria embraced her daughter and kissed the top of her head. "Get ready for bed."

Adsila drowsily stretched her arms overhead and pushed herself up. "Okay, goodnight, Mom."

"Goodnight, Honey." She watched Adsila sleepwalk up the stairs to her bedroom.

Gloria took the empty popcorn bowl to the kitchen sink and leafed through the mail on the counter. She saw the large envelope from the US Attorney's office. She ripped it open and read the transmittal letter listing the discovery documents that had been turned over. The government's evidence against her husband consisted of four hundred and twenty-three documents. She paged through them.

Most of it consisted of the real estate and vehicles purchased by McElroy under the name of Shiquita DeBonnet, along with the statements taken from the realtors and car salesmen. Following that came the plea agreement, mug shot, and rap sheet for McElroy and Tamika's statement. The last document was an FBI 302 report from the debriefing of confidential informant 36-115.

Gloria read the debriefing of the FBI informant.

McElroy is known to frequent a bar at 16th Street and Pulaski called Hainey's Place. It is a known drug dealers' hang out. He can be found there at 4:00 a.m. on Saturdays and Sundays, when he picks up cash proceeds from the sale of heroin and crack cocaine from his street pushers.

"What the hell? This shouldn't be in the discovery." She slammed the report down on the counter and went to bed. She tossed and turned, haunted by the information received from the informant.

She was disconnected from the case on orders to recuse herself. Then why was the discovery sent here? Was another package sent to wherever Robert and Darius are living?

Unable to sleep, at midnight she called Lauren.

"Sorry to wake you."

"No problem. What's up?"

Gloria explained to Lauren about the FBI 302 regarding the confidential informant memo, and that it should not have been included in discovery.

"If they sent the discovery to you, maybe Robert didn't receive a copy," Lauren said.

"That's probably what happened. Doesn't really make any difference, because we can't get in touch with anyone until tomorrow, or maybe not even until Monday. I just had to talk to someone about it. Sorry if I woke you."

"You didn't. It's the start of another wild weekend for me. I was reading *The Narrows*. It's another of Michael Connelly's really good Harry Bosch novels."

"When you finish, give it to me. I could use a distraction. Anyway, sorry to bug you. Goodnight."

Carlton had dinner with Darius and watched the Bulls game. "What a way to start the season, double overtime loss to the Nets. I've got to run out for a few minutes. Be back in a little while," Carlton said.

The judge went down the street to the mail drop at the UPS store and checked his box. It was stuffed with a large envelope, the one thing he had been waiting for, the government's discovery. He unlocked the box, yanked it out, leaned against a counter in the store, and ripped it open.

Carlton paged through the first couple of documents. *Fucking plea agreement for that son of a bitch McElroy. Probably get probation. My lovely daughter Tamika's statement, signed by my wife. Talk about irony.*

He flipped through the business records and the statements from the realtors and car salesmen. "All these prove is that McElroy laundered his money," he mumbled.

Then he saw the rap sheet and mug shot. "Perfect, I can show these to Darius, so he'll know what the punk looks like."

Robert got to the FBI 302 with the informant interview. His head tipped back, and with a total lack of self-consciousness, he turned his face to the ceiling, and roared with laughter. He noticed the clerk look his way, and he stuffed the documents back in the envelope. He mumbled, "Thank you, FBI. Four o'clock in the morning. We've got a date."

Gloria's sleeplessness continued. Every time she looked at the clock, only fifteen minutes had passed. At three o'clock, she decided there was only one thing to do. She dressed, loaded her Sig with a fourteen-round extended magazine, chambered a round, and topped off the magazine with one more. She added her double-stack magazine holder with two more fourteen-round magazines. That gave her forty-three rounds. If she ever needed more ammo than that, it would not be a happy outcome. Then she slid her handcuffs into her belt and strapped on her bullet proof vest.

She hopped into the black Blazer, clicked the seat belt, and headed to Hainey's Bar. It was in one of the highest crime areas on the west side of Chicago. On the ride down the Eisenhower Expressway, she was startled to find herself praying to a God she had seldom sought out.

Carlton went to Darius' bedroom at two forty-five in the morning. He put his hand on his son's shoulder. "Darius, wake up. I need your help, son. This will be the most important night of our lives."

Darius lurched awake, startled out of the kind of deep sleep only the young enjoy. "What is it, Dad? What's wrong?"

"Nothing's wrong. Tonight, we're going to make things right. You and me, father and son, the way things ought to be. Put on your jeans and this. I bought it for you." He laid a black hoodie on the bed.

They left the hotel, and Carlton led his son to another rental car, a 2001 green Toyota Camry.

"Whose car is this? Why aren't we taking your Lexus?" Darius asked.

"We have some undercover work to do."

They slid into the car and headed west on the Eisenhower. At three ten, Carlton parked a half-block south of Hainey's on the east side of Pulaski.

"Son, I need your help tonight like I never needed you before. We have to get rid of that lying son of bitch." He handed McElroy's photo to Darius. "He won't be hard to pick out. He's six two and weighs about two eighty."

"What are we going to do?"

Carlton lifted the Beretta out of his waistband, grasped it by the barrel, and handed it toward Darius.

Darius kept his hands in the pockets of the hoodie and drew back. "What's that for?"

"We have to take care of the dope dealer."

Darius backed against the passenger door. "Are you crazy? I can't do that."

"Son, I'd do it, but I can't take the chance that someone could identify me."

Darius was breathing heavily, his chest visibly expanding and contracting. "What about me?"

"You haven't had your picture in the newspapers or on TV like me."

"How can you expect me to kill someone?"

"You're the only one I can trust, Darius. The only one that can save me from spending the next ten years in jail."

Darius slowly extended his clammy, shaking hand.

The pistol grips went *whap* when they hit Darius's palm. "The government wins ninety five percent of its cases. Juries want to believe that the government is telling the truth. That they wouldn't indict someone if it wasn't true," Carlton said.

"Is it true, Dad? Did you tell McElroy how to launder his money?"

"No, son, I swear to you I didn't, but I can't risk spending the next ten years in jail for something I didn't do. I'd have so many enemies from all the convicts I sentenced that sooner or later one of them would slice me up with a shiv. It's either that or be locked up twenty-three hours a day in solitary. Either way, to me it's a death sentence. Please, son, only you can save me."

Darius tightened his fingers around the pistol.

"The magazine is topped off, and there's a round in the chamber. The safety's off. You don't have to aim down the sights. Just point it at him and pull the trigger."

———◇———

Gloria drove past Hainey's at three thirty. The traffic coming in and out of the bar was heavy. The cars parked on Pulaski presented an impressive array, including a late-model Mercedes, a few BMWs, and even an Excalibur. She found a parking spot on the west side of the street a half-block north of the bar and settled in. She muttered under her breath. *Please God, let this be a waste of my time.*

At three forty-five, a Chevrolet Cavalier parked two spots in front of her under a streetlight. McElroy got out of the car and looked up and down Pulaski for anything that shouldn't be there. He trotted across the street like a defensive tackle looking to pound a quarterback.

———◇———

"There he is," Carlton said. "Wait for him to go into the bar. It closes at four, so I don't think he'll be in there long. All you have to do is get on the sidewalk side of his car. Hide behind the fender. When he returns to his car, stand up and pop him! I'll drive up the street to you. Hop in and we're gone. The cops will think it's just a dope dealer getting ripped off. It happens every day in this city."

Darius flipped his hood up, tightened his grip on the pistol in the pocket of his hoodie, and dithered out of the car. He crossed Pulaski to the west side of the street and went up the sidewalk, approaching the Chevy Cavalier.

Gloria saw a youngster approaching McElroy's car. He looked like a typical gangbanger and who else would be out at four in the morning—Jordan basketball shoes, baggy jeans, and a hoodie?

"Oh no. Please let this boy walk on by." She pulled her Sig out of her holster. The boy crouched down behind the front fender of the Cavalier on the sidewalk side. He pulled something out of his waistband. *Gun*, she said to herself.

She saw McElroy leaving the bar, grasping a paper bag in his hand. He hurried across Pulaski and reached for the car door handle.

Gloria rushed out of the Blazer and ran down the sidewalk as the boy rose to his feet, pushed the hoodie down, and pointed the Beretta at McElroy. The boy's hand was shaking.

McElroy looked up from the car door. He laughed at the nonexistent threat the boy posed and pulled a pistol out from under his coat.

The boy's posture and gait looked familiar. Now, with the streetlight shining on him, she recognized him. It was her son. "Darius, get down," she screamed.

Darius dropped the pistol and crashed to the ground.

McElroy held his pistol at an angle pointing downward over the hood of the car. The muzzle flash blasted into the night, again and again. Round after round exploded ripping into the hood and fender, lodging in the engine block.

Gloria veered behind the trunk of the Cavalier and pointed her Sig at the doper. The first shot hit him in the side of his head. His momentum turned him toward Gloria. The second shot hit his mouth. He collapsed to the pavement.

The paper bag McElroy was holding flew out of his hand, ripping apart. Singles, fives, tens, and twenty-dollar bills were blowing down Pulaski. Within seconds after the shooting, hangers-on from the bar were chasing the bills.

The high rollers got into the Mercedes, BMWs, and the Excalibur and squealed away, not wanting any part of what had happened.

She dropped her arms to her side and rushed to Darius. He stood and they embraced each other. "Honey, what are you doing here?"

Another figure ran across Pulaski toward the Cavalier. "Look what you did for me," Robert smirked.

Gloria shoved him against the side of the car and handcuffed him. "What kind of father are you!"

"Let me go. You just killed the main witness against me."

"Not a chance, you bastard. You put my son, our son, at risk to save your sorry ass. Your day in court is still in front of you. Darius, give me the pistol, and lie down in the back of the Blazer. Stay out of sight."

She shoved the pistol into her waistband and watched her son get into the SUV. She grabbed the back of the collar of her husband's shirt and pushed him over the hood of the Cavalier. "It's in everyone's best interest—you, me, and Darius—that our son was never here. I'm sure you agree."

The judge nodded.

"Say it!" Gloria screamed.

"I agree."

"Open your right hand." She rubbed the Beretta vigorously against her pants, wiping off Darius' fingerprints, and then put the pistol in her husband's right palm. "Close your hand."

He did. She grabbed the barrel and slide, jerked the pistol out of his hand, and shoved it back in her waistband.

"You agree to plead guilty to all counts, or I testify how you attempted to manipulate your son to kill McElroy. How do you think that would sound to a jury? A father trying to get his son to commit murder."

"You can't prove that."

Sirens grew louder as squad cars rushed to the scene of the shooting.

"The cops are on their way. You agree or not?" She held the handcuffs by the links and twisted them upward.

"Ow! OK, OK, agreed."

Three squad cars, sirens screaming, came to a screeching halt and surrounded the Cavalier. Their flashing blue lights bathed the street. Six uniformed cops jumped out of their cars, guns drawn.

Gloria pulled out her badge, holding it in the palm of her hand, high above her head. "Police, police," she shouted.

One of them approached her. She explained the situation. She had shot the dope dealer who was supposed to testify against her husband, a federal judge, whom she had arrested. The cop had a bewildered look on his face. Gloria didn't mention Darius.

The cop pulled his hand down his face. "That's one you don't hear every day."

An unmarked car stopped near the squads. Two detectives stepped out, met with the patrolmen for ten minutes before they approached Gloria. "I'm Detective Lenti, this is Fuelling. Who're you with?"

Gloria opened her credentials, "IRS, Criminal Investigation."

Lenti examined her creds, "The patrolman said you said 'Police'."

"I did. It takes too long to say IRS, Criminal Investigation."

An ambulance pulled up. Apparently, they got the call that the victim was DOA. The paramedics scooped up McElroy's body up into a body bag and left.

"I got your story from the guys," Fuelling said, pointing at the patrolman. "Never heard that one before. Anyway, they're bagging and tagging the shell casings. We've got to take your weapon as evidence and need you to come to the station so we can take your statement."

She handed the Sig over and pulled the Beretta from her waistband. "This is what he was carrying."

"Follow us to the station, tenth district, 2259 S. Damen. We'll take your husband into the lockup at our place," Fuelling said.

Gloria got in the Blazer. "Darius, the only people that know you were here are your father and me, and that's the way it's got to stay. You keep down and don't let anyone see you. Your father's going to cooperate to make sure you don't get in any trouble. You understand?"

"Yeah. What's going to happen to Dad?"

"He'll have to deal with the situation he created."

"I'm sorry, Mom. I just wanted to help, but I couldn't pull the trigger, and I failed him. I hope I didn't screw up."

"What he wanted you to do was terribly wrong. You did the right thing. Now you have to do what I say, okay?" Gloria said.

"Yeah, Mom. Thanks…Mom, I love you."

"I love you too." She pulled into the CPD parking lot. "Remember, stay down. It'll probably be an hour before I'm out."

Gloria called Stephens and Lauren and told them what happened as she walked toward the police department, excluding any involvement by Darius. By five thirty in the morning, she had finished her statement to the cops and Stephens and Lauren were waiting for her. They met at the sergeant's desk and were ready to leave when FBI agents Axelrod and Fanelli walked into the PD.

"You killed McElroy. There goes the case," Fanelli said.

"No, he's going to plead guilty," Gloria told him.

Fanelli crossed his arms. "Ha, fat chance. What makes you say that?"

Gloria gave a half-shrug, keeping her secret. "He agreed to."

The veins in Fanelli's neck popped. "Lady, that's not going to happen."

"I guess we'll see."

Fanelli's knuckles whitened as he clenched his fist. "You know we're going to take over the investigation of the shooting. Looks mighty suspicious when the defendant's wife kills the main witness."

"Good. I'm sure you'll be very thorough. Make sure your report includes the fact that your 302 in the discovery package informed the defendant the time and place where the principal witness would be. It's been a long night and not really a good one. The first time I killed anyone was in Iraq. I didn't like it then and I didn't like it tonight. I'm going home. Should get there just in time to see my kids off to school. They're the most important people in my life." Gloria realized; *I need them just as much, if not more, than they need me.*

The End